The Memory of Animals

By the same author

Unsettled Ground
Bitter Orange
Swimming Lessons
Our Endless Numbered Days

The Memory of Animals

CLAIRE FULLER

FIG TREE

an imprint of

PENGUIN BOOKS

FIG TREE

UK | USA | Canada | Ireland | Australia
India | New Zealand | South Africa

Fig Tree is part of the Penguin Random House group of companies
whose addresses can be found at global.penguinrandomhouse.com.

Penguin
Random House
UK

First published 2023
001

Copyright © Claire Fuller, 2023

Image credit: *Strong Arm* by Nathaniel Smith from Noun Project

The moral right of the author has been asserted

Set in 12/14.75pt Dante MT Std
Typeset by Jouve (UK), Milton Keynes
Printed and bound in Great Britain by Clays Ltd, Elcograf S.p.A.

The authorized representative in the EEA is Penguin Random House Ireland,
Morrison Chambers, 32 Nassau Street, Dublin D02 YH68

A CIP catalogue record for this book is available from the British Library

HARDBACK ISBN: 978–0–241–61482–2
TRADE PAPERBACK ISBN: 978–0–241–61484–6

www.greenpenguin.co.uk

MIX
Paper from
responsible sources
FSC
www.fsc.org   FSC® C018179

Penguin Random House is committed to a
sustainable future for our business, our readers
and our planet. This book is made from Forest
Stewardship Council® certified paper.

For Jane Finigan

Falkirk Council	
30124 03182040 2	
Askews & Holts	
AF	£16.99
MK	

Dearest H,

Is it possible to fall in love at twelve? With an octopus? I met him in the Ionian Sea when I was snorkelling off the beach where my father had his hotel. I like to think he loved me back, as you maybe did too. I wonder often where you are and how you're doing. Are you dead or alive? Was it wrong, what I did? And is it better to live a small life, contained and enclosed where everything is provided and the unexpected rarely happens? A safe life. Or one where you swim out into the unknown and risk everything. I chose for you since the choice wasn't yours to make. But, I wanted to write ~~to apologize to ask your forgiveness~~ *to explain myself.*

Neffy

Day Zero Minus Two

A nurse collects me from the ground-floor lobby and takes me and my wheeled suitcase up in the lift. I smell the familiar odours of disinfectant and industrial cleaner, mixed with a kind of hopeful hopelessness. The nurse, whose head is level with my chest, is wearing the ubiquitous hospital top and loose trousers; the same as the nurses wore in the clinic in the hills above Big Sur and in the hospital in Athens. She's also got on a medical face mask like me but, above her brown eyes, neatly drawn eyebrows arch. She asks whether I had a good journey even though she must know they sent a car and that I sat in the back with a plastic screen between me and the driver. What she doesn't know is that I was smarting from the argument with Justin while the phone in my pocket vibrated with messages from him and Mum – apologies at first, rising to warnings and then angry admonishments to turn back now. Part of me worried I'd made another bad decision but the more my phone buzzed the more determined I became. I tried to calm myself by watching the empty streets of central London go by and counting the number of pedestrians we passed. When the car pulled up outside the unit, I was up to thirty-three.

The nurse has an accent; Thai, I guess. The lift stops on the second floor, the top floor. She tells me sixteen other volunteers will be arriving, and that I'm the first. 'Volunteers' is the word she uses although we are being paid. That, for me, is the point.

'We'll get you settled in,' the nurse says. 'No need to be nervous.'

'I'm fine,' I say, although I'm not sure I am.

The lift doors open to a windowless reception with a long desk behind which sits a young woman in a white uniform. VACCINE BIOPHARM is displayed in large letters on the wall, with YOUR DREAMS, OUR REALITY beneath. An extravagant flower arrangement is at one end of the desk, a dozen tall stalks with orange flowers in a glass vase, and beside the lift there is some soft seating and a low table with glossy magazines fanned across it. The place looks like an advertising company from some American television series.

'Good afternoon,' the receptionist says from behind her mask.

'This is Nefeli,' the nurse says.

'Hello, Nefeli.' The receptionist speaks like a children's TV presenter, too gleeful.

'It's Neffy,' I say. 'Hello.'

The receptionist's nails click on her keyboard as she checks me in.

'Room one?' the nurse asks.

'Room one,' the receptionist says as though this is the best room.

The nurse leads me to a wide corridor of closed doors and recessed lighting, a nurses' station, hand sanitation units at intervals along the wall, and glove dispensers. Our shoes squeak on the vinyl flooring, which is patterned with a sweep of a different colour as though to guide our way. My first name is already on the whiteboard attached to the door of room one.

'I'll change it to Neffy,' the nurse says as she swings the door open and lets me go in first, like an estate agent

3

showing me around. One of those tricks to make sure I'm impressed.

I'm relieved to see a picture window the full length of the far wall beyond the bed. Three weeks isn't so long if I can see more than four walls. I can do this. Outside is a view of roofs across to the east, and opposite, an old red-brick building which looks as though it's been converted into apartments. Behind a row of square-framed windows – what's the architectural term for them? Justin told me once – a woman shrugs herself into a raincoat and disappears into the depths of her flat. Separating us below is an alleyway and when I peer to the right I can see a sliver of the main road, with a bollard stopping any traffic from turning in. Leftwards, beyond the end of the unit, the alley meets a dead-end road, which turns the corner around the building opposite and out of sight.

Everything in my room might have come from an identi-kit upmarket-hospital-room catalogue. I don't doubt that the other rooms are furnished the same: hospital bed, wardrobe with full-length mirror, desk, large-screen TV attached to the wall and two easy chairs facing each other in front of the window as though I might be allowed to receive visitors and offer them coffee. And to my right a door leads through to a tiled shower room.

'I need to go over some things with you,' the nurse says. She unconsciously turns the gold band on her wedding-ring finger. 'And then I'll leave you to unpack. You can take off your mask if you like. Volunteers don't need to wear one.'

'Okay,' I say. I've read through the 'what to expect' email many times. My phone pings again as I remove my mask.

'Do you want to look at that?' As though suddenly conscious of her habit, she lets go of her wedding ring.

'No, it's fine.' I'm here now, I don't care what Justin and Mum are telling me to do or not to do.

'You just have one case?' The nurse's nametag says 'Boosri' and when she sees me looking, she says, 'You can call me Boo.'

'I don't need much,' I say. The wheeled suitcase is an old one which Mum bought for my first solo trip to visit my father – Baba – in Greece, the summer I turned twelve. Before that, Baba had bought plane tickets for her and for me, and Mum would travel with me, handing me and one of her old suitcases over to Margot at Corfu Arrivals with hardly a word spoken. I would be embarrassed on Mum's behalf, fidgeting while she hugged and kissed me and tidied my collar, which wasn't untidy. I never turned to look at her as I skipped out into the wall of Greek heat with Margot; never once thought about what it must have been like for her to walk straight back into Departures and catch the next plane home to England, alone. When I was twelve either Mum decided I could do the trip alone, supervised by a cabin attendant, or maybe Baba questioned why he was buying two tickets when one would do.

Boo takes a screen from a wide pocket in her uniform, taps to wake it up. 'So, I need to check, you don't have alcohol in your bag?' I shake my head. 'No cigarettes, no tobacco?'

'No.'

'No drugs, prescription or anything else, except birth-control pills? No food of any kind? Sweets, snacks? Coffee, tea?'

I shake my head at each item.

She asks me to read the disclaimer one last time and indicates where I should sign with the stylus. I skim the information and scrawl a signature. She scans the barcode on a white wristband and has me confirm my name and date of birth, and then attaches it to my right wrist. She asks if I've had any symptoms in the last five days, and she lists them. 'No,' I answer to each one. Have I kept myself isolated, apart from contact with my immediate household in the last seven days? 'Yes.' I haven't been near anyone except Justin for more than a week.

Boo snaps on a pair of blue plastic gloves and swabs the back of my nose. I can't help but pull away and she apologizes. 'This will be tested overnight to make sure you're not asymptomatic.' She puts it in a plastic tube, labels it, tucks it back into her pocket. 'The doses of the vaccine will be given in staggered intervals,' she explains. 'You're in the first group, tomorrow afternoon. Okay?'

She shows me how to turn on the television and how to lower and raise the blinds on the external window using the voice service, and she explains that the venetian blind on the interior window which overlooks the corridor must always remain up, even at night, and she tells me how to access the alarms in the bedroom and the shower room.

'Mike will bring your dinner at seven. Vegetarian, yes?' She has hold of her wedding ring again even through the gloves.

'Yes, thanks.'

'If I can get you anything else, let me know.' I realize she hasn't touched anything in the room. 'I'll see you in the morning.'

'Some paper.'

'Pardon me?'

'Could you get me some paper, please? My laptop broke and I meant to bring a notebook but I ran out of time.'

This morning, when Justin and I were arguing, I'd stepped

6

with my full weight on to my laptop where I'd left it on the floor beside the bed. He was always telling me to put it away but I never listened. I'd been staying with him in his West London flat, paid for by his father, Clive, and taking whatever jobs I could find – bar work, waitressing – determined to pay my way, and then the virus swept through the city, swept through everywhere, and the pubs and the cafes closed. I sat in Justin's apartment, eating his food, using his electricity. He said, of course, that it didn't matter but my zero-hours contracts hadn't qualified me for any furlough scheme and I had debts to pay, or at least one big debt. Justin said he'd pay it off and I should come with him to Dorset, but I'd already signed up for the trial. That's what this morning's argument and ultimately every argument had been about. I'd heard the call for paid volunteers on the radio and had filled in an online form and passed all the tests before I even told him I'd agreed to be given a vaccine which was untested on humans, and then the virus which everyone was terrified of catching, and to sit in a room on my own for three weeks. 'I'll be fine,' I told him. 'It's not that different from sitting in your flat. Only this time they're paying for me to do nothing.' He didn't think it was funny.

This morning should have been a tender goodbye. Both of us were leaving – Justin in a hired van down to his father's house in Dorset, me to the unit in East London. He'd begged me again to go with him but I told him to stop trying to live my life for me and that I could make my own choices.

'A notebook?' Boo asks.

'Please. And a pen?'

'No problem.' At the door she pauses. 'I want to say thank you for volunteering. It's a very generous thing you're doing.'

I wonder if the words are scripted, a phrase she's been told to say to every volunteer, but they sound genuine.

Alone in my room, I look at my phone. The last message is from Justin: *I'm in Dorset. This is where I'll be waiting for you when you change your mind.*

I put the phone back in my pocket and watch another nurse escort a woman to the room beyond mine. I didn't see the name on her door but I catch a glimpse of her fine blonde hair and freckled skin before the enormous rucksack she carries obscures her face. The layout of her room must be the mirror image of mine with our beds back to back because, once the nurse has left, through the wall I can hear the girl speaking on her phone. She sounds Irish and her tone is bright and she laughs a lot. Other volunteers arrive, including a man who is shown to the room opposite mine. 'Yahiko' it says on his door. Later, I see the blue flicker of a screen through his corridor window.

In the evening, Mike delivers my dinner – sweet potato and aubergine curry with lemon rice – from a trolley he parks outside my room. He's fiftyish and balding.

'Make sure you order extra for tomorrow,' he says as he hands me a menu card. 'Everyone always complains they don't get enough. Management think that just because you're sitting around doing nothing you won't be hungry but in my experience it's the opposite. All you want to do is eat when you're bored.' Mike is large, soft-bodied. 'I'll collect the card when I've delivered the rest of the meals.' I wonder about the other volunteers, who they are and why they signed up. Even if I asked, I know Mike wouldn't be allowed to tell me. The options are porridge or yogurt and granola for breakfast, sandwiches, crisps and fruit for lunch, and for me either vegetable lasagne or mushroom risotto for dinner. I tick two sorts of sandwiches and both vegetarian options.

I get another text from Mum while I'm eating.

Please don't do this again. I know you think you have to because of what happened with your father but none of that is your fault. No one will think any less of you if you change your mind and leave. Please, darling, just think about it.

She's written more but I turn off the screen and put the phone face down on my bedside table. I want the trial to start so that I don't have time for second thoughts or to analyse my decision any further. I have coated the idea that I might be doing the wrong thing with a thin layer of self-assurance, brittle and flaking where I've picked and rubbed at it, so I know if I read the rest of her message the veneer will crumble, and if I reply to Justin he'll offer to come and get me and I'll say yes.

I've finished eating and I'm still hungry when Mike comes back in. 'Nearly forgot,' he says. 'From Boo.' He puts a pen and two spiral-bound notebooks on the bed.

That evening, I open one and pick up the pen.

Dearest H,

Day Zero Minus One

At the window, early, I feel more resilient than I did last night, and I compose a reply on my phone to Justin which sounds like an angry apology when I read it back. Before I press send, I'm distracted by the woman from the building opposite coming down the alleyway in a wide-collared trench coat, belted around her middle. She's like a character in a film, something noirish, maybe a French black-and-white detective story. The sun is just up, so where has she been? With her lover overnight? On a stake-out? She uses a key at her street door and goes inside. I wait for her to appear upstairs and, when she does, she comes to the window opposite mine so that we are only a few feet apart. If we were to both open our windows – if my window opened at all – and we leaned as far as we could, stretching out our hands, our fingertips might touch. I can see the cushions on her windowsill and a blue Roberts radio. Her profile is placed centrally in one of the black-edged square panes as she speaks into her phone. Crittall windows, that's what they're called. I reread the reply I've written to Justin and delete it. One-handed, the woman undoes her belt and swaps the phone to her left hand to shake off the coat. Underneath, she's wearing what seem to be scrubs, similar to Boo's. That's my answer. She finishes talking and flings the phone behind her, on to a chair or sofa, and sees me watching. The woman raises a hand in a quick salutation of despair, an acknowledgement of what the world is like outside.

'You didn't want the blind down?' Boo asks, rotating her wedding ring. 'For sleeping?'

'I couldn't make it work,' I say. I'm sitting in one of the chairs by the window, still in my pyjamas and a white robe the unit has provided. I didn't point out to her that it was having the blind raised on the interior window which kept me awake even when the lighting in the corridor was dimmed for the night.

'Blind down,' Boo says, and the mechanism starts. 'Blind up.' It reverses. 'How did you sleep?' she asks.

I hesitate. It feels rude to say that I didn't sleep well, as though this is her place and I'm a guest.

'No one sleeps well their first night. Strange bed. Nerves. It's normal. Don't worry.' She puts on a plastic apron and the snap of her gloves is like gunshots. 'You tested negative, so that's good.' I'm only half relieved. Maybe it would have been better to have an easy excuse to leave. 'I need to do some checks, take some blood.' She asks my name and my date of birth, and then, on a stand which she's wheeled in, she takes my weight and height, recording everything on her tablet. She takes my blood pressure, and then I look away, squeezing my eyes tight shut as she finds a vein and inserts a needle into the crook of my arm to take a tube of blood. She sticks another long swab up my nose and my eyes water. 'Sorry,' she says. 'It's not nice but I must do it every day.'

She gives me a clipboard with sheets attached where three times a day I have to record how I'm feeling. They include columns for mood, pain and its location, bowels, urine, sleep, energy, appetite, smell, taste and other. I'm a scientist, or rather, I was a scientist; I know we're here to be observed and recorded. When Boo has labelled everything she's taken from me and cleared away the paraphernalia, she says on her way out that Mike will be here soon with my breakfast.

The blinds are down now in the apartment opposite in what I imagine is the woman's sitting room. I decide to give her a name: Sophia. I've only ever known one Sophia and she would have grown, I think, into someone strong and brave.

I write to H some more, and then when I see the blinds go up in Sophia's apartment, I tear four pages from my notebook and write on them in block capitals, going over and over the lines with my pen. HELLO, I write. YOU ARE DOING AMAZING WORK. Using dots of toothpaste on each corner, I stick the pages to the window.

I sit in bed with my new notebook and think about H and what to say, how to explain my actions. When I glance up, I see that Sophia has replied and I clap my hands, delighted. The telly comes on to a programme about a race around the world that must have been made last year before the lockdowns. In black marker pen, Sophia has written: TY. SO ARE YOU. HOW ARE YOU FEELING?

How does she know what I'm doing? But of course she knows, the whole world knows, and since she lives opposite the unit she must have worked out that it's happening here. How should I answer? That I'm having second thoughts and I'm homesick although I don't know which home to be homesick for. That I'm here because I'm only decisive when someone tells me I shouldn't do something, and that's an idiotic reason.

'Off,' I say to the telly, but it doesn't change. I wonder if it's been set to Boo's voice. 'TV off,' I say, but it won't obey me. A news programme is on with a scrolling tape along the bottom, and when I pay attention, I realize that it's this clinical drug trial they're talking about. They show stock footage of the Vaccine BioPharm logo as a presenter says, 'Today sees the start of the world's first human challenge trial to attempt to find a vaccine for the so-called Dropsy virus responsible for the current pandemic, which causes a range of symptoms including swelling in some organs. Healthy, young volunteers between the ages of eighteen and thirty will be exposed to the virus in a safe and controlled environment at a secret location, while doctors monitor their health around the clock.' *Dropsy*. What a silly name. I don't understand why they can't keep to its proper scientific title. Some tabloid came up with it and it's stuck. It sounds like a Disney character and, as if to confirm this, behind the presenter on a giant screen are cartoonish images of viruses as alien life forms in dayglo colours bumping into each other and pulsing. 'The trial, which is due to finish in three weeks' time, is being delivered by a private clinical drug trial organization. We can talk now to Lawrence Barrett, CEO of Vaccine BioPharm.'

A man appears with the company's logo behind him as though he might be sitting in reception, except that every time he moves his head, we get a glimpse of what seems to be a child's bedroom. Lawrence Barrett is a double-chinned

American in a suit and green tie with the distracting circles of a ring light reflected in his eyes. He talks about how safe the trial is, how Vaccine BioPharm considers the volunteers' health as a priority, and he praises us for our altruism. I remember this human challenge study stuff from a lecture in my one year of medical school. No placebos, no double-blind testing; instead we'll all be given the vaccine and we'll all be given the virus. Sink or swim. That's why they're paying us so much money. The presenter goes on about informed consent, risk mitigation, whether the chance of success is high enough and if the potential outcome is worth the danger.

During the pre-tests, I was told repeatedly, and once more by Boo, that before I'm given the virus I can leave at any time, but something in the way she said it made me sense a subtle pressure to stay. And, naturally, she also meant that after I'm given the virus I'm not allowed to leave; I have to sit out the twenty-one days in my room. How will they keep us in, I wonder, if we threaten to leave? Will they lock us in, and how ethical would that be? I *will* have both the vaccine and the virus, and I will stay. I could kid myself that I'm doing it to save the human race, but honestly? I'm doing it for the money. The money I owe to the aquarium for their octopus.

While I'm trying to turn the telly off again, my phone pings. It's Justin and I'm flooded with relief that he hasn't given up on me. Now he'll tell me one last time that I shouldn't go through with the trial, and I can agree to give in.

Justin: *Have you arrived safely? Settled in?*

Me: *I'm here. All good*

We're being polite after yesterday's argument, careful to get the measure of each other before apologizing. Another ping. Another message. Please say you're coming to get me, I think.

Justin: *Have you used room service yet?*

Me: *Just the porno channels*

I'm too late, I'm beyond rescue. It seems that we're going for light banter.

Justin: *Careful you don't get addicted. I know how easy it can be. Did you see you made the news?*

Me: *I was waving but they must have cut it. Would you have waved back?*

Justin: *Madly*

Justin: *I'm sorry about your laptop*

Justin: *I'm sorry we didn't get to say goodbye properly*

Me: *Me too*

Justin: *I know what you're doing is important to you. I get that now*

I sit cross-legged on my bed and feel dejected. The girl in the room next door is laughing again.

Me: *It's ok*

Justin: *You're going to save the human race*

Me: *Hardly. And who needs a laptop? I've gone back to pen and paper*

Justin: *Did you decide what you're going to write about?*

Me: *Sort of*

Justin: *Write drunk, edit sober*

Me: *Alcohol is forbidden*

Justin: *Or you could just put the telly on*

Before I reply that the telly is on all the time because it has a mind of its own, I'm distracted by a segment about a new variant. Mutation, I think. That's what the sci-fi books and films used to call it. Maybe mutation is too scary, or not politically correct, or probably it's scientifically incorrect. I'll have to google it. I tune back into the programme. Just a few cases have been identified so far in the UK, but they say it appears that the new variant is affecting the brain as well as the other organs. A scientist talks about brain swelling or cerebral oedema and symptoms ranging from severe headache to fever, confusion and memory loss.

I'm aware that Justin will be checking his phone, waiting for my response and trying to resist messaging me again when I haven't answered. He once admitted that he would sometimes masturbate to my most mundane messages.

I wonder for the zillionth time whether what I am doing is right, if I should get up and leave.

Me: *Have you heard about the new variant? Can't remember what the symptoms are*

I want him to come back with a joke, something flippant, a picture of googly eyes, but he writes: *I think it's going to be bad. Seriously. Dad is on at me again to go to Denmark. Reckons it's safer there.*

'Television off,' I bark. It continues. A scientist is saying the new strain is more infectious than previously thought and can cause seizures and even coma within hours. He recommends four days' isolation minimum for anyone showing symptoms or testing positive. 'Off!' The presenter asks whether he would recommend that the government impose a nationwide curfew. 'Fucking turn off!' I shout, and the telly goes silent as though I've hurt its feelings. The images of empty supermarket shelves continue.

I read Justin's message twice to make sure I've understood. I can't believe he would go and leave me here. I write three replies, deleting each one:

Wow. Really?

Are you actually going to go?

If that's what you want

I've always assumed he will be here, like he said, waiting for me in Dorset, when the trial is over. The vaccine will work, the whole world will be cured and we'll go back to normal. Justin will carry on doing architecture and I'll pay off my debt and take whatever job I can get. For the first time it occurs to me that maybe this pandemic might not work out that way but my brain cannot imagine what sort of world we'll be left with.

The television flickers in the corner of my vision. Distracting, annoying. I get off the bed and feel around the edges of the screen for an off button or a cable which leads to a socket and plug, but the cable I find disappears into the unit the TV hangs on. I sit on my bed with my back to the screen and read Justin's message once more.

Six minutes later he writes: *I don't think you should do this trial. I know I've said it before. Plz plz plz think again. It's not too late to leave*

You should go to Denmark, I type, fast. *Be safe. Say hello to Mum and Clive.* The screen blurs from my tears and I blink them hard away.

You can't save everyone, he writes, even though he's just told me I can. *I love you*

I love you too, I type and send him, my stepbrother, Justin, a picture of a yellow face blowing a kiss.

Dearest H,

The water around Paxos turns cobalt as the sun goes down – the best time to see an octopus – and in the summer the sea stays warm. The first one I saw was an Octopus vulgaris, a common octopus, and it lived in a crevice in a rock with a messy collection of empty shells in front which gave away its hiding place. An octopus, as you know, can squeeze into a space as small as its beak, and it brings its food home to its den to eat, afterwards using the shells as a barricade. I went back to the crevice the next day and the octopus stretched out an arm and I reached out a finger, and it put its suckers on me and drew me in to see if I were good to eat. I might have gone with the creature, shrinking to the size of a fist and squeezing into its den, except I wanted to tell Baba that I'd met it. Every day I took the octopus a gift: a morsel of food, a silver spoon, a small mirror I stole from Margot's handbag. The octopus examined each one briefly and rejected them in favour of me. It was like getting to know an alien, one that is intelligent, inquisitive and eventually trusting. He – I'm pretty sure now that he was male – came out of his den when I arrived each evening as though I were expected, anticipated even, and I let him taste me with his suckers. We played with his empty shells and then one day when I arrived I saw that they were scattered and he didn't appear from his crevice in the rock. Had I encouraged him to become too trusting so that something took him – an eel, a bird, a human? Whichever it was, the octopus was gone. As you are also gone.

Neffy

'Name? Date of birth?' The two questions I'm asked before anything is done to me, before anything is taken or given to me, asked of me. This much I can do. I give my full Greek name – the names my father gave me. After the tests and checks, Boo asks if I've had my lunch, how I'm feeling, and confirms that I've been writing in my symptoms diary, even though I have no symptoms. 'Fine', I have written at 7 a.m. and 12 noon.

How am I feeling? 'Fine,' I tell her and smile. She cocks her head, gives a little squint like a bird trying to work me out. How am I really feeling? Like I've been deserted, like all my family have gone where it's safe, like this is my own stupid fault, like I should get up and leave, but I'm angry and sad and have nowhere to go.

'You're sure?'

'I'm sure.' I try to work out what she's expecting me to be feeling and how I can make that show on my face in order to reassure her. Pride? Terror? I can only smile harder.

'You're nervous?' she says. 'It's usual to be nervous. Everything will be okay.'

'Usual' seems a peculiar word to use, as though this specific trial with this virus and vaccine has been trialled before and it worked out fine. Fine.

Boo inserts cannulas, one each into the insides of my elbows, flushes them with saline and hitches my left arm to a drip. It has the vaccine in it, but it doesn't look like anything important. She chats while she works, about the weather, about how her daughter has always liked the rain, how she got married last year and is expecting a baby. I ask her what the second cannula is for.

'Protocol,' she says. It's not a Boo word, it's a word from a manual she had to read during training. 'Nothing to worry about.'

'Yes, but why?'

'In case of an unforeseen event,' she says and the smile behind her mask reaches her eyes.

'Is the girl in the room next door getting a second cannula too? Is she getting the vaccine now as well?' I gesture towards the adjoining wall. 'The Irish girl?'

'I can't give details about other volunteers,' Boo says. I know that, but I was hoping to catch her out, discover the girl's name at least.

For two and a half hours I lie on my bed, write to H and watch a drug – a vaccine which hasn't been tested on humans – drip into my vein. I fall asleep and only wake when a different nurse comes to take out the tube. There's some disturbance in the corridor and the nurse looks out. One of her colleagues jogs by and she raps on the window, but perhaps she isn't needed because she comes back to me and carries on with her work. She wouldn't tell me what was going on even if I asked.

I write and I work on my reply to Sophia:
FINE. WHAT'S IT LIKE OUT THERE?

Dearest H,

Traditionally in Greece, octopuses are caught in earthenware pots laid out on the seabed. The animals are killed with a knife between the eyes. They will writhe for a while, maybe shoot out some ink, clouding and swirling like blood in the seawater, and then their colouring will turn white and their arms will become limp. I'm sorry to be so graphic but I'm apologizing on behalf of all of us humans. You should brace yourself, there's worse to come.

Neffy

Day Zero

I write until my notebook is a quarter full. I eat my pot of yogurt, compote and granola standing at the window. It looks nice outside, that cool beginning of day which you know is going to turn into a scorcher in a couple of hours. I'm grateful for the air conditioning, or maybe I'm getting a temperature. I put the pot down and place my palm against my forehead. Impossible to tell. I wonder if Justin has left for Denmark, whether he remembered where he put his passport. I think about his passport picture, so serious, so sweet.

A woman – not Sophia – is coming down the alley. Even from a distance I can see she is elderly with a lead-footed gait – how I remember the way my grandmother walked when I was a child, with that rolling motion before she'd had her hip replaced. As the woman comes closer, almost under my window two floors down, I see she's wearing a cardigan and sensible shoes but between the shoes and the bottom of the cardigan there are only tights. Light-tan tights. As she goes past, I can see the shape and a suggestion of the colour of her large knickers. And as she reels towards the road, I see that something is wrong with the dimensions of her legs – they don't go in at the knees or the ankles but instead are nearly the same thickness all the way down, like an elephant's legs. I raise my hand as if to bang on the glass but, not knowing what good it would do, I stop myself and watch until the woman turns the corner on to the main street.

Later, after lunch, I look out into the unit's corridor. I can see Yahiko's room, but I can't see him, only the flicker of his TV. Further along, three nurses are behind their desk, laughing. One pats Boo on the back as though in appreciation of a joke. It is as if I'm watching them on a screen with the sound turned low. If I pressed rewind, I could make it happen all over again. The sense of unreality, of being in a box within a floor of boxes within a building of boxes, makes me go to the exterior window and press my palms flat against the cool glass.

Sophia has replied:

IT'S BAD. HOPE YOUR VACCINE WORKS.

On a daytime TV show, two presenters, a woman and a man, lounge at either end of a long, curved sofa. The TV came on in the late morning after Boo had done her checks and gone. I must have coughed or flicked a page in my notebook. I try everything to turn it off but it won't listen so I leave it on while I work on my reply to Sophia: YOU CAN'T SAVE EVERYONE. It takes me a long time to make the letters dark enough with my biro. I remove the previous sheets and put the new ones up. Writing to her is using a lot of the pages of my notebook but I have a second one. Mike comes in with my lunch and he laughs when I tell him the TV won't obey me.

'Television off,' he says, and even though he's speaking through his mask the telly shuts down.

'Actually, I think I'd like it on while I'm eating,' I say.

'Television on,' he says.

I sit on the bed with the plate of sandwiches on my lap.

Behind the two presenters is the logo of the World Health Organization. The woman presenter says the WHO has confirmed that the new variant is causing disorientation, memory loss, seizures and coma. The Minister for Health is due to give a press conference shortly, and the Prime Minister will give an address after that. They chat about the speculation that the UK will close its borders and other countries are likely to do the same.

I pick up my phone and message Justin: *When is your flight, if you have decided to go?* Maybe, I hope, the border will close before he can leave.

I should try again to switch the telly off, but I am stuck, inclined forward, eyes glued. They show footage of pushing and shoving at what seems to be a ferry terminal, with those doing the policing in full hazmat suits, and then an aerial shot of miles of traffic on what a voice says is the approach to Dover. Cars and caravans are queued as the drone – I presume – passes overhead. The voice says the queue has been at a standstill for three days and that there are concerns about dehydration and the unsanitary conditions. No ambulances or help have been able to get through. The drone lifts higher and I can see the line of traffic stretching for miles and then at the side of the road a few specks moving, others stationary. One or two raise their arms and wave, and I see that they're people who have abandoned their cars and are walking, a slow trek along the verge. Some of the shapes become people sitting or lying on their sides. I lean closer. Are those bodies? 'Oh my God,' I say aloud. The picture switches back to the studio.

'A spokesperson for the ambulance service calls this a

humanitarian crisis,' the female presenter says. 'And now, I'd like to bring in –' She pauses, glances down at her notes on the sofa beside her but can't seem to find her place. She looks up at the camera, and then behind her at the screen showing a still of the line of traffic, as though she's surprised to find herself there. 'We have . . .' Her eyes are wide in the moment of forgetting on live TV.

'Oh, come off it!' I shout at the screen, my mouth full of cream cheese and roast vegetable sandwich. 'This isn't a joke.'

The TV goes off.

'On!' I shout. 'On!' And the picture reluctantly returns. The male presenter is interviewing someone at home, sitting in front of an image of a bluebell wood. The female presenter is gone from the sofa, and Justin hasn't replied.

I'm lying on my bed, hands and face disinfected, with the doctor on her way, when I hear a message arrive on my phone. I've been told not to use it – possible contamination or something. But I take it out of my pocket and read.

Justin: *Plane diverted to Malmo, Sweden. They're not letting us off. Sitting outside terminal now, waiting for info. I think it's bad*

I can't believe he's gone already, no longer in the country, but then in a lurch of hope I wonder if not being allowed off means the plane will be turned around and he'll have to come back to England. Another message arrives before I've had time to reply.

Justin: *Very bad*

Me: *What kind of bad?*

I wait for his answer but it doesn't come. I shake the phone in frustration, then open Google, and I'm thinking about what to search for – *Bad things at Malmö airport? Trouble in Sweden?* – when Dr Tyler and Boo, both in hazmat suits, step into my room, and I shove the phone under my pillow out of sight. Boo's colleagues have moved my bed so that the top end is against the interior window, and they've put a pillow under my neck so my head is tilted back, and they have attached a plastic antechamber to the outside of my door. I have an upside-down view through the window to the corridor: the spotlights and ceiling with a pale-yellow stain in the shape of Antipaxos – an old boot, wrinkled and baggy, stamping westward across the Ionian Sea. And four masked and goggled faces appear at the window, upside down. I hear a hum from the motors clipped to the belts of the hazmat suits, which keep the air flowing and the hoods inflated. 'Hello again, Neffy,' Dr Tyler says. Her voice comes from underwater. She visited yesterday to explain what was going to happen today. She smiles at me – the smile of a zookeeper reassuring the tiger while making sure the bars are safely between them. I smile back and wonder if she thinks I'm insane to allow them to do this to me and whether I am insane, and then what kind of chit-chat one should have when being given a virus which will either slay one or maybe even save the world. I almost laugh but Boo asks my name, my date of birth. I say them, the answers coming without thinking. She asks if the procedure for giving me the virus has been explained to me. I say, 'Yes, fine,' and she places the safety goggles over my eyes.

My head is adjusted by blue hands. Dr Tyler and Boo are foreshortened, their chests enormous and their heads small even with the hoods. Boo says the name of the trial, reads out the name of the virus, and writes it on her screen. A method is followed, items are passed between her and the doctor. I like a good process, a method, boxes ticked. Dr Tyler puts a pipette filled with clear fluid up – or is it down? – one of my nostrils. Two drops, I have been told, although I can't tell. It's just cold, uncomfortable, like when seawater would get in under my snorkelling mask. Two drops in the other nostril. I can hear Mum remonstrating: Is your body worth so little that you'd sell it for a few thousand pounds? Are you so short-sighted that you'd do this again? Let yourself be a testing ground? A Petri dish? *Don't you remember what happened last time?* is what she really means. I remember what happened in California, I say to the mother in my head and she vanishes.

I want to sneeze, blow the liquid out, but Boo fits a giant white peg to the end of my nose and tells me that I must lie on my back for ten minutes and then keep the peg on for another half an hour. She makes a note of the time, starts a timer which she leaves with me, removes my goggles. They catch on my hair and the tug hurts. Boo apologizes. I watch the doctor and Boo through the interior window, taking it in turns to go into the temporary antechamber and remove their suits, bundling them up in a specific order and stuffing them in a bag while another nurse watches each of their actions to make sure they've followed the correct procedure. What have I done? I ask myself. Is the Irish girl next? Will they put on new suits to give it to her?

When the first bell sounds on the timer, I sit up and swing my legs to the side of the bed, take my phone to the bathroom to stare at myself in the mirror above the sink. The peg is a clamp with circular rubber discs which press my nose closed. I look like a clown wearing a bulldog clip. I take a selfie in the mirror and I don't mind it too much even with the clamp: my round face, brown eyes and dark unruly eyebrows which are finally in fashion. But who to send it to? Justin? He wouldn't find it funny, and he hasn't replied to my question about his delay. Surely they won't keep the plane waiting too long? And of all people, I send it to Margot.

I push my bed back to its usual position, up against the Irish girl's wall. It's still quiet in her room but through the interior window I see the guy opposite properly for the first time. Yahiko. He has dyed blond hair, very black at the roots, and is wearing oversized glasses with chunky blue frames. The nurses are standing in the corridor talking animatedly; it doesn't look as though they've gone into the room next door yet, where the Irish girl must be lying on her bed with her head tilted back, waiting. Unless she got too scared and left – she looked like someone who would scare easily. I can feel a pressure at the top of my nose and behind my eyes. Yahiko and I smile at each other and I flap the plastic bag I've been given to collect used tissues. It will be weighed, I suppose, analysed in some way. He waves back at me and we smile, and then we begin to laugh. I can't hear him through my window, across the corridor, through his window, but I can see the pink interior of his mouth and the way his eyes keep shutting and I laugh so hard my sides ache and I have to bend over, and each time I stand upright he's there, mouth open, eyes streaming. I'm not even sure why it's funny, but I laugh until I have to hold my nose clip on, worried I'll dislodge it and they'll have to reinfect me. The laughing makes my chest hurt and the pressure behind my eyes worsen. I want to go and look in the mirror to check my face again but, suddenly, taking one step feels like too much and it is all

I can do to cling on to the windowsill. Yahiko isn't laughing now. I can't see him very well but I think he's trying to ask me something, or he's shouting. He raps on his window with his knuckles, and I think I just need to lie down for a minute, and I retreat further into my room and climb on my bed. The tightness in my eyes has spread to my chest.

My phone, which I'm still holding, buzzes in my hand. I'm expecting a reply from Margot but it's not from her, it's a video from Justin. Lying on my side, I press play. I have to hold the phone close to my face to see it at all. The picture is dark and then glaringly bright, shapes moving about, and I hear noise – men shouting and a baby crying. The quality is poor, grainy, the image shaking. A group of three or four men seem to be standing in the aisle of a plane arguing with a member of the flight crew. I can see pushing and shoving, and someone falls. The shouting is louder. The camera pans jerkily to the window and takes a moment to adjust to the light. Justin's hand wipes at the condensation. People are outside on the runway, but it is too unclear to make out what's going on. I hear him though: 'They're not letting us off. They won't let us out and we can't go back. They've got guns.' The background noise blasts out and it's hard to hear his words. The camera swings again, quickly past his face to the seats behind him, where once more it takes a moment for the picture to lighten. But I see two or three people, slumped, someone half in the aisle. None are moving. 'Don't –' he starts, and the next words are scrambled. All I hear is 'the virus' before the film cuts out. I try to find his number, but my fingers won't press the right buttons, and the words I'm saying aloud to myself – 'phone Justin, phone Justin' – sound as though my tongue is too big for my mouth. Nothing is working. If I do make the call, Justin doesn't answer.

Dearest H,

An octopus has half a billion neurons located not just in its brain but throughout its body. This level of intelligence puts an octopus in the same category as a dog or a three-year-old human. Reading around my subject, I learned that the existence of nociceptors in cephalopods – or their ability to feel pain, including in laboratories – is circumstantial. Ironically, more research is required.

Neffy

Day One

Boo, in a hazmat suit, comes into my room. I think it is her. I hear noises in the corridor, something falling and someone shouting. My door is open and Boo is yelling back, hood off, hair whipping. Thai and English muddled together. The door falls shut. Boo is gone. Boo is holding my arm, fiddling with a syringe, too fast, and she fumbles, pinching skin. I am expanding, my tongue fills my mouth, pressed against the back of my teeth, my pyjama shorts are tight around my thighs and waist, strapping me to the bed. My blood dances in a Brownian motion.

'Has there been an unforeseen event?'

'What?' Boo bends close, no longer in her suit. I want to tell her to fetch it and I struggle, tugging my arm out of her hands. 'Yes,' she says, her breath on my face. 'An unforeseen event.' She turns her wedding ring round and round her finger.

I sleep.

I am eight or nine and I have been given a gift of a pair of jelly shoes. Clear rubbery plastic with a buckle on the side. I am up to my knees in the sea and I know Baba's hotel, the Hotel Ammos, is behind me on the hillside where he and Margot are resting through the afternoon heat. The Ionian extends out before me, blue to the horizon, where a milky line separates it from the sky. When I look down, I see my bare feet through the water, rippling with light, streaking and distorting. The jelly shoes are on a rock that sticks up out of the water, and as the shoes begin to move I understand why they are so special: within the soles are the parts of an octopus, its three hearts and beak, ovary, crop and siphon – words I know and understand although I'm a child – all still connected via the cephalic vein, tubes and intestines, so that the octopus, without mantle, skin or arms, still lives. I understand that it is a test, a trial to mix shoes with the parts of an octopus to create a new kind of underwater locomotion. That the parts of an octopus have been separated like this for our benefit is abhorrent and I'm overwhelmed by horror at what humans can do. I slide off the side of my bed, stagger to the toilet to vomit salt water.

The walls are too white, too bright. My pupils constrict to the shape of a miniature letterbox, swivelling independently towards the darkest corners of the room. The slow shutting of a door and the suction sound as it pulls closed. Shaking with cold. Throwing off my covers from the heat. Pills on my tongue. 'Swallow, Neffy,' Boo says, her hand cool and ungloved, behind my neck. The touch of a human. My head is lifted above the waves for a mouthful of air. I am rolled by the sea, one way and then the other, my stinking sheet tugged out from under me and replaced. The interior blind is lowered like curtains drawn around a death bed.

'I've got to go, Neffy. I'm sorry,' Boo whispers up against my ear. Me too, I think. Me too. 'Take these but not too many. Eat this when you can. Drink.' Brown eyes above her blue cloth mouth. I watch the words on the side of a Vaccine BioPharm mug, jiggling.

Picnic comic bench

       Vibra phone

   Chomper

                Bacchi

Panoramic caveman

                    Chimeric amphibian

'Someone will come, soon,' Boo says, bringing me back. 'Someone.' She looks over her shoulder at the door, unsure who it might be. The interior blind is still lowered. I close my eyes. I don't say thank you. I cannot speak. I don't watch Boo leave. I cannot see. The words on the mug dance and jump: *imp, obv, cam.* An alarm sounds but not mine, shouting in the street, screams; a blue light turns and turns across the ceiling of my room.

In the night I slither off the side of the bed again and crawl to the toilet. I don't make it in time, and I lie on the floor and cry. I want my mum to come and look after me, I want an adult to take control and tell me what to do although I am an adult. I wet a towel in toilet water and wipe myself the best I can. I will be in trouble for not measuring my personal output. It is important to be precise with data collection. Observe, record. The emergency line with its red triangle that I tied out of my way on my first day here, when it knocked irritatingly against my shoulder, is high and taunting.

The octopus drags me back. Hauls me up on to the bed. Each sucker can lift five pounds! Or is it thirty? She lays an arm across my forehead, clammy, damp, cooling. She shouldn't be here, in bed with me. She can only survive for twenty minutes out of water, thirty at the most. And besides, my raft is only big enough for one. I push at her mantle and she flashes blue, blue, blue, the light moving across her skin and her eye blinking, a black dash in an opalescent marble, knowing, remembering. Drink, she says. Take these, she says. I open my mouth, swallow. I've never heard you talk before, I say. Tell me what you see. But she slinks off the side of the raft, lowers herself into the inky waters below the bed and is gone.

Later she comes again, making my sheets salty wet. She lifts my head, puts something in my mouth, water and a tiny piece of crab – her favourite. It's good of her to share, I think. I shove back the duvet; my shorts and vest top are sodden. The octopus circles my wrist with an arm, her suckers moving along my skin, tasting me, clasping me. Her grip tightens, another on the top of my thigh, a third on my ankle. 'Stand back,' I say to my students who are gathered around the tank. 'A fully grown common octopus can crush the shells of crabs and crack a shark's spine in half.' I might have made up that last fact but they are impressed. 'Stand back. See!' I say, and she pulls me over the lip, headfirst into the green water, and I go willingly, slipping over the edge and down, the water exquisitely fresh, streaming against my face and my body. We go down, she and I, to the bottom where the light falls in beams and all is jade. Our skin is the colour and texture of the sand and the rocks. We are invisible.

She doesn't ask my name, I have no date of birth. I am a ring of white paper around a wrist, a felt-tipped X above an absent kidney, a label tied about a toe. So wonderfully cool.

Day ?

I gulp down the rest of the water in my glass, edge myself upright to try to fill it from the plastic jug. I miss and water runs down the side of the little cupboard and on to the floor. Using two hands, I tilt the jug up to my mouth and drink. The room is too cold. A plate with a slice of toast is on the bedside table. I can't remember Boo leaving it. White sliced bread, margarine. I eat a quarter, made a long time ago and the bread pressed flat by the knife. It peels from the roof of my mouth like PVA glue pasted on a palm. It smells of nothing, tastes of less than nothing. Next to the plate is a plastic drugs box, pills in each compartment. I take out two and swallow them with half a cup of cold tea – the milk settled thickly at the top – and I lie down again. The air conditioning hums. I'm sure there is something I should be worrying about but the effort to remember is too great. The corridor is silent, the interior blind still lowered, the room dark. I hear distant city noises: car horns, a police siren, shouting; and nearer or in my head a persistent knocking. I sleep. Hours, a day, a week. When I wake, the toast hasn't moved. I eat two more quarters, still tasteless, finish the tea, and sleep again. People in the corridor now, an argument, swearing and the slam of a door, another. I turn over, close my eyes and sink once more.

My phone has run out of battery. I lean out of the bed, almost at falling point, following the wire to plug it in. Rest. I swing my legs over the edge of the bed and search around for the TV remote, pat the bedcovers, remember that there isn't one. I see a glimpse of my skin between top and shorts, purple bruising on my sides and belly as though I have been kicked repeatedly. It's sore when I press it. My shorts are wet and the sheet is wet too but I don't smell anything. I tug the sheet off, resting after each movement, and push it under the bed with my toes. The plastic mattress is clammy. It will do. I sit. 'Telly on,' I say, and it comes out as a croak, but the screen on the wall miraculously wakes, perhaps only to be polite. Some sitcom is showing with canned laughter. 'Channel one,' I say. The television power button flashes but the programme doesn't change. 'Channel three,' I say, and the picture switches to an almost identical sitcom except the characters are black and American. Channel four is showing horses, those white ones from the Camargue galloping through water. I skip through the channels, Sky and even CNN, which has a static picture of a CNN building and scrolling text that reads, *An update will follow shortly*. I leave it on this.

The blinds on the exterior window are still up and it's day outside. Is it morning or afternoon? All the toast and tea has been eaten and drunk although I don't recall finishing it, and the plate and the cup are still there. I pause on the side of the bed, gathering strength, then stand and go to the window, and when I look to the east the sun is rising over London. At the end of the alley I see movement and I tense for what might be coming, but as I watch, a fallow deer trots around the corner. It's young and long-legged, the spots on its orange coat easy to see. It stops below my window to look about and scratch behind its ear with a hind hoof and then something must scare it because, with a flick of its tail, it's off.

Across the alleyway Sophia's blinds are up but her apartment is dark. She has written me a message: YES, I AM HEAR. I register the spelling mistake but I'm confused by what she's written until I read the last one I stuck up which I don't remember writing: ARE YOU THERE? I rest against the wall, legs weak and shaky, and turn back to my room to see the muddled duvet, a pillow under the bed with my dirty sheet, my water jug empty. A towel lies on the bathroom floor, my toothbrush beside it. No one has been in to clean, to take my pulse or my blood, to bring me food, to ask me my name and date of birth.

Dearest H,

Margot continued to serve octopus in the hotel's restaurant even when I begged her not to. They say an octopus must be tenderized before it can be cooked and eaten. Greek fishermen will beat the creatures on the harbour stones up to one hundred times to make them edible. Alternatively, some restaurants put the dead octopuses in a washing machine used only for the purpose of tenderization. I don't know which cycle they use.

South Korea has an octopus dish – sannakji – where the animal is eaten alive, either whole or sliced and served with its arms still squirming on the plate. Octopus arms continue to be active after amputation as I later discovered. There have been several reports of choking and death from those eating sannakji due to the suckers sticking to the inside of the diner's throat. I'm sure you can imagine what I think about that.

Neffy

Day ?

When I wake properly for the second time, I feel better: cooler, more rested. In fact, the room is chilly and I pull the duvet up to my chin. The items on the bedside table still haven't changed position: the empty water jug and the plate, the mug with *Vaccine BioPharm* on the side. The box of pills is there and the interior blind is still down. The picture of the CNN building has gone from the TV screen and now shows only white text on a black background: *Sorry, something has gone wrong.*

I lower myself off the bed and go back to the exterior window, dragging the duvet with me. The air conditioning is blasting out a fresh breeze but it's sunny outside, maybe midday, and when I stare again towards the east, the sun is still rising, only now with a cloud of dark smoke above it. I look and I look but there's nothing else to see and no one is in the alleyway – not even any more deer – and no cars or people pass the far end, no sirens sound. Sophia's blinds and message haven't changed position. Using the wall as a prop, I go to the bathroom and stick my head under the tap and drink, gulping down air and water, stopping to belch and then drinking again. I grip the edges of the sink and look in the mirror. I am shocked to see a whole, real human being as though I were expecting to no longer have a structure, no skin containing bones but instead something more fluid, slippery; a liquid body that could flow into a dark corner or a desk drawer, a shoe, a drain.

My face is even rounder than usual and my skin is dry. I have dark circles around my puffy eyes and the flesh here is tender when I prod it, and when I pull up my top, the colour of my chest is yellowish-green, my stomach too, as though a bruise from a fight I have forgotten about is disappearing, one that covered my entire body. Back in my bedroom I press my ear to the adjoining wall, listening for the Irish girl laughing or the sound of her TV. But I don't hear anything.

How long is it since I've been outside this room or someone has come in? Time has folded in on itself, corners and triangles overlapping and forming dark pockets, and now that I am trying to uncrease it, it is flattening into a different shape. I make my way around the bed to the door and I press down on the handle, slowly, silently. I don't know what I'm expecting on the other side, I only know that something is very wrong – there is no noise in the corridor, no chatter of the nurses at their station, no rattle of Mike's trolley. The handle depresses but the door won't open. I turn the twist lock and its clunk is loud but still the door doesn't release. I give it a final tug and then let go. I try to remember how the door is accessed from the outside; it seems so long since I came in here with Boo. Did she have a key card which she waved in front of a reader or pushed into a slot? Have they locked me in because I was given the virus and tried to leave? That can't be right – I would be given food, I would be checked on.

'Hello?' I say, my cheek pressed to the door, too quietly for anyone to hear. No answer.

I pull the duvet closer around my neck and consider pushing the emergency button above the bed or shouting, banging on the door. My fist is raised, about to thump, when the thought arrives – not that I'm unsure about who might come but that no one will. I lower my hand.

I pull at one of the slats of the interior blind and peep out at the corridor. From this position I can only see up in one direction and everything appears normal, although there's not much to see. No one is about. The blind to Yahiko's room opposite is also down. Did I stand at this window and laugh with him or did I dream it? Both cannulas are still in my arms. Should I remove them? Has the unforeseen event happened while I was sleeping? I let the slat go and return to my phone. It's partly charged but I still don't have any Wi-Fi, no 3G or 4G, and no little row of bars for a phone signal. With a final scrap of energy, I take the phone to the window and move it around – high and low – but nothing changes. No messages from Justin or Mum or Margot, or anyone else. The timer signal for a connection to the internet spins and spins, and outside in the east I can no longer see red, just plumes of smoke carried off towards the Thames estuary. Perhaps we're in another lockdown, I think, and no one is allowed to leave their homes. I go back to bed and put my hand on my heart, where it still beats, too fast.

Day ?

I rise from sleep and then, curling up, let myself become heavy and sink. I rise and I sink. On one rise, one morning or afternoon, I open my eyes. I'm lying in bed, facing the corridor, and I see, in front of my door, just inside my room, a tray. It seems to float a few centimetres off the floor, carried by a swell and then gently deposited on the shore. As it settles, I see that on the tray is one of the unit's meals, still in its microwave dish rather than served up on a plate as Mike always gave it to me. Alongside it is a jug of water, a carton of orange juice and a bag of crisps, the same expensive brand I would get with my lunch. I am suddenly starving. I get out of bed, dragging the duvet with me again because the room is still cold, and I hover my hand above the dish. It's pasta and it must have been here for a while. Who delivered it? Who opened my door and pushed the tray inside? The food doesn't smell of anything – the label is gone with the plastic film, but it could be cannelloni, probably spinach and ricotta, possibly vegetarian, but I put it down and open the crisps and eat three, one after the other. Their saltiness is good although I can't smell them. I stick the straw into the orange juice carton and drink it all, suck after suck, and it rushes to my legs and arms as though vitamin C and sugar is what they have been craving and what will make them work. On the floor, with my legs flopped out, I eat all the crisps and rip open the packet to lick the silver insides and dig out the salty corners with my tongue, although I have to look at the packet to see that they're salt and vinegar. I don't touch the cannelloni, just in case, and besides, I'm already full. Above my head is the door handle and I reach for it, pulling on it slowly, unsure whether I want the door to be locked or unlocked. What would be worse? To be kept captive by some unknown person – surely not anyone official, Mike or Boo or even Dr Tyler, because they would simply put on a suit to deliver my food if I were that infectious – or to have to go out into the corridor and discover what has happened?

The door is locked.

Dearest H,

An octopus is believed to be the only invertebrate aware of being in captivity. They will repeatedly squirt water at lights to make them short circuit. They will grow depressed and listless if they aren't provided with enough stimulus to occupy themselves and many will try to escape, climbing out of their tanks and heading for different waters. Others have been known to chew off one of their own arms or climb to the top of their tanks and allow themselves to dry out until they die. Would I be brave enough to do the same if it came to that?

Neffy

Day Seven

In my room, a man is sitting in one of the chairs beside the window reading a thin book. As well as jeans and a jumper, he has on one of the white towelling robes which the unit put in our rooms and over the top a blue plastic apron like the one Boo would wear. Hooked around his ears and scrunched under his chin – patchy with islands of dark beard – is one of the unit's masks. The man's boots with their dirty soles are up on the arm of my other chair. I am in that detached state between sleeping and waking, content for now to examine him without thought about who he is or what he's doing, and it is only when the man, maybe two or three years younger than me, turns a page, that I recognize with a flare of anger that it's my notebook he's reading. Perhaps I make a noise or move because he looks at me with surprise and then a smile – wide and genuine across his brown face. 'You're awake,' he says, taking his feet off the chair and bending towards me, elbows on knees. 'How you feeling?' His voice is low, his accent, London.

'That's private. My letters. Important.' My voice doesn't sound like my own, too deep and raspy. I shuffle to sit up.

He closes the notebook. 'Sorry.' He backs away as though it might explode. 'Will an octopus really chew off its own arm?'

'Arm?' My head is fuzzy, slow. I try to think where I'm up

to, whether it's a trick question. Whether this is a trick man. 'Yes.' I pull the duvet closer to my chin, sink back down in the bed.

My eyes begin to close, but he says, 'I'm Leon. Room nine.' He holds up a hand in a clownish wave. 'Oh shit,' he says, noticing his hands, and pulls out gloves from his robe pocket and snaps them on. He remembers the mask and lifts it over his mouth and nose. 'I'm sure you're not infectious now, though. Just pleased you're awake and that Yahiko spotted it.'

'Who isn't infectious? Yahiko?' I don't understand and I don't like what he seems to be saying.

'*You* aren't infectious. Probably. Most likely,' the man says. 'It's been seven days.'

I look around, still disorientated. The room seems solid; on the bedside table are the familiar dirty plate and cup.

'You want some food?' he says. 'I could bring you some food.'

'Why are you in my room?'

'Yahiko saw your blind, yesterday.' The man nods towards the interior window where one of the blind's slats is askew. Did I leave it like that?

I'd like him to go and have him replaced by a familiar face. 'Where's Boo?'

'She left and didn't come back but some of us stayed. Nowhere else to go. Or too –' he looks outside briefly – 'scared.'

I glance towards the window as well and I remember a fire in the east, a skirtless woman in the empty street and a deer. The sheets of paper with my message to Sophia have gone from my window. I should write to her but what to say? The television is off. I'd like to check my phone but I don't want to appear rude. Absurd. 'Outside,' I start, but the words won't form into a question.

The man puts his hands on his head, squashes down the ragged spirals of his hair. 'Don't you remember? It's been –' He stops again. 'It's been crazy, man.'

'I don't think you should be in here.' I'm decisive. 'We aren't supposed to leave our rooms. Cross-contamination. The trial will be compromised.' When have I ever worried about this kind of thing? I swing my legs out from the duvet, put my feet on the floor – I'm still wearing the same top and shorts as before. The room is chilly and my legs feel too hollow to be able to hold me up. 'I'm going to get Boo or someone.'

He reaches out an arm, withdraws it without touching me. 'You should stay in bed. There isn't anyone to get. Only us. Boo didn't come back.'

I don't know what he means. Something is turning in the centre of me, gathering speed and cohering into a mass I'd like to cough up. 'A doctor, then. Have you pulled the alarm cord?'

'None of them came back. Or they ran off. Home, wherever. It's just us.'

'Us?' My mind is foggy and won't clear.

'Yahiko – in the room opposite yours – Piper – she and Rachel are in the corridor on the other side of reception – and I'm down the end. That's it.'

'Who are you?'

'Leon,' he says, patiently.

I try hard to concentrate, understand what Leon is saying. 'This is stupid. How long have I been in bed for? Where has everyone gone?' The ball inside me sits just above my stomach, under my ribs. All the rest of me – my fingertips, my bladder, sphincter, heart – knows it is there.

44

'You've been out for seven days.'

'And when did I get here?'

'Two days before you were given the virus.'

'Nine days!' I try to recall what had been happening on the news the last time I saw it. 'I don't understand. Why didn't you get someone?'

Leon shakes his head. 'There isn't anyone, and it's not safe outside.' He stands, and I see that he's tall, much taller than I thought he was when he was sitting down. He seems nervous, like he's afraid of me, and I realize he's another volunteer. Maybe he reacted badly to the drug and he's hallucinating or paranoid and he's left his room without anyone knowing. Relief spreads through me and the ball inside dissolves in an instant. I nearly laugh, and then I think, what the hell is this place doing, letting volunteers wander the corridors and get into other people's rooms? I decide to be calm, play along with his psychosis until I can get some help.

'Why don't I just go and see?' I say as though I'm talking to an unpredictable child. 'Maybe someone at the nurses' station can help?'

I move towards the door, testing out my legs, which seem to want to bend in random directions like tubes of cooked pasta. I keep one hand on the bed, give Leon a reassuring smile. And then I remember the door had been locked when I tried it last time. The distance from the bed seems enormous but I make it to the door handle, cling on and press down, wondering if it will open. It opens, and a girl of maybe twenty-one, twenty-two, is just the other side. Both of us jump and yell, and she steps back from me, two large paces. She's wearing layers of clothes like Leon and a green beanie, and I can't imagine where she got it from in August.

'God,' she says, her hand on her chest. 'You scared me. So you are awake.' She looks over my shoulder to Leon. 'Is she okay? Safe?'

'I think so,' he says.

'What day is it today?' she asks me.

I squint at her. 'I don't know.' I could maybe work it out – the date I came in, plus nine days, but right now that's beyond me.

'Where are we?'

It's a test, a different kind of test. She's worried I'm forgetting things. 'London,' I say.

She purses her lips, undecided. 'What sort of place?'

I can't work out if this woman is crazy or I am crazy. 'A medical unit run by Vaccine BioPharm. I'm on the clinical drug trial. Or at least I was.'

It seems I've passed because she turns and shouts into the corridor behind her. 'Guys! She's up!' I follow her out, keeping the fingers of one hand on the wall, as if this structure is the only reality I can trust. And although nothing feels real yet, I am relieved to be out of that room, that the door opened and I was able to step out. Two others come quickly, standing a little way from me, staring: like Leon said – four in total. And the sight of them, wrapped in layers of clothing with the unit's robes over the top, makes the object inside me reassemble itself in an instant. An enormous hailstone gathering ice, a giant hairball, a fist of half-baked bread which I have swallowed whole. I would be freezing if it wasn't for the energy the thing is generating.

'You made it. You actually made it,' the man who I recognize as Yahiko says, and I think I can see tears in his eyes behind his large glasses. They introduce themselves: Piper, the girl in the hat who is tiny now that I see her standing next to the others; Rachel, with a perfectly made-up face – foundation, lipstick, filled-in eyebrows – beautiful in a doll-like way that I find difficult to draw my eyes from; and, of course, Yahiko. 'From the room opposite?' he says.

'Opposite,' I echo.

'Opposite.' He points to where his name is written on the door, and I remember him laughing.

And then Leon, who has followed me out to the corridor. I'd guess they're all in their twenties like me, and it's clear none are nurses or doctors.

Leon, pulling down his mask, says, 'See. This is us.' He rolls back the sleeve of his robe and shows me his white hospital bracelet and then Rachel shows me hers, and Yahiko and Piper. I hold out my own wrist and show them mine.

'Everyone else has left,' Yahiko says. 'Or they're –' He pauses as though he doesn't know how to say it.

'Dead,' Rachel whispers.

I look from one to the other as they each speak.

'No,' Piper says. 'We don't know that. We're alive. Other people will be alive. And they'll come to get us.'

'Dead!' Rachel shouts the word and we flinch collectively. Leon puts his arm around her shoulders as though he's seen this behaviour before.

'Look,' he says, and now he's the one talking to a child. 'Neffy has survived.' And they stare at me again like I'm some kind of miracle. Rachel is gulping, trying to control herself.

'Maybe Neffy will be our saviour,' Yahiko says, and I can tell he's joking as a way of also calming Rachel.

'Maybe,' Piper says as though she means it.

'Your saviour?' I give a hollow laugh. 'Is this part of the trial? Was there an extra sheet in the paperwork I forgot to read? What's going on?' The muscles in my legs are shaking as I stand in the chilled air, trying to make everything slot together. I stare back at them but I know from their faces and from what I saw outside and from what I remember, that the world has turned without me.

'A pandemic and stuff,' Yahiko says, as though explaining it to an idiot.

'Are you going to stay?' Rachel asks. She has a child's voice, high and plaintive. A strand of her long hair is caught in her lipstick. I might have got her age wrong and she could be still a teenager.

'Give her a chance,' Leon says. 'She's only just out of bed.'

'Have you all been ill too?' I ask, staring beyond them down the lit corridor to the nurses' station. It's a mess of folders and charts; a computer keyboard is hanging off the side of the desk, dangling from its cable. They watch me without answering as though they haven't heard my question, and beyond the nurses' station I see that all the doors are closed, and I sense the vacancy of the other rooms. The only sounds are from these four as they watch to see what I will do. I go unsteadily past the room next to mine – Orla, the name says on the door – and the one after that which has no name, to the nurses' station. I stretch over the counter and pick up the telephone. I watch them standing and waiting as I hold it to my ear. No dial tone. No sound at all.

'Say you'll stay,' Rachel says.

My brain is sending messages to my legs, telling me to run. But I'm not sure they're capable of running. And where would I go?

48

Dearest H,

Octopuses are walkers. They usually only 'swim' to escape from danger or to catch prey. They are generally seabed or reef dwellers and their locomotion of choice is walking on their arms. Out of the water some species will use their suckers to drag themselves from rock pool to rock pool. In New Zealand, at the national aquarium, a Common New Zealand octopus escaped from his tank one night when the lid was accidentally left ajar and he disappeared. It's believed he went down the drain in the floor and escaped out to sea. I like to imagine him drawing in the water from the drain and pushing it out through his syphon in order to move forward, his body elongating to the width of the pipe in the way that humans and their possessions will expand or contract to the size of the space we're given.

Neffy

I follow the sound of talking to the staffroom. The door is behind the nurses' station, and it feels as though I'm violating some nurse/patient code to push it open and go in. The room is small and windowless with four lit panels in the ceiling. I take in an aluminium sink and drainer, a full-size fridge, a toaster, kettle, mugs hanging from hooks below a cupboard, and the four people I've just met seated around a central table, eating and discussing something urgent. It's cold in here too, the air conditioning blowing down, but the atmosphere is heated with a mood of disagreement, not anger, but vehemence and rivalry, and when they see me in the doorway they pause, spoons raised to their mouths as though guilty at having been caught in the act of making decisions without me.

'Neffy,' Leon says quickly, standing, the legs of his chair squeaking against the floor. 'How are you feeling?'

I've removed the cannulas from my arms and I've showered. Under the water, inside the blast and noise, I was able to calm myself a little, the flow removing the feeling of anticipation, the butterflies, the tingling in my fingertips, the lump in my throat, that damn cat-sized furball in my chest. But as soon as I stepped out, it came racing back. I'd found clean clothes and I'd made the bed with a clean sheet and duvet cover, which Yahiko had brought me. And now I am also dressed in several layers, and on top of it all the unit's robe with *Vaccine BioPharm* and *Your Dreams, Our Reality* embroidered across my left breast.

'A bit better, thanks,' I say. I'm not sure I do feel better, but I am my father's child, always polite in the face of illness.

'Do you want some breakfast?' Piper says and Rachel takes hold of the sleeve of my robe and pulls me down to the empty seat beside her.

'Sit here. Sit with me.' She has gel nails, pink with blue flames twisting up from her cuticles. Close to, her skin is smooth and flawless, and her eyes are lined expertly in black with a smoky blue blended across her lids.

Yahiko picks up the cardboard pot in front of him and eats a spoonful. He waggles the pot at me, cheerily. 'Porridge with maple syrup.'

'Maple-*style* syrup,' Rachel says, wrapping her hands around her pot, fingernails clicking. 'There was yogurt and porridge with berries, but Leon ate them all.' She says it like he's been a naughty boy.

'I didn't want to get scurvy,' Leon says, scraping out the last of his pot. 'And there were only four.'

'I'll get you some.' Piper goes through a door marked KITCHEN.

'The orange juice has gone too.' Rachel leans in. 'One of us,' she says the words with emphasis and eye-rolling, 'had more than their fair share in the first few days.'

'Piper is food monitor now, apparently,' Yahiko says.

'The staff left all sorts of things in their fridge,' Rachel chatters on. 'Bread and margarine, chocolate. But,' she points a decorated nail at Yahiko, 'he ate it.'

'Wait. What? Why are you talking about food when . . .' I say.

'It's breakfast?' Yahiko says, looking to the other two for their reactions.

'No, I mean . . .' I shake my head to clear it. 'I don't understand. What the fuck has happened?'

Piper has returned silently with another pot of porridge and there is a moment of stillness, each waiting, it seems, for someone else to explain.

Leon starts. 'The new variant? Didn't you hear about that before you got ill?'

'The one that causes memory loss?'

'Memory loss because of brain swelling,' he says.

'And everyone who gets it dies,' Rachel says, dramatically.

'It seems to be incredibly virulent and very infectious.' The way Piper stares at me is intense and I look away.

'And it's still out there,' Rachel says, waving towards the window.

'But couldn't someone have done something? The government, the police?'

'They imposed a twenty-four-hour curfew and the army

51

tried to clear the streets of cars and bodies, in the cities at least,' Leon says.

'Bodies?' I say. 'In the streets?' And I remember the pictures on the news of the people beside the road near Dover.

'And riots in the supermarkets, hospitals that couldn't cope with the people who were sick, or dead, or forgetting.'

'I saw a video of people banging on the doors of a hospital wanting to get in but I don't know why they would have wanted to go in there.' Rachel shudders.

'It happened so fast,' Leon says.

'Everyone was told to stay indoors,' Rachel adds. 'They said people would get food deliveries, but no one ever came.'

'I can't believe it,' I say.

Piper puts water in the kettle and switches it on. 'You didn't hear the fights, or the sirens? None of it?' she asks.

'I remember a blue light flashing,' I say. 'That's it.'

'And then it was silent and that was worse,' Leon says. 'We watched it online until the technology died, and then we watched it out of the window.'

'Not even Leon could get the Wi-Fi working,' Rachel says.

'Gangs of men, stuff you wouldn't believe. Didn't you hear the dogs?' he asks. I shake my head. 'Well, they've nearly all moved off somewhere else now. Anyway, the nurses in the unit left – Boo, did you have Boo? – and the next shift didn't come in.'

'And all the volunteers went too, apart from us,' Piper adds.

Yahiko, who hasn't said anything, lays his spoon on the table next to his empty pot. He looks traumatized. We're all traumatized.

One wall of the staffroom has a row of lockers and on another is a large whiteboard on the left of which someone has written *Day Zero* in black marker. Below that are seven vertical strokes. A large 21 is circled. Leon, sitting the other side of me and seeing me looking, says, 'Day Zero is virus day, when everything went to shit.'

'I can't believe it,' I say again.

'I still can't believe it either,' Rachel says and gives a sob. Leon reaches across and squeezes her hand.

'What's the twenty-one?' I ask.

'Day Twenty-one is when we'll be rescued,' Piper says. Yahiko raises his eyebrows high above the frames of his glasses. Piper puts the porridge in front of me. Her fingers are the size of a child's, each nail clean and squarely filed. 'Careful, it's hot. Give it a stir.' I'm not sure I'm hungry. Leon rests on the back legs of his chair and reaches into a drawer for a spoon. 'It's when the trial ends,' Piper continues. 'When the army or the government come to get us.'

I hold the pot of porridge to my nose to smell it; there's no smell. 'What? Really? They're coming?'

'No, obviously they're not,' Yahiko says. 'The army and the government will all be dead by now or in some bunker somewhere without an internet connection, wanking over old porn mags because there's nothing else to do.'

'God, Yahiko!' Rachel says.

And I have a glimpse of how fragile their little grouping is. Fraying threads tied together by calamity and shared need, each tugging on an end hoping to make the knot firmer but risking undoing the messy tangle. I take a spoonful of porridge but taste only sweetness, no maple syrup, no oatiness.

'I think I've lost my sense of taste,' I say.

'What about smell?' Piper asks and the others wait for my answer.

I lift my nose and sniff the room and then sniff at the pot of porridge again. 'Nope, nothing.'

'It's one of the symptoms, nothing to worry about.'

'I suppose it'll come back.'

'I'm sure,' she says.

On the right-hand side of the whiteboard is a list of food items including curries, pasta dishes, porridge, and a number beside each one: 2, 5, 7. Porridge is the highest at 33.

'Is that everything you have to eat?' I nod towards the list.

Yahiko picks up his spoon and licks the arched bowl of it. 'Piper won't let us go near the food or the industrial microwave she's got in there.' He waves his spoon towards the kitchen. 'She parcels it out like a dinner lady.'

After only three spoons of porridge my stomach is full and I could do with going back to bed to think, to look at everything they've told me from all angles. It's like the first night I spent with Justin – in the morning I needed time away from him to process what had happened, who I'd just met and what I thought about it all. But now I already have a feeling that I might need to be part of this group, attach myself to them even if only for a short while. I don't want to be alone.

'Piper was going to be on *Bake Off*,' Rachel says.

'I only applied,' Piper corrects her. 'Then the pandemic started.'

'And yes, that's all the food we've got,' Leon says. 'We're already on rations. Two meals a day.'

'How long will it last?'

'Until the army arrives.' Piper taps on ㉑ and rubs out the number 33 beside *porridge* and writes 29. Yahiko tuts.

'I hope you've updated your calculations to include Neffy,' Leon says, and Piper's expression moves through horror to embarrassment. She changes 29 to 28. 'If you're staying,' Leon says to me in a way that lets me know he wants me to stay.

'I don't know,' I say, but no one hears.

Yahiko is shaking his head and saying, 'Piper was hoping you wouldn't make it so she could have more to eat.'

'Don't be ludicrous,' she snaps.

'That's not even funny, Yahiko,' Rachel says.

I try to work out what the dynamics and alliances are, not ready to pick a side if I should need to: Yahiko v. Piper? Leon and Rachel?

'Fourteen days with four of us,' Leon says. 'And eleven point two days with five. Or actually eleven days, four hours and forty-eight minutes.'

'How many days until the army comes?' Rachel looks from one to the other.

'Fourteen,' I say to her quietly.

'They're not coming,' Yahiko says in a moronic voice. 'No one's coming.'

'So what are we going to eat for the last however many days before the army comes?' Rachel asks the room in her baby voice.

'We'll have to eat less,' Leon says. 'It'll have to last longer.'

'Or someone could go outside and get some more,' Yahiko says. 'Just saying.'

'It won't be necessary for anyone to go outside,' Piper says. 'We've got enough food if we're careful.' She reminds me of a GP I had in Plymouth who I'd been to see about something routine – straight-talking, no nonsense. The appointment was meant to last fifteen minutes and she had me out in five with my prescription in my hand.

'But the food will run out eventually.' Yahiko emphasizes

the last three words individually as though Piper won't understand them.

'The army will have found us by then.'

He breathes out theatrically.

'Do you want some tea, Neffy?' Rachel gets up with a lot of noise. She fetches a mug and pours weak tea from the pot on the table before I've answered. 'We haven't got any milk left but we might have some sugar in the cupboard.'

'How do you know what it's like outside if you haven't been out?' I say. 'Maybe it's not as bad as you think.' No one speaks and I keep going. 'Aren't there shops, down the main road? I'm sure I saw some when I arrived.' I don't actually remember what shops are outside but don't all London streets have mini-markets?

'You wouldn't want to go outside, not if you can help it. Not for a while,' Rachel says. 'The big supermarkets were emptied in a couple of hours. I saw it on Instagram.' She closes her eyes as though to shut it out. She groans and I put my hand on hers and she grips mine.

'A few more days and it'll probably be safe enough,' Yahiko says. 'But no turning on the lights in your room,' he tells me. 'Don't move the blind on your outside window and no more sticking up messages.'

'What?' I say. 'Why?'

'I'd take the light bulbs out if I could but I need a special tool to get into the light fittings.'

'People might be watching.' Rachel's fingers tighten around my hand. 'Yahiko put some tape over my light switches so I don't forget. He could do the same on yours, if you want.'

'Who might be watching?'

'Gangs of men, outside.' She whispers it in horror. 'Breaking into places. Yahiko saw them.'

After I'd first met the four of them in the corridor, when I'd gone back into my room to shower, I'd tried to turn the TV on. 'Television on,' I said. 'TV on!' It stayed dark. I checked my phone but I still didn't have any messages, and no internet connection, no signal, although the power was working. And I looked out of my window down to the alleyway again but saw nothing. The street was empty and, although I stayed watching for five minutes, maybe more, no vehicles or people passed the junction with the main road. Across from my room, the lights were still off in Sophia's flat and I didn't see any movement. I'd seen her message again, though: YES, I'M HEAR, with its typo in big bold letters.

The air-conditioning vent in the ceiling blows down on us in the staffroom.

'My mum,' Piper says, pouring herself some more tea, 'cooks my dad a fried egg every morning for breakfast. A fried egg every morning before work.'

It feels as though we're all aware that she says *cooks* and not *cooked*. I don't feel it's my place to ask, not yet.

Rachel makes a face. 'Urgh! Eggs. No way. All that slippery slimy stuff.'

'I wonder if she can still get eggs,' Piper murmurs.

'They're all right if you flip them,' Yahiko says.

'Sunny side over,' Leon says.

'Still disgusting,' Rachel says.

'It's over easy,' Piper says.

'What?' Leon asks.

'Over easy,' Piper repeats.

'Not sunny side over,' Yahiko joins in.

'But it's sunny side up,' Leon says.

'Yes, but it's over easy for when you turn them,' Yahiko says.

'Please can we stop talking about eggs.' Rachel tucks her chin into her neck and turns her mouth down.

'It's sunny side down,' Leon says. 'Isn't it?'

'It's over easy,' Yahiko and Piper both say at the same time.

'I'm not sure,' Rachel says. 'I hate eggs.'

I think about the meals Margot made for me in Greece and the ripe tomatoes and the thick slabs of salty feta, and I remember the roast chicken and the shepherd's pies Mum would cook, and I wonder with a stab of something that feels physical whether maybe Justin did make it back somehow. He said he would wait for me in Dorset and surely he'd hope I would make my way there too. How long would it take me to walk? Days perhaps. Maybe there are taxis. The others don't really know. The cost would be horrendous but Clive would pay. How long would it take to drive, three or four hours? Mum and Clive and Justin are probably in Dorset now, worrying about how to reach me.

'Neffy?' Leon says.

'What? Sorry?' I rest my spoon on the table; I've eaten enough although I haven't finished the porridge. They're looking at me.

'What do you think? Is it over easy or sunny side down?' Rachel says.

'Oh.' I shake my head to focus and then pretend to think. 'Yes,' I say, definitively, and Rachel sways into me, laughs and puts her head on my shoulder. I like the feel of it, the friendly weight of it. I take a sip of tea from the mug with the company's name. Someone has scratched out the *p* and it reads *Vaccine Bio harm*. 'Tea's warm,' I say. 'But why is this place so fricking cold?' It's meant to be a joke, but Rachel immediately sits upright and we're all quiet until Piper and

Leon start talking at the same time. Piper stops and Leon says, 'Yahiko fiddled with the air con, he took the cover off the control box and now it's stuck on arctic. Fucking idiot.'

Without looking up, Yahiko raises his middle finger and Leon laughs. The atmosphere in the room relaxes and they get up, Piper to wash the spoons and the mugs, Leon to collect the rubbish into a bag which he puts down a chute in the wall. I see that in only seven days the in-jokes and banter have been sorted; who is friends with who, and where they sit around the table, as though we've started at a new school but I arrived a week late and they're working out whether I might make an advantageous friend, even one worth swapping for the previous friend they'd made.

'Great that your appetite is returning.' Yahiko is eyeing my porridge and I slide the pot across the table.

Piper intercepts and pushes it back to me. 'You should eat it,' she says. 'Get your strength up, and there won't be anything else until this evening.'

'I think my stomach has shrunk.'

'Take it and finish it later.' She stands with her legs apart and her arms folded, a Peter Pan figure, with neat, boyish features.

Rachel wipes the table and jokes about something with Leon, their heads close. I wonder whether they're getting together or are already there. In this room without windows, it's easy to imagine we're on some kind of self-help weekend retreat with a schedule of therapy and classes we've signed up for where we're encouraged to share our feelings, meals together around the table, and then on Sunday evening before we go home, we'll swap numbers, hug each other and promise to keep in touch, but we probably never will.

'What about the water and electricity?' The porridge is swelling in my stomach, my digestion is telling me I need to sleep. 'How come they're still on if the whole world has gone to shit?'

'There's a generator in the basement. Leon and Yahiko went down to see,' Piper says. 'You can hear it through the waste chute.'

'You went down to the basement?'

'The emergency stairs are in reception,' Rachel says. 'Leon and Yahiko checked out the first-floor offices too – sounded really spooky.' She waits – a prompt for one of them to tell me.

'Well, yeah,' Yahiko starts. 'Leon and I went down to see, the generator looks like pretty state-of-the-art stuff. New, I'd say. Seems to be running okay, not that I know much about generators.'

'Tell her about the offices,' Rachel says, as though a brilliant story is coming.

Yahiko is at the door, leaving. He pauses, looks out into the corridor. 'See you later,' he says, and he's away, leaving Leon to tell.

Leon seems to falter. 'Everyone had gone in a hurry. Chairs knocked over, stuff left behind.'

Before I was accepted on the trial, I'd come twice to the offices on the first floor to go through various tests, physical and mental, to see whether I was a suitable candidate. I wasn't asked about my work history, I was vague about my father, and a scan of my body wasn't required. Clearly, since I'm here, I passed. I can't work out yet if I was lucky or not. I hadn't paid much attention to the offices.

'But the birds, tell her about the birds,' Rachel says excitedly.

60

'A couple of crows had got in,' Leon says without enthusiasm.

'What?' Rachel is disappointed. 'Yahiko told me it was parakeets. A whole flock of them.'

'It might have been parakeets. I'm no good with birds,' Leon says, and Rachel cuffs him playfully.

'Yahiko's such a liar.'

Piper cuts in. 'We're not sure about the water. Yahiko reckons it could stop at any time or it might already be polluted. We're boiling it – you shouldn't drink any straight from your bathroom tap.'

Maybe the disbelief at all this, at how calm and organized they seem, shows on my face, because Leon says, 'Yeah, it took us a while to get used to the idea of it but you can't live in a state of shock for very long. You'll adapt quickly enough. Unless you're Rachel, in which case you'll blub at any opportunity.' She pokes her tongue out at him.

'Is there anything you need?' Piper taps with her finger on my shoulder. 'You should still take it easy for a while. Drink lots of water.' Her hand squeezes and there is something overprotective about it, but I smile up at her, probably more of a grimace.

'I'm fine, thanks. I think I'll go back to bed for a bit.'

'Good girl. See you all later.' She leaves, but the warmth and the heaviness of her hand remains.

Rachel is at the door now. 'You coming?' she says to Leon.

'Soon,' he says, and she looks from Leon to me and back again. He's sitting at the table opposite me and hasn't moved. She tuts, says something under her breath and leaves. As soon as she's gone, he stands and picks up one of the jugs of water and a glass. He hands me the rest of my porridge. 'Come on. Piper's right, you need to take it easy.'

Back in my room, Leon waits for me to sit on the bed and then he pours some water. My stomach muscles are trembling either from the food or from a nervous energy. He goes to leave, but I say, 'Tell me something normal.'

'Normal?'

I wave towards the window. 'Something from before.'

'Normal.' He shoves his hands deep inside his robe pockets. 'I don't know if I can remember normal.'

'Anything. Please.'

He thinks. 'I once saw Nina Simone at the Barbican.'

'Nina Simone?'

'My mum took me.'

'That must have been amazing.'

'She saved up for two tickets for months and then when we got there it turned out I was allowed in for free.'

'For free?'

'I was one year old and strapped to her in a baby carrier.' I smile.

'Apparently it *was* amazing. Everyone stood up and sang "We Shall Overcome". Nina too. Just a shame I slept through it.'

'So you didn't exactly get to see Nina Simone at the Barbican.'

'No, I suppose not.' He sounds sad.

'And more recently? What were you doing?'

'Uni, mostly. Some tech stuff too. Actually, it is quite interesting. I'll tell you sometime, show you maybe, but not now. You look exhausted.'

'It's too hard to take in. It feels so surreal. Like you're all playing some shitty joke on me or it's part of the trial.'

He lets his head hang. 'For the first couple of days I just

looked out of the window, checked my phone, thought about going outside to see what was really happening.'

'I had these weird dreams when I was ill and I keep thinking maybe I'm still dreaming.'

'Got as far as the lift and then went back to my room.'

'It's really happened, though, hasn't it?'

'It's probably worse for you because you woke up in the aftermath.'

'Did you all have the same reaction as me to the virus?'

'Didn't you know? We weren't given it, we never even got the vaccine.'

'You didn't get the vaccine? None of you?'

'Yeah, well, there was a delay.' He shifts about, doesn't seem to want to explain. 'And then Yahiko saw the reaction you were having and they stopped the trial.'

'Really? They stopped the trial? I don't remember that.'

'He said you were pretty out of it, from what he saw.'

'I remember Boo coming in.'

'Everyone started leaving at about the same time. It was chaos. You'll have to ask him. You should sleep now.'

'But if I was given the virus and survived, that means the vaccine worked.'

Leon is at the door. 'We've all been wondering about that.' He doesn't look at me as he speaks. 'You were pretty sick, and anyway, we searched for it but it's not here. They must have brought in exactly the right amount or else taken the spares away. You should sleep.' He opens the door. 'See you later. Piper gets dinner ready at eight.'

'Leon,' I say, and he stops. 'Why didn't you leave?'

He blinks for a moment and I think maybe my question was too blunt. 'My mum died,' he says. 'Early on, you know, at the start of the pandemic.' He sounds like he's trying to tough it out. 'No brothers or sisters. Neighbours and friends, yeah, but no one I'd risk going through that for.' He nods to the window, puffs his cheeks, blows out air. 'At least she missed all this.' He looks at me. 'I don't know how you survived it, but you did. You actually fucking did.'

Dearest H,

I read a scientific paper a few years ago in General and Comparative Endocrinology *about the olfactory sense in the octopus. The paper suggested the animal's well-developed sense of smell happens via two dimples in its mantle. For most of an octopus's life these are used to help with the hunt for food but at a certain point in a female's maturation the sense is switched off as are some of her optic abilities, when she moves from concern for sustenance to that of mating. She's no longer interested in food, and therefore no longer needs her magnificent eyesight or her sense of smell if she is only going to be protecting her eggs at the bottom of a dark ocean. The giving up of a life for the continuation of the species.*

Neffy

When I wake, my mouth is parched from the air conditioning, and my face – the only thing sticking out from under the duvet – is cold, the tip of my nose a chilly point. My sleep has been restless. I kept thinking I could hear a distant siren, warning of some imminent catastrophe: tsunami, fireball, earthquake. Like the outdoor warning system that I heard broadcast on a Tuesday at noon in San Francisco. The seemingly inexorable rise of that echoing bellow and my internal alarm rising with it, the temporary relief of the fall. And then the male voice from a 1950s B-movie: 'This is a test, this is only a test.' But in London there's no siren, it seems there was never time.

I'm still in bed, the warmest place, when Rachel's shouting gets me up – something about people being outside. It must be around midday looking at the light, and I pull on more clothes and my robe and go to reception. I can't run – even walking makes my stomach muscles ache. The others arrive too and Rachel hurries us into her room and to the window, where the four of them crouch below the sill. Her room is nearer the front of the building than mine, and she has a clear view of the main road across to a mobile phone shop with a smashed window and three shuttered shops: Charlie's Casual Wear, Miz Nails and Easy Carpets & Flooring. It seems so open and exposed after the limited view from my window. On the corner, in the middle of the road, a red double-decker has smashed into the front of a car, concertinaing the bonnet and shattering the windscreen. An ambulance is stopped beside them, and its back doors are open. The car doors are also open, but I can see that it's empty, the blue light on the ambulance is not flashing and no one is about, no drivers, no passengers, no bystanders. The advert on the side of the bus has a line drawing of a pair of clasped hands under running water. *Save Lives. Wash Your Hands* the advert says as if that is all it would have taken.

'My God,' I say. 'Is anyone hurt? Where are they?'

'Not that,' Yahiko says. 'That happened days ago.' When he sees I'm standing, still looking out, he grabs the bottom of my robe and tugs. 'Get down,' he hisses as though the non-existent people outside might hear him and look up. I kneel between Rachel and Leon.

'There,' Rachel says. She points down to the right and we see in the distance two people walking in our direction: a child and an adult. The child is in front and during the few minutes it takes them to come closer it becomes clear that she or he is leading the man by the hand. When I look out at the alley below my own window, I can fool myself into thinking that nothing has happened, that everything is going on as before in the world and the alleyway is empty because no one uses it much, whereas here, in Rachel's room, the smashed shop window, the abandoned crash and the empty street make it horribly clear that everything has changed. I start to shake. Reality confronting me makes me remember that Justin is probably on a plane in Sweden and that Mum and Clive are still in Denmark. I remember Rachel – was it only this morning? – shouting, 'Dead!'

Rachel, I can tell, is ready to duck if the people on the street should look up. The child – a girl, I decide, of eight or nine, in shorts and a loose top and hair that looks ratty even from here – is walking with purpose down the middle of the road, tugging the man along behind. He is too big for his short-sleeved shirt, which strains around the buttons, and he is spilling out of his jeans. He waddles and dawdles, looking about him and up at the sky. 'Memory loss *and* Dropsy,' Leon says.

'New variant,' Piper adds.

The two are beside our building, nearly directly below us, when the man stops, pulls his hand out from the girl's and searches for something in his jeans' front pocket and then the back as though he's realized he's forgotten his wallet or phone. I can see his swollen face and protuberant eyes. The girl is patient, waiting, looking with curiosity at the accident, the ambulance, the empty car.

'Don't go in the bus,' Rachel whispers like a prayer. 'Please don't go in the bus.' The girl turns to the man, catches hold of his hand, gives it a tug, and they continue down the road.

I put my palm flat on the window. 'Wait,' I say.

'No!' Yahiko reaches across Leon and grabs my wrist to pull my hand down, and with only a little resistance I let him.

'We're not going to get them?'

'Of course we're not,' Piper says, standing. The girl and the man have moved past our building now. 'They've gone, it's fine.' And I realize we hadn't been watching in order to bring them up here but crouching to hide.

Leon stands too and I sense him looking at me, but I stay kneeling beside Rachel, and he leaves with Yahiko and Piper. When the girl and the man have disappeared completely from view, Rachel says, 'Do you want a mug of boiled water? We aren't supposed to make tea in the middle of the day, but I like to pretend it's tea.'

'That would be nice,' I say.

When she brings the mugs from the kitchen we sit side by side in her bed, tucked close together under her duvet. 'I heard the accident happen,' Rachel says. We're both looking straight ahead at her dark TV screen. Below it is her desk covered with neat clusters of pots and tubes of make-up. 'It was early in the morning. It woke me up. There was this crunch of metal and a horn, and I got out of bed and went to the window. I hid under it like we did just then, so they wouldn't see me. There'd been some other stuff going on that night, noises and screams, and I'd put my head under my pillow. Is that terrible? It is terrible, isn't it? I was still deciding whether I should leave, you know, get out. This was a day or so after you'd been given the virus. I just couldn't make my mind up about anything. But anyway, when I heard the crash I got up to watch.' She sips some of her hot water. 'The passenger in the car and the bus driver got out and started shouting at each other. I was worried about the car driver because he didn't get out at first although I could see that the airbag had gone off. Then a couple of people got off the bus and stood around watching like people do after an accident, just gawping. And then they eventually walked away, checking their phones. Then an ambulance arrived soon after that but I could see straight away, like, that the paramedics had something wrong with them. God knows why they were at work. Their bodies were swollen, you know, and one of them, it was so bad it was like someone was squeezing him round the waist.' She lifts her elbows and clutches her mug with both hands. 'His neck and his head were kind of squeezing out of the top of his uniform. Like, I don't know, toothpaste from a tube.'

'Oh, Rachel,' I say. 'I'm sorry.'

She runs her fingernails down through her straightened hair. 'They were both just really confused about what they were meant to be doing. It was like a Harold Lloyd movie.' She looks at me sideways. 'I was doing Film Studies at Sussex before all this. Like it was slapstick except it wasn't funny. The driver of the car got out in the end and he didn't seem too badly hurt. No police came. No one else came either. After about half an hour of trying to get the paramedics to do something, the car driver and the passenger tried to flag down a taxi. And that was weaving along the road, nearly crashing into the bus. But it didn't stop and they just walked away. Other cars came past and they didn't stop either, and someone was running and screaming and screaming while she was running, you know. The bus driver and the paramedics left when it was getting dark but not in their cars, like, they just wandered off too.'

'That must have been terrible to see.'

'Oh, that's not it,' Rachel says. 'That's just the start. The next day, I looked out again and the car, the ambulance and the bus were all there, and then I saw one passenger still sitting on the bus, on the top deck at the front where I used to sit with my dad when I was little. This woman was staring out and then she turned her head, and I swear she looked in here. Right into my room and smiled at me.' Rachel gulps. I take her mug from her and put it on the bedside table. 'Her eyes were really bulging and she just kept turning her head and looking at me.' Rachel's voice is breaking. 'I didn't know what to do. What was I supposed to do? I wanted to put the blind down but I knew Yahiko would kill me if I did after what he saw out the window.' She bites her lip. 'Oh God. So I tried to stop looking. I went into Piper's room and made paper cranes with her, and I only came back in here when it was dark. But then in the morning when it got light I saw the woman was still there and when I was standing watching, she just disappeared. Honest to God. It was like she'd been waiting all night for me to look out and she just bent over as though she'd leaned down to pick something up off the floor. Some bit of rubbish, you know. I waited for her to get off the bus, cos the doors were still wide open. I watched for ages, for more than an hour. I didn't take my eyes off that bus but that woman never came downstairs. She never got off.' Rachel is crying as she finishes, rocking backwards and forwards, and I put my hand on her arm, willing to hold her if she turns to me, but perhaps we aren't ready for that because she doesn't turn or open her arms; instead we stay in that position and I cannot think what I can do to make it better.

'Please don't leave,' she says between sobs.

I don't answer, and I don't ask her why she didn't go outside to see if she could help, because I didn't rap with my knuckles on the glass for the child and the man to look up, I didn't run downstairs and invite them in. A hand on a window is not enough.

When her crying subsides, Rachel picks up her phone and holds it out in front of us, slightly higher than our eyes, and rests her head on my shoulder like she did in the staffroom. She's taken a dozen pictures by the time I've realized what she's doing and I've arranged my face. She flicks through them, selecting one and changing it to a silver-tinted noir. I look startled and my face is still wider, puffier than it should be, my eyes still slightly protruding, but the greyscale has brought out Rachel's freckles. She must have taken off her orange-coloured foundation earlier in the day but her lips seem plumper from crying and her eyes, under perfectly plucked and drawn eyebrows, are magnified and liquid, and a single tear rests below one of them. She saves the picture, seems satisfied.

'Instagram will come back one day, don't you think?' she says. 'Or something else. Something better.'

'Maybe.' I don't know what to say. I haven't thought about

social media at all. I never had a profile on any of the places, I was only ever a lurker.

'Leon's really techie. He says it'll come back.'

She flicks through other pictures on her phone, mostly of herself wearing different outfits, which seem to be taken in the full-length mirror on her wardrobe door. She flicks further back in time, colours and shapes blurring. She stops the run and moves more slowly through photos of herself in a black swimming costume with an indoor pool in the background, a diving board, people in the water. 'I was getting to be a good swimmer,' she says.

'You'll be able to go swimming again, I'm sure.' I think about what swimming pools might be like without anyone to maintain them, put the chemicals in, clean them. 'In the sea, at least.'

'It's okay, I suppose, you knowing.' I can tell she wants to say something and that she has some pride in it, whatever it is. 'I had this thing, an affair, an intimate relationship, a whatever, with my swimming coach. Apparently, it was inappropriate because he was so much older than me.' She emphasizes *inappropriate*, makes it into a joke. 'Only fourteen years but he turned out to be a shit anyway.'

'I'm sorry,' I say. Fourteen years was the age gap between Margot and my father. It had never seemed much to me. I pass Rachel her mug. 'Here,' I say. 'Have some more tea while it's still warm. It's Earl Grey with a slice of lemon.' She smiles, takes the mug and drinks, holding her hands around it with their painted fiery talons. I see that one of them has peeled off to reveal an ordinary pale-pink nail underneath.

'Have you got someone?' she asks. 'You know, to go home to?'

'I'm not sure.'

I expect her to ask more but like a child she turns the conversation back to herself. 'I'm not sure either. Maybe my dad. I saw the international space station go past last night.' She licks the side of a finger and wipes carefully under both eyes. 'He used to tell me about it. The people in it and what they were probably doing, you know, how they have to poo into a bag that gets sucked away, how they don't sit down when they eat – all that space stuff, he loved it. *Star Wars*, *Star Trek*, he was such a geek. When I saw it go past I tried to imagine what it's like for them, the astronauts. Knowing something is happening down on earth but not being able to do anything about it. Maybe they don't even know what it is. They just have to wait until the air runs out or the food.'

'I can't imagine,' I say, but I am picturing Justin and the plane on the tarmac in Malmö.

'It's so awful.' She sounds as though she's going to cry again.

'I've been thinking about what's happened to the animals,' I say, to distract her. 'My friend Nicos works in a zoo.'

'Oh God. London Zoo?'

'In Australia.'

'I hadn't thought about the zoos. What'll happen to the animals? Maybe they'll be able to jump their fences and escape cos the electricity's off.'

'I used to work with octopuses before I came on the trial.'

'We might look out the window and see some giraffes and tigers strolling down the road. That would be mad.'

'I'm not sure giraffes and tigers really socialize together, and I think they might be kept in by more than just electric fences.'

'At least we *can* leave, I suppose.' She doesn't sound like she wants to. 'No one's keeping us here, are they?'

'They're not.' I thought about how a cage made of glass is still a cage but that the glass can be shattered if you have the strength and the courage. Or maybe you don't need to break it, maybe you only need to find the door, slide it open and step out.

'Neffy,' Rachel says, bringing me back to her and her room. 'If you do leave, will you take me with you?'

Dearest H,

My first job out of uni was as a Laboratory Research Assistant. I didn't think deeply about what I was applying for, I needed a job and I wanted to work with octopuses. I'm not going to say which institution I was employed by for fear of reprisals, confidentiality, and because of the Non-Disclosure Agreement they made me sign when I left. It was a prestigious study and I had been recommended by my tutor. I was too much of a coward to say I didn't want the job once I'd found out what it entailed.

Neffy

Day Eight

I wake at what could be two or three in the morning with my heart racing and some panicked dream about trying to run through water fading too quickly for me to grasp. No artificial lights show from my window but the sky is clear, the moon is a sliver and stars are scattered across the dark; pinpricks of light which can't have been seen in London for how long? Fifty years? A hundred? There's a meteor too, or more likely a satellite, moving slowly across my range of vision. The satellites will probably remain in the sky for years, circling the earth, taking their power from the sun, continuing to transmit their messages with nobody listening. I think of the conversation I had with Rachel about the space station and the zoos. Maybe some of the animals might have got out, but I know that most, if not all of the lab octopuses won't have been so lucky. And I begin to list the animals I can think of that live in aquariums: the sea urchins, and rays, and the starfish, and on and on until I make myself stop, and I think instead about what Rachel asked me. I can't take her with me if I do decide to go. I can't save her; I can barely save myself.

I wait for the pain of that awful list to dissipate so I can sleep but I'm restless, too contained by these four walls, and I put on my robe and silently go into the corridor. The only sound is the blowing of the air conditioning. The unit's blue low-level lighting is on, illuminating my socks and making an indigo tunnel of the corridor. If I were to turn left, I would come almost immediately to the reception area. But I turn right, holding out my hand so that my fingers graze the bumps of door frames and walls, past Yahiko's room and the Irish girl's, empty now. At the end I turn left now, sliding past Leon's closed door. Left once more, and I take the corridor that runs parallel to mine so that I have walked around the unit's central block, which contains two windowless bedrooms – one of which is Yahiko's – as well as the staffroom, kitchen, sluice and treatment room. Piper's and Rachel's rooms are on this corridor, two empty rooms between them. I think about the woman in the bus and Justin on his plane. Is he still on it or is he at his father's house, waiting? We weren't allowed to tell people the address of the unit and although he could probably work it out, if he made it back to England I don't think he'd come to London to look for me. He would wait in Dorset for me to come to him. If he's there at all.

My head is heavy, and the walk tiring. If I can't walk around a corridor how would I even make it to Dorset? Perhaps I should stay and build up my strength for a little longer? Last night, at dinner in the staffroom, they seemed happy to learn that I was vegetarian so that they could eat the meat dishes, and Piper heated up some cannelloni for me. I ate it because I thought I should, even though it was like eating tasteless pap. We sat in the same seats we'd sat in at breakfast and we talked about birthdays – Rachel is turning twenty soon – and the parties we'd had when we were children. Yahiko said his parents used to hire party planners for him and his brothers' birthdays. 'Everything coordinated, fancy food and party bags with gifts that cost more than the presents the other kids brought. I used to be so embarrassed. It was all too much, even for me, and when I was ten, I wouldn't eat the food. I got under the table and refused to come out. And my dad was so mad. He sent all the kids home and me up to my room with all the food. All the food from the table.'

'Oh God,' Rachel said.

'He made me lay it out on the floor and go to bed.'

'And?' Leon said.

'And in the morning it was gone and we never spoke about it and I never had another birthday party.'

'That's terrible,' Rachel said.

'I don't understand,' Leon said.

Yahiko looked like he regretted starting this story.

'Why did your dad do that, though?' Leon insisted.

'Shut up, Leon,' Rachel hissed.

When we left the staffroom, I saw that Leon and Rachel went in separate directions.

The end of Piper's and Rachel's corridor takes me back to reception and the long desk with the vase of flowers surrounded by dropped petals. The doors of the lift opposite the desk are kept ajar by a closed Apple Mac wedged in the gap. Yahiko has put it there for security to keep the carriage, or whatever it's called, on our floor. He's disabled the interior light, or it's burned out from being on for so long. Simply out of curiosity, I press the button on the intercom beside the lift and with a buzz and a flicker the little screen is illuminated and an overhead light comes on outside so that tiny patch of street is illuminated too. I release the button quickly, shocked by the artificial light, worrying about the warning the others gave of someone knowing we're here. But I cannot resist, and I press the button again to have another look at the outside: a fake world, grainy and grey. The fuzzy lines somehow suggest movement and the ground is shining as though it's been raining. I look in closer, my ear near the grille where the nurses once spoke to the volunteers when they arrived – where Boo must have first seen and spoken to me. Something moves past, a dark shape, gone in a second together with its sound like the single sweep of a broom through a puddle of water. I rear back, heart exploding, and let go of the button. Are people still roaming the streets, in the dark? And then another sound from behind me: the flip-flop of backless slippers coming up the corridor.

'Neffy? Are you okay?' It's Piper.

'I was just . . .' I start, but I don't want to be told off about putting on the outside light. 'I'm fine,' I finish. I take my hand from my throat. I'm not completely convinced by her tone of surprise at finding me here; I wonder if she heard me go past her room and followed.

'What are you doing up? Couldn't sleep?' In the dimness of reception I see her brush a few of the flowers' fallen petals into her palm.

'Can anyone?'

She comes closer as though to work out what I was doing. Piper is small with sharp edges, a definite line to her jaw as though drawn in charcoal, square corners on her eyebrows, which are now puckered together, and tiny sticking-out ears. She still wears a woolly hat and she seems to have on proper pyjamas under her robe.

'You weren't about to leave, were you?' she asks.

'No, of course not.'

'Not flitting off in the night without telling anyone.'

'No, I wouldn't do that.'

'Does that mean you're going to stay?'

'I'm not sure.'

'You know we'd love it if you stayed.'

'Thank you.' It feels as though she means it but also that she has another agenda which I can't work out.

'You have somewhere to go to?'

'Maybe my stepfather's house in Dorset although I don't know if anyone will be there.'

'That's a long way.'

'What were you doing up?' I ask to deflect her questions. I don't want to provide answers to Piper when I don't know the answer myself: whether to stay or to go.

'Just prowling. Checking the windows are closed and the doors are locked, metaphorically speaking. Silly, really. After Day Zero, I didn't sleep for four nights in a row and, when I did, I woke up not believing it, every time.' She clenches and unclenches her fist, watching the petals fold and crease, and I expect to smell their sharp decay but there's nothing.

'I found a corner of the seating,' she says, 'where the air conditioning doesn't blow.' She sits down, shuffles along. 'Here,' she pronounces and pats the space beside her, and I go and sit. 'I've also got somewhere I could go, if I wanted.'

I pull my knees up, my feet on the seat, and wrap my robe around them, although she's right, we're not being blown on. It's almost warm.

'But you haven't gone?'

Piper shuffles back and with her spine against the seat her feet don't touch the floor. 'Yahiko has a theory that we were all accepted for the trial because none of us has anyone close, no partners, and therefore no one available to sue Vaccine BioPharm' – she lifts her eyes to the sign behind the desk – 'if it all went wrong. It's an interesting idea, but he isn't right.' She looks at me without turning her head, giving me an opportunity to explain my own situation and who might be waiting for me in Dorset. When I don't, she carries on. 'My parents are at home in West London. Parents whom I love, and love me, and know how important this trial is.'

'They didn't come to get you?' I'm thinking, clearly they couldn't, and wondering if she hasn't admitted this to herself yet.

'They knew I wouldn't have gone with them. Not like most of the other volunteers who just upped and left, as though their little lives – our little lives – are more important than what we're doing here.' She taps out the words *we're, doing, here*, with her forefinger on my knee.

'Aren't we just sitting it out? Trying to survive?' I move my legs, tucking them under me in a way that I hope looks as though I'm getting more comfortable. The irritating rhythm of her little tattoo remains on my skin long after she's removed her finger.

She looks incredulous. 'The trial is still ongoing. Someone *will* come.'

'What?' I've turned sideways and have been staring at her trim profile but she only now turns and looks at me.

'To collect the data,' she says. 'I've carried on recording my symptoms. Inputs, outputs. It's what we're being paid for.'

I hide my laugh. 'But you weren't even given the vaccine or the virus. Leon told me, none of you were given them. The trial is over. There's no data worth collecting and certainly no one to collect it. And we're not going to be paid, Piper, there won't be any bank accounts. No cards, no card readers, no money.' No debts, I think.

'No, well, okay. But someone will want to understand about how you were given them and survived.'

'Leon said they stopped the trial because Yahiko saw I was having a bad reaction.'

'And because everyone was leaving. But you did survive and someone will want to understand how you're immune. Maybe they'll want to use your antibodies to create a vaccine that definitely works. You'll be someone worth studying.'

'Am I immune, though? If I am, I'm not necessarily immune to the new variant.'

'Well –'

'Wouldn't it just be better to try and find where the vaccine they gave me is stored? At least that one worked, since I'm alive.'

'We're sure it's not in the unit. If it was going to be anywhere it would be in the treatment room where the drugs are stored. But that's just paracetamol and plasters. And downstairs is only offices. Anyway, you're here!' She slaps her thighs with her tiny hands as though I have solved everything. 'I'm not a scientist, though. I was studying Business and Human Resources Management at university. I don't know how these things work but we do need to keep going. It's important for the rest of the human race, don't you think?' She tips her pointed chin down to look at me.

'You really believe the army is coming?' I can hear the sarcasm in my voice.

'Look, lots of people stay at their post even when everything around them is collapsing. Soldiers, doctors, nurses.' She flutters a hand as though that covers everyone. 'All those people who carried on doing their jobs right through to the end, right up to Day Zero.' Her voice is getting higher and louder and she moves around on the sofa in agitation. 'It's a shame the doctors and nurses in this unit decided to leave and not come back. I don't understand why you would give up on this trial. No, actually, I'll tell you why – because you were doing it for yourselves, for the money.' That's right, I think, absolutely right. I was doing it for the money. Piper stops, pauses as though to get control back, and steadies her breathing. 'And in answer to your question, I don't know who will be coming: scientists, doctors, the government, the army. Someone *will come*. The trial ends on day twenty-one and it's your duty, Neffy, to keep yourself well. Eat all the food you're given. Keep your symptom diary up to date. They'll want that. Are you still menstruating?'

'What?' I laugh, unsure if I heard her correctly.

'Have you had a period since you've been in the unit?' she says as though I don't understand the word 'menstruating'. 'You're not on the pill, are you?'

'Well, I –'

'You're not pregnant?' Her little hand touches my arm with what might be excitement.

I laugh again. 'No, definitely not pregnant.' My last period had arrived on time and I'd been on the pill – the one drug the trial allowed volunteers to continue to take – although I suddenly realized I'd forgotten to take any since I was given the virus.

'Rachel says she thinks she's stopped menstruating, too little food or too much stress. Or maybe you've always been irregular. You strike me as one of those women who are irregular.'

'I'm sorry?'

'Oh dear.' She smiles. I see she has rolled the flower petals into a small damp ball in her palm. 'People often take the things I say in the wrong way. I'm only ever trying to do what's best. That's important, don't you think? Sometimes you just need to step back and think first before you act. Take the heat out of the situation.'

'In what way?'

'Oh, I'm just thinking about the others. Sometimes they can be a little impetuous. Rachel's so emotional, Yahiko too in his way. And Leon, well, Leon is in a little band of his own.'

I make a noise, demurring. Although I'm still working everyone out, I know I don't want to be in a gang of two with Piper.

She clears her throat, maybe disappointed that I haven't jumped to sign up to Team Piper, and hurries on. 'But anyway, if you didn't bring any sanitary products with you, you can just ask Yahiko – he has a store of everything. Or me. Ask me, and I'll get some for you. And put it in your symptom diary. I'm sure whoever comes will want to know that too.' She's been smiling all the time she's been talking but I can only stare, and then she gets off the sofa, wriggling her bottom forward until her feet touch the floor and she can stand.

She goes back to the desk and places the ball of petals beside the vase. 'I'll clean it up in the morning,' she says to herself and then turns to me. 'You could sleep here, if you want. It's a nice place to sleep, out of the way of the air conditioning.'

I can just make out the shape of her, the arch of her hat. 'Goodnight, then.'

When she has flip-flopped her way back to her room and her door has closed, I go across reception to my room. Remembering not to switch on my light, I go to my beside table and scrabble about in the cupboard for the mooncup I'm sure I brought with me. I look amongst my clothes in the drawers, in the pocket of my suitcase under the bed and in my toiletry bag in the bathroom, and it isn't in any of those places.

Dearest H,

*The lab took delivery of eight specimens of Octopus vulgaris and
kept them in marine aquaria, one animal per tank. Each tank
had a layer of sand and a couple of large concrete blocks in a
corner to form a cave. They were filled with artificial seawater
(ASW) and kept at 18°C on a 12-hour light/dark cycle. The
animals were left to adapt for ten days during which time it was
my job to check their chemical/physical water parameters, note
the colour and condition of their skin, and write down what they
ate and how often. Observe, record. Lucky octopuses, I might say:
ten days to adapt to their tanks; I had one.*

Neffy

Leon doesn't come to the staffroom for breakfast. The rest
of us sit in our customary seats around the table, with pots
of porridge.

Rachel and I speak at the same time.

'I've been thinking about whether I should leave,' I say.

Rachel says, 'Don't you think this place is like a cross
between *Groundhog Day* and the *Stepford Wives*? All of us
doing the same tidy little things over and over.'

I want to sound them out, see how they react. If I'm honest, I've become scared about the idea of setting one foot
outside the front door; horrified by the things Rachel told
me about the bus, what the others said about the dogs and
groups of men, and what if I do make it all the way to Dorset and I'm alone? The unit, with its solid walls, thick glass

windows and concrete floors, is beginning to feel safe, safer than outside. But the dynamics between the others, the way they always seem to change the subject when I come into the staffroom, is unsettling. I can sense a sub-plan, a more secret plan than the sit-it-out-and-wait-to-be-rescued plan, which they aren't letting me in on.

'Oh no!' Rachel says. 'Please don't go. I can eat less, we can all eat less, can't we?' She appeals to Piper and Yahiko, who is eyeing up Leon's unclaimed porridge.

Yahiko makes a noise that's a cross between disappointment at my announcement and, I suspect, anticipation for more food.

'Don't you think you should wait, a few days at least, until you're fully recovered?' Piper says.

'I'm feeling much better.' I'm not feeling that much better. I still need long periods of sleep, and everything aches when I move. But it's Piper who I'm most suspicious of although I don't know why.

'Where would you go?' Yahiko says.

'Dorset, where my mum lives.'

'How would you get there?'

'I'm not sure. Maybe I'll be able to, I don't know, hire a car?' As soon as I've said it, I know it was ludicrous to think that it might be possible.

'Hire a car?' Rachel says, finishing her question with her mouth open. Yahiko simply laughs.

'I don't think there will be any cars for hire,' Piper says.

'Okay, then,' I say. 'I'll find a car. Steal a car.' I've not been above stealing in the past but it was nothing like a car, and I have no idea about hot-wiring or whatever it's called.

'I'd think you can just take one,' Yahiko says. 'No one's going to mind. They're too busy being dead.' We ignore him as he does an impersonation of a zombie, arms out, head jerking, saying, 'Come back with my car.'

'I don't think you should go,' Rachel says. 'It's not safe. Not yet.'

'I wanted to ask Leon too, see what he thinks. Has anyone seen him?'

We look at Rachel, but she shrugs. 'Don't ask me. He's probably messing about with that freaky tech shit of his.' Perhaps it's over between her and Leon, perhaps it never was. 'I suppose someone should go and check? See if he's okay.' She isn't volunteering. There's a moment where none of us move.

'I'll go,' I say.

'What if he's sick?' The overhead light flares in Yahiko's glasses and I can't see his eyes.

'No, I'll go.' Piper half rises, sits.

'I'm going.' I stand and pick up Leon's pot of porridge and stick a spoon in it. I'm sure I see the three of them lean in together over the table before the door closes but almost immediately Piper comes out and follows me to the nurses' station.

'Let me know how he is,' she says.

When I'm halfway down the corridor I look behind me and she's still watching. I turn the corner at the end.

I knock on Leon's door and when there's no answer, I knock again. What if he is sick? What then? If I go in will Piper make me stay, lock me in my room until the bloody army get here? I open the door. His outside blinds are up and the lights are off as expected but this end of the building faces north and the room is shadowy. Still, I can see that it's a mess with belongings strewn across the chairs and floor, and then I hear a sound, and I can make out Leon in bed, turning over to face me. I am relieved at the movement but worried he hasn't got up yet. 'Are you ill?' I take my hand off the doorknob, remind myself not to touch anything, not to touch my face. I should have worn a mask and gloves.

He groans. 'What?' he says.

'Are you sick?' I ask. He shuffles up in the bed. 'Leon?'

'Rach?' he says, his voice sleepy.

'No, it's Neffy. Are you ill?' I stay in the doorway, keeping the door open with a foot.

'What time is it?'

'Just after eleven. How are you feeling? Do you have any symptoms?'

'No.' He sounds aggrieved. 'I was sleeping.'

'Are you sure?'

'I don't have it. I was asleep.'

I pick my way through the room, negotiating the clothes on the floor. On his desk is a collection of items: a tube of Pritt Stick with the glue removed, a couple of spoons and a kitchen knife, two pencils and a large heap of cables, some of which have had the insulation stripped, and a notebook, the same type as the two Boo brought me. I forget already that I told myself not to touch anything in Leon's room and I open it – after all, Leon read my notebook – but it's not diary entries or letters, instead it's filled with tightly packed writing, interspersed with symbols and words written in uppercase.

'I missed breakfast,' he says.

'I brought it for you.' I hold out the pot of porridge, still looking at the notebook, and feel him take it from me. When I look up, he's sitting on the side of his bed in jeans, a hoodie, socks.

'I'm not ill,' he says. 'I was just up all night.' He yawns for full effect, his gaping mouth enormous. 'Sorry.'

'What's all this?'

'I'm trying to make a radio. It's not going to work but it's something to do. No soldering iron, no way to get the antenna high enough –'

'No, this?' I flick another page in the book.

'That's private. My notes. Important.'

I laugh. 'Very clever.'

'I felt the urge to write last night. Some stuff. Ideas. Code.'

'How have you got the same notebook as –'

'I had to get it down before I forgot it.'

'– me?'

He stirs the porridge and eats a spoonful. 'I couldn't find any paper. This is cold.' He eats another.

'You didn't come to breakfast. You're lucky Yahiko didn't have it.'

'How can we have no paper in the whole of the unit? I'm sure there used to be paper in the nurses' station. Probably Yahiko took it. Did you know, he's taken everything from all the other rooms? All the stuff that everyone left behind, and stashed it in his? It's like a car boot sale in there, except you can't buy any of it because money is useless now. He spends his days sorting it into different piles, counting it.'

'The notebook?' I remind him.

Leon has a mouthful of porridge. 'So I knocked on your door.'

'You knocked?'

'But you were asleep. I went in, and it was just on your desk.'

'You went in?'

'Like I went in when you were ill. Going into your room wasn't a problem then.'

'But I'm not ill any more. It's my room. I was asleep. You can't just come in and take things. This is my paper.' I put my hand down flat on the page with a slap.

He holds up the spoon like it's a gun he's surrendering. 'I'm sorry. I'm sorry. I know.' He hangs his head for a moment and then lifts it again. 'Is it, though?'

'What?'

'Yours?' He shovels in more porridge. 'You might ask whether we're going to own things in our brave new world, and it's a good question. Maybe we should start afresh and everything should be shared? Discuss.' He continues to eat and speak. 'I just had to get it down. I was writing it in Notepad on my laptop but then I started worrying about it disappearing when or if the electricity goes off. No electricity, can't charge my laptop, no code. I'll find you some more paper. I promise. And I'm sorry I came in when you were sleeping.' He scrapes out the porridge pot and puts it on his bedside table amongst the other detritus.

'What's it code for?'

'Just some modifications. Ideas for something. I don't think I've ever written code by hand.' He considers for a moment as though it's important.

'And what computer are you planning on putting it into?'

'Well, yeah. No servers, no mainframes, no internet, no apps, no users. But it'll all come back. One day, don't you think?'

It seems he's as naive as Rachel suggested, with her hope for Instagram.

'Surely if we're starting again with technology it could go in directions we've never dreamed of? Like octopuses and humans. Did you know we share a common ancestor from seven hundred and fifty million years ago – a flat worm – but they went off on a completely different evolutionary path to us. Shells instead of backbones, which then got internalized.'

He smiles. 'That's your subject, isn't it? That's what you're writing about. Octopuses.'

'I was a marine biologist, once.'

'And you love your subject, don't you?' he says.

Before I can tell him to piss off, we hear a muffled voice calling my name from the corridor. 'Neffy! Are you in there?'

'Shit,' I say. 'Piper.' I go to the door and look out. She's at the corner in full PPE and when she sees me she takes a step back. 'It's all right,' I say. 'He was sleeping. Overslept. Not ill. Still alive.'

'Really?' she says, frowning.

'He's okay. Tell Rachel not to worry. He'll be up soon, I'm sure.' Piper hesitates. 'Really,' I say. 'He's fine. He's eaten his breakfast. He's here and alive, and not sick.'

'I'm good, Piper!' Leon shouts from behind me. 'Tip-top!'

She leaves reluctantly and I turn back to the room. Leon is out of bed and putting on his robe. He leans on the windowsill and looks out.

'I'll leave you to it, then, you might as well keep the note –' I say, but he cuts in with, 'I don't know if it's better to see a little bit of the main road like you can, or the cats and the rats and the bins like me.'

I walk to the window and below us, two floors down, is a gated yard with brick walls.

'My mum and me lived in the Draper building. You know it?' Leon shoves his hands into the pockets of his robe.

I shake my head. 'Elephant and Castle. Eighteenth floor. We could see everything and nothing from up there. I loved it, except the lift was always breaking down.'

'That's a lot of stairs.'

'Yeah, my mum couldn't do it. She was stuck indoors a lot of the time.'

'You looked after her?'

'I suppose.' We look down again, outside. Several large industrial bins, all with their lids open, crowd the space; one is tipped on to its side. Rubbish is strewn about, most of it blown into the corners.

'Cats and rats didn't do all that,' I say.

'No.' He breathes in, holds it. Exhales his story. 'A woman climbed the gate on one of those days you were ill. I don't know if she was searching for food or somewhere to sleep or what. She looked in each bin but didn't find anything she was interested in.' He speaks in a dead voice and I want him to stop. I know it's going to be another story like Rachel's. 'And then a man climbed the gate after her. I think they might have been together, I don't know. They knew each other, cos they started fighting. Shouting and screaming. Maybe she'd found something after all and he wanted it. I couldn't tell. He tipped the bin over so she was trapped in a corner and I was about to knock on the window but she managed to climb on to the side of the bin and then the top of the gate, and I was like, *Yes! She's got away*, but at the last minute he got hold of her foot and she fell forward, out on to the road, the other side of the gate. She was wearing this yellow skirt, which flew up when she fell. She had bare legs and she was wearing boots. DMs. Pink DMs. And no underwear.' I look out at the road, the silver gate with its square bars. I don't want to hear the rest of the story, but I know

90

he's going to tell it anyway. 'And she had the virus, I knew from the colour of her skin, the bruising. She lay face down, not moving. The man climbed the gate and he stood looking at her for ages, looking at her bare arse without lowering her skirt. He kept putting his fingers on his head and bending and looking away, and then bending towards her and straightening up, and I couldn't work out what was going on. And then I thought it looked like he couldn't remember what he was meant to do. Check her pulse, lower her skirt, call a fucking ambulance on a phone that doesn't work any more, something, man. And he didn't do anything. So, I knocked on the window.' Leon puts a closed fist against the glass. 'And the guy looked up at me and I thought, *Fuck, what have I done? He's going to come in here and we're all finished*. I ran to the intercom and watched the front door through the camera but he didn't come. I was shitting myself, and I stood with my ear pressed to the emergency exit in reception waiting to hear the door downstairs opening. I remember thinking, *Piper's going to kill me*.' He laughs sourly. 'You probably can't open it from the outside anyway. I stood for like five minutes, plenty of time for the guy to make it around the building, and then after a bit I came back here and looked out the window again. Creeping up so he wouldn't see me, you know. He'd gone but the girl hadn't moved. I thought about going outside, but I didn't. Too fucking chicken. I waited and she still didn't move, and then in the night I heard the dogs.' He shakes his head as though to shake away the sound.

'I don't know why you're telling me this.'

'Because I think you're planning on leaving and you need to hear what it's like outside.'

'What it *was* like.'

'What it's still like.'

'If I go, you'll have more food. You'll be able to stay inside for longer.'

'Till the fucking army get here? I don't think so.'

'Someone, maybe.'

We stare out of the window side by side without speaking until eventually Leon says, 'Who is it you want to go home to?'

I turn my back to the glass and Leon stands up straight. He faces the room with me.

'There are people, but I don't know if they made it.'

'In Dorset?' He pulls his duvet off the bed, wraps it around his shoulders and sits in one of the bucket armchairs. And now I know they've been talking about me, of course they have.

'Probably.'

'Who are the people?'

'Which people?'

'The people you want to see.'

'That's a lot of questions.' I rest on the window, fold my arms, tucking my hands into my armpits.

He laughs. 'Fair enough.' He brings his feet up on to the seat of the chair and then lifts himself up until he's sitting on the chair's back. 'If you could see anyone again, who would it be?'

'I don't know. Lots of people.'

'Just one, though, if you had to choose.'

'I'm not sure I like this game.'

'It's not a game. I want to try something out.' He frowns. 'Just one person. A person in a place. Go on.'

'My father,' I say, quickly. I know Leon wants me to name someone who's missing but out of all my family the one person who isn't missing is my father. I know exactly where he is.

'Okay,' Leon says. 'Now you have to think of your father in a precise place. A memory you have of him somewhere. A good memory. Close your eyes and think of him.'

I laugh, doubtful. 'What?'

'Don't you trust me?'

'I don't know you, so not really.'

He smiles. 'It probably won't work anyway.'

'What won't work?'

'Do it, close your eyes just for a moment, and then if you think it's a load of bullshit you can leave. It doesn't work on most people.'

'You do this with most people?' Is he flirting with me? I'm not sure.

'In fact, why don't you lie on the bed and close your eyes and think of your father.'

I'm laughing as I shake my head. 'Is that the best you can do?'

'It's in case you fall.'

'Fall from where?' He doesn't answer and I plump his pillow and lie out on his bed with my trainers on, thumping one heel down and then the other. I look at him again but he hasn't moved from the chair. I close my eyes.

'All you have to do is think of a time and place you'd like to go back to. A memory. Something vivid. Something good.'

It's easier when I can't see his face. Leon's voice is normal, ordinary. 'Okay.'

'You've thought of somewhere, something?'

I try to keep my mind on one memory of Baba but my thoughts flit about from one moment to another. I hear

Leon move and when I open my eyes I see him bring out a silver case from under his bed.

'Eyes closed,' he says when he turns back to me. 'Keep remembering. But keep your eyes closed. I promise it won't hurt.' As I feel his hands moving about my head and neck, their warmth just above my skin, without touching, I worry that I haven't settled on one memory of Baba. Should I be thinking of Justin, I wonder? 'Put your arms by your sides, palms up.' He puts something smooth and round in the centre of each palm, cool to the touch like beach pebbles.

I look up at him, next to my bed, like a doctor. And I do trust him although doctors have never done too much for me or my family.

'Close your eyes,' he says. 'You've got to let go. Utterly let go, you know, like falling asleep or jumping off a cliff. Like drowning.'

I hear electronics – a background buzz, white noise. See nothing.

It is the smells that come first. Or a memory of the smells. Not exactly through the nose; rather, inside the head. Odd but beautiful. The smell of the dry Paxos earth I recognize, the bougainvillea, the sea, and something cooking: bacon. And then the heat, God, how I've missed heat. I think of the stone garden with the path winding up through the olives and the terraces and a low orange sun casting its long shadows and, like an image emerging on a photograph pulled from an instant camera, it is there. I am there. All of it, the time of it, the age I was then.

A piece of grit was caught between my foot and my flip-flop and I paused to shake it loose. With astonishment, I feel it: the quick pain under my sole, the annoyance, the wobble on one leg, the small moment of satisfaction as the pebble falls free. I am my twenty-seven-year-old self inhabiting my twelve-year-old body in a damp bikini. I laugh at how fantastical this is but there is no one to hear me. In one hand were my goggles and snorkel, and I was in a hurry because today I had touched an octopus in the sea and the octopus had touched me, and I wanted to tell someone. I understand my – this young girl's – thoughts, desires, loves, hates, without being conscious of them, because they were mine too, but I also know I am me, now. It is like stepping into an old family video to inhabit the body of the person I was, reading the mind, being that mind. Behind me was the swish and rattle of waves on stones. I am here and I am not. The colours of the olive trees are greener than I remember; each blade of grass is accentuated, crisp, heightened. And, for the first time in nearly a year, I hear Baba call my name: 'Neffy!' and then he returns to his singing, something grand and sweeping, operatic. The pain of it, that I could be back, made me look up at the hotel too fast in anticipation of seeing him, and now the pixels showed – the white edges of the building jagged, his voice caught like a scratch on vinyl – and it took a second, less than a second, to catch up with the movement of my head. I stumbled, I jerked.

'Watch it. Careful,' Leon says, his voice cutting in, and I feel hands on my shoulders, pressing something, removing something else.

'Not yet!'

But I rise, a rushing sensation upwards through foaming blue, until I am back on Leon's bed, beached and winded. His room is claustrophobic, too small to contain us both and all the furniture, as well as the mess of clothes and cables strewn about.

I am dazed, exhausted.

'Oh my God,' I say, half sitting up to watch as he packs things away into tiny boxes and then into a small silver suitcase, moulded hollows for each one – the kind woodwind musicians use for the separate parts of their instrument.

'It worked, didn't it?' he says, looking up at me.

'How did you do that? How did that happen?' The need to sleep is overwhelming but I have to know. 'How is that even possible?'

'It doesn't work for most people.' He grins.

'Shit, it worked for me.' I flop back on the pillows and he laughs, delighted.

'Revisiting can be pretty intense the first time. You can sleep if you need to and then we can talk. Fuck.' He shakes his head. 'I can't believe it worked.'

I have that feeling you get when returning from a holiday or a few days away, as though your house is not your own house although everything is familiar. As though it's a film set made to look exactly like your place, and you, an actor, are playing yourself travelling through it, the colours a considered palette, movement choreographed, sounds applied later. 'Revisiting – is that what it's called?' My words sound rehearsed.

'Revisiting is what you do. It is a Revisitor. Our marketing guy named it.' I hear Leon close the case and slide it under the bed, and I shuffle backwards until I'm sitting up. He rubs his hands together and blows on them. He's trying to hide

96

it but I see an expression on his face – a sheepish pride, or satisfaction.

'How does it work?' I ask. 'Why doesn't everyone have a Revisitor?'

'Like I said, it doesn't work on most people.' He sits on the end of the bed.

'Have you tried it on the others?'

'Nothing happened.'

'I nearly saw my father again. I have to go back. I could smell!'

'It worked well, then?' He can't stop smiling.

'I want to go back, now!'

'It can be pretty exhausting, the first few times.'

'Now!' I shove his side playfully with my foot and he sways exaggeratedly.

'Ouch!' He holds up his hands, laughing. 'Okay, okay, man. How long were you there for?'

'I don't know, three or four minutes?'

His face falls. 'Is that all?'

'How long did it take?'

'Thirty seconds.'

'Wow,' I say.

'I still have to do some adjustments.'

'I heard my father. He was singing. Oh my God, I heard Baba singing.' I bring my hands to my cheeks and laugh at the shock of it. 'Opera. He was singing opera and I was back on Paxos where he had his hotel. And the beach was just behind me, and I could smell the earth and I heard the noise of the water on the stones. The actual fucking sea was behind me.' I move my head as though to look, expecting it, but see only Leon's messy room and the door to the corridor. 'I don't know how you did it but I need to go back. I have to see him.' I hold on to Leon's wrist. 'It was so real. I was there. Please.'

And he laughs again. 'I'm not sure I've ever seen it work so well. All right. A quick one, just to see if you can do it a second time.'

'Okay,' I say, and when he gets off the bed I lie back and close my eyes. 'I'm ready.'

'Christ, let me get the thing out first.' I hear him open the case.

'I'm going to see my father,' I say as I feel the same warmth pass over my face and throat.

He pauses. 'It's your memory you're Revisiting, it's not time travel, right? And we have to be careful. You shouldn't really do it so soon after the last time.'

I don't really listen. 'Right,' I say.

'Your cue has to be something good, a nice memory, okay?' he says, and I try to imagine the Hotel Ammos, Baba singing.

And then I hear the same white noise and I let myself sink down into it, through the blue, forgetting my body on this bed in this room in a clinic in London.

This time when I look behind me, I see the path down between the olive trees, the sea flashing and glittering. I have a sensation of balance: that if I am too aware of the technology it will bounce me out. I let myself float with the memory, rising and falling. Ahead was the terrace and the white hotel, and a smell of cigarettes. I heard Baba singing from an upstairs room and I was just as impatient to tell him the news of the octopus, and I hurried up the path. In the kitchen Margot was sitting on the counter next to the sink, wearing a pink top and her jeans shorts. She was smoking one of her cigarettes, hand-rolled using liquorice paper, and the smell now is intense, complex, as though I can separate the chemicals and sugar and tobacco, one from the other. She was kicking the heels of her canary-coloured espadrilles against a cupboard door and the yellow hurts my eyes, but her face . . . her face is a miracle. I was twelve, and Margot . . . Margot must have been twenty-six. Twenty-six! A year younger than I am now.

'Hey, Neffy,' she said in her Californian drawl and hugged me, one-armed, as I twisted into her. I held back the news of the octopus, saving it for my father. Even over her cigarette smoke, I could smell the bacon she must have just finished cooking and the musty damp of her shoes where she'd got the rope sole wet in the sea yesterday. My twenty-seven-year-old self remembers that, soon, the rope will unravel and she'll go barefoot, until in about a week's time she'll step on a thorn and get me to extract it from her dirty heel with her eyebrow tweezers.

Breakfast was finished and the hotel guests had scattered, down to the beach, to sit on the terrace and read, or to walk the island's dusty spine, all seven miles of it. Margot may have packed some lunch for the guests if they'd asked, including a free bottle of red wine wrapped in a checked picnic sheet with a couple of glasses – a trick to stop them complaining about the lines of ants which trekked from kitchen through dining room, to a crack in the back step, the bathroom towels which were beginning to fray, or the noise of the building site next door where a hotel, bigger and fancier than ours, was being built. If Margot was lucky the guests wouldn't find out that she bought the wine by the barrel and decanted it into bottles which she used over and over. If they asked about the worn labels, I was to tell them that they had been rubbed away because of the time the wine had spent in the cellar, maturing.

Two breakfast trays lay on the central kitchen table. One with coffee, pastries and a blue bowl of yogurt with honey. The other with a plate of congealing fried eggs, as well as black pudding and bacon which I had been asked to bring from England in my suitcase. The meat turned my stomach. I imagined sweet English pigs nosing through straw, jumping through mud.

'One-nineteen didn't eat his breakfast again,' Margot said – Margot said her numbers differently to my father. 'Didn't even touch his coffee.'

The Hotel Ammos had only twelve rooms but Baba had numbered them 115 to 127 to make the place appear more impressive on its rudimentary website. A single man was staying in one-nineteen – I liked to copy Margot, mostly to annoy my father – and although we knew his name, Margot and I didn't use it. Using his room number was like a secret code between us. One-nineteen was the only guest whom Margot didn't insist come down to the dining room for breakfast and this was because he always booked for the next summer on the last day of his holiday. His dates were written carefully in the diary kept in the reception table drawer and his deposit taken in cash, folded away by my father.

'I'll take Baba's,' I said, picking up the tray with the plate of bacon and eggs. My adult heart hammers at the thought of seeing him again and I try to tell myself to hurry before Leon turns off the machine, but the child can't hear me, doesn't know I am here, eavesdropping. I wanted to ask

Baba whether he knew that octopuses and pigs were cleverer than dogs, cleverer even than three-year-old children.

'Cleverer than twelve-year-olds?' he will ask.

I'll take him the meat and I'll try to make sure he doesn't eat it.

'Wait a minute,' Margot said. 'Tell him . . .' She paused, her voice soft. I paused too with the tray. 'Oh, tell him to fuck off.' She sounded weary. Margot and my father were always arguing.

'Fuck off?' I said.

'Yes,' she said. 'Or piss off, if you like.' She said *piss off* with an exaggerated English accent. 'And then check on one-nineteen for me, would you? Make sure he didn't die in his sleep or something. Pretend you've come to make the bed but put some more clothes on first.' She ran the tap and held her cigarette under the flow. I adjusted the tray –

'That's enough,' Leon says, removing something from my forehead.

I rise upwards, wanting to be furious, but I am drained. I want to ask how it works but I am too weak to form the words. It's as though I've been playing some mental game which has lasted days and something physical in my brain has been wrenched out of alignment. I'm too tired to even get off the bed, too tired to get under Leon's duvet, so I let him remove my shoes and roll me one way and then the other to cover me up.

'Wait,' I say, trying to push the covers back. 'What about Rachel?' I can't even open my eyes.

'What about Rachel?'

'Aren't you and her, you know? Won't she mind, me being in your bed?'

'Me and Rach?' I think he says and then I am asleep.

Dearest H,

When I was a student, I wrote an essay on the effects of underwater noise pollution on cephalopods. I was an undergraduate, enjoying learning for the sake of learning, making friends and sleeping with whoever I liked. I had an on-off thing with Ed for the whole three years. I could have fallen in love with him, made it a proper relationship – I think he would have liked that too – if it weren't for his singing. Ed liked to sing to himself, tunelessly, in a piercing voice that went through me like a harpoon. I'd ask him to stop, and he would for a while, until he forgot. And we would split up until I forgot how bad the sound he made was, and I would sleep with him again. I didn't do any empirical research for that essay, I think I wrote it in my first year when we weren't allowed near the animals, but I did discover that low-frequency sounds from shipping or oil and gas drilling will cause lesions on an octopus's statocysts, the fluid-filled, balloon-like structures that help them balance. The damage will become worse even when the sound is turned off, until the animal eventually dies.

Neffy

When I return to my room, a folded towel has been placed on my bed. It's white and fluffy and I put my hand on it and already it seems like something from another time. Nothing in the world will be as clean and as soft as this again. But it being there means someone else has been in my room while I was Revisiting. Shouldn't this be one of Piper's rules? No entering other people's rooms without an invitation. I think maybe I should bring it up at one of the group meetings she apparently holds. I look at the towel suspiciously, knowing from what Leon and Piper said that it must be Yahiko who has left it. Maybe I should ignore it and use the hand towel for my showers to make a point about how Yahiko has all the stuff. I know it would be a pointless point. Before my first shower just after I'd met the others, I'd found my foul bath towel on the floor. I must have used it to mop up when I was ill, although I didn't remember. But it was beyond washing and I'd shoved it down the waste chute in the kitchen. The towel on my bed reminds me of the towels in the Hotel Ammos, taken away by a laundry service during the trouble-free times and delivered back to us like new, all our dirt and mess removed without us having to confront it. Whoever has thought about a bath towel for so long? I pick it up and press my face into its softness and inhale. I long for that newly laundered scent of the hotel towels, which would smell so pleasingly of nothing, like fresh air. This one I can't smell at all.

I was going to do some writing but the towel tempts me with a shower instead, and I find, in the cubicle, that Yahiko has removed the Tesco own-brand toiletries I brought with me and replaced them with plastic sample pots. 'Jo Malone: Lime, Basil and Mandarin Shampoo' he has written on the label on the side. 'Not for consumption' he has added. In another is Aesop Nurturing Conditioner, in a third, body-wash by Chanel. Despite the fancy toiletries, I long for a bath to immerse myself in. I think of the bath Justin and I shared in his father's house, an end each with the taps in the middle.

When I come out, wrapped in the new white towel,

Yahiko is sitting in one of the armchairs by the window. He covers his glasses with his hand, head tilted, overplaying coyness, but maybe he is looking, because when I step to the window to lower the blind to the outside he jumps up to stop me. 'No,' he says, and I let go of the cord. 'You must never move the outside blind. And you mustn't put the lights on.'

'For the same reason someone removed my message?' I remember what Rachel said about people outside, watching. Yahiko keeps his head down and his hand shading his eyes while I get dressed.

'Do you want any clean underwear?' he says.

'Underwear?' I still haven't got the measure of Yahiko and can't tell when he's joking. Everything he says is salted with a little sarcasm or innuendo.

'If you tell me your size, I can see what I can do. You'll need clean underwear for your little trip down to Dorset.'

It sounds like he's imagining I'd be going on a jaunt, a long weekend to the seaside.

'I think I'm going to stay, for the time being.'

'Oh, I am pleased,' he says, and he sounds like he is. 'I don't think it's safe yet for a woman travelling on her own. What times we're living in, eh?' While I'm towelling my hair, he stands up. 'Here,' he says, holding out another specimen pot with both hands.

'What's this?'

'A gift. It was going to be a leaving gift but maybe it can be a staying gift.'

I take it from him. Inside are two knobbly sticks. I give the pot a shake and then turn it between my fingers to read the label. 'Matchmaker' it says on the side, 'For consumption'. I can't help myself, and I laugh, then take off the lid and sniff.

'Imagine intense chocolate and mint.'

I pretend to swoon. 'No, nothing,' I say.

'They're my mum's favourite.' He puts two hands on the bar at the end of my bed.

'You have chocolate as well as towels? And I want to know who the heck brings Chanel bodywash to a drug trial?'

He turns down the corners of his mouth, lifts an eyebrow above the frames of his glasses, making that already familiar Yahiko absurdist face. 'What can I say? Jade in room seven had expensive taste.' I sniff them again. 'Are you going to eat them or inhale them?'

'It depends on whether you have any more.'

'What if I told you these are two halves of the last Matchmaker?'

'The last Matchmaker in the world or the last one you have?'

'The last Matchmaker in the world.'

I put the lid back on and think about it. 'I would eat one half now and save the other until I find the person I want to give it to.'

'It's clearly not me then since I'm standing here.'

'It's not you because you, no doubt, have a box of them under your bed.'

'And it's not the lovely Leon either since you've found him already.' The eyebrows again.

'Are you implying I've made a match?' I try to do the eyebrow thing back.

'Don't worry, it's only me who knows. I saw you leaving his room looking, how shall I put it, rather dishevelled?'

'What?' I'm shocked at his snooping more than his assumptions.

We share a moment, squinting at each other until he says,

'Ah, my mistake. Wrong apparatus. Unfortunately, Revisiting didn't work on me. Didn't work on any of us. Poor Leon was desperately disappointed and naturally none of us believed that it did actually work.'

'Well, I can tell you, it absolutely fucking works.'

'I can see that. Just look at you. Positively glowing.'

'I nearly got to see my father.'

He raises an eyebrow again. 'If I could go back to any memory, I'd pick plenty of other men before I chose my father.' He tilts his head at the pot. 'Go on, then.'

'Not right now. Not in front of you. I want to nibble it in private.' Actually, I don't want the disappointment of not being able to taste it. I sit on the bed, pulling the duvet around me. 'Anyway, maybe you should save it for your mum.' I unscrew the bottle, waft it under my nose and put the lid back on.

'I don't think so.' He says this solemnly, honestly.

'Oh, I'm sorry.'

He sits on the other end of my bed. 'We've all got a story, otherwise why would we still be here? Apart from Piper. No story there, or not an interesting one she'll admit to. Lovely mum, lovely dad, who love their lovely daughter. Whereas I'm finding this rather like the school holidays when only me and a few other sad fucks didn't have family to go home to and had to stay with a guardian who was only doing it for the money.'

'You were at boarding school?'

'Winchester. It was hell. All those boys.' Eyebrows.

'Where's home?'

'London, I suppose. I was deciding what to do with my life, hanging out, having fun. Taking too long about it my mum always said, so I signed up for the trial to show her I was doing something. I didn't expect them to accept me. Mum and Dad and my brothers were in Tokyo when all the shit happened. My dad's Japanese.' He seems to want to tell. 'Mum called me the evening before Day Zero. She said to stay here, in the unit. She thought it would be safest. She said, she and Dad and the twins were getting on the next flight to Heathrow and they'd come and get me. She's a force, my mum – everyone does what she says. If there'd been a flight, she would have been on it. "Sit tight. I'm coming to get you." Those were the last words she said to me.' He puts his palm on his chest to compose himself. 'I doubt they even made it to the airport. If they'd got here they would have come.'

'I'm sorry.' Once again my words feel useless. I am sorry, though, for all our pain and loss, and sometimes I am sorry for the moments of hope we allow ourselves. Wouldn't it be easier to have a body – bodies – and to know for certain? Even though nine days have passed since I last heard from him, I sometimes imagine Justin's plane taking off from Malmö. An air steward places a tray of breakfast food on the fold-down table in front of him. He peels off the foil lid on his cup of orange juice, folds it into four and puts it in his pocket so he can recycle it when he gets home. This is what I think in the daytime but in the night the horrors of that plane stuck on the tarmac haunt me. And then, like a shot of adrenaline, I realize that it's not only my father I can Revisit with Leon's apparatus, as Yahiko called it, but Justin. I can go back to when we went to Cornwall and swam in the sea in April, or to when we spent a whole weekend in bed, only getting up to make toast and Marmite and coffee and to go to the loo, and to when he said he loved me. I try hard not to smile.

'I can't go to the flat,' Yahiko says. 'All their things. And anyway, there won't be anything useful – no food. We never really ate at home. So here I am.' He opens his arms.

'Here we all are.'

'Sharing a space with four other fuckers, running out of food, too petrified to put on the lights. It's no way to live, is it?'

'Who do you think is watching?'

He glances out of the window. 'It's just a precaution. I try not to say it too much in front of Rachel. She's such a baby, easily spooked. Likes to have her little breakdowns.'

It seems to me that Yahiko is the one who is easily spooked.

'I was thinking,' he continues, trying and failing to make the words sound spontaneous, and I know that whatever it is, this is the thing he has come to my room to say. 'If you're staying, maybe you could pop out to the shops. Get a few things. Restock our larder. Man – or woman – cannot live on Matchmakers alone.'

'What?'

He picks up the bottle with the Matchmaker in it from the bed and gives it a little shake, and now I understand the towel, the expensive toiletries, the chocolate. 'You're immune, Neffy. You do realize that's what they're talking about every time you leave the room? All they ever do is talk about what that means, for us, for everyone. Piper's especially excited. She has *plans*, you know.'

'She told me that's what you all think. I hadn't even realized I was the only one given the vaccine and the virus.'

'Oh, you weren't the only one.'

I frown, confused, and he quickly shuts his mouth and closes his eyes, although I'm not sure whether at the pain of remembering or trying to forget. When he opens them again, he continues. 'Orla and Stephan were given both too. Orla was in the room next to you and then it's the empty room and Stephan's room after that. It took the doctors that long to realize something was up and stop the trial. I was banging on my window to try and get their attention, but then suddenly volunteers started coming out into the corridor with their bags and saying they were leaving. And I was trying to watch the TV and my phone at the same time, and things were going crazy outside, some of the nurses were leaving and more of the volunteers. He pauses, looks away. 'Orla and Stephan left then too.'

'Did they get ill like me?'

'Yes, they were sick.'

I can tell he doesn't want to talk about it but still I ask. 'How did they seem?'

'I don't know. Pretty ill, I suppose. Loads of people were leaving. They left together, I thought they must have known each other. I just kept my head down, most of the time.'

'When did they go? Maybe they survived. If I'm immune, they could be too.'

'Well, we'll never know, will we?' His voice is fierce. 'They left when everyone else did. And then we locked their doors because of the risk of infection. It was Piper's idea. She found one of the doctors' key cards and locked their doors and opened up everywhere else.'

'She locked my door too,' I say.

'For everyone's safety. We gave you food and something to drink. Leon volunteered to put the tray in.'

I remember the saltiness of the crisps, the restorative orange juice, and the locked door. What if they'd all caught the virus while I was still locked in, or what if they'd lost the key card? I could have died in here, alone. Most of those seven days, before I saw Leon sitting in my chair reading my letters, are dream-like – too hard to grasp with any surety. All that remains are impressions: noises and silence, sensations and emotions, light and dark. 'But anyway, if I'm immune, like I said to Piper, it'll be against the original virus, not the one that causes brain swelling, memory loss. Not the new variant that's wiped out the rest of the fucking world.' I gesture towards the window.

'You don't know that. The thing is, I don't believe in Piper's hare-brained idea about the army coming. There's no one left, or hardly anyone. No one's coming. At some point we're going to have to go out and get more food and other stuff, or one of us is. Surely it's better if the person who does that has the best chance of not catching it?'

I think of what I saw from Rachel's window, the smashed shops, the double-decker, and the story that Leon told me about the woman, and then the dogs. Being kept inside, maybe even locked inside, feels safer. 'I don't know,' I say. 'I'm not that into shopping or home visits.'

'For fuck's sake, Neffy, this isn't a joke! You had the vaccine. You're immune.' Yahiko launches himself off the bed and I flinch at the surprise of it. 'You're just going to sit in here and eat our food or leave, and that's it? You can go outside! Jesus fucking Christ.' He grabs the bar at the end of the bed and shakes it violently, and I jolt, stiffly, frozen in place, scared by his bared teeth and wild eyes, and by the fact that he's right. Of course I should go outside for them, for these people who are maybe a little strange – aren't we all a little strange right now – but are beginning to be my friends. And just as suddenly Yahiko lets go and spins around to face the other way. He breathes deeply, calming himself. I sit and wait, still shocked. He turns back.

'I'm sorry. I'm really sorry.'

'No, I'm sorry,' I say and my chin begins to shake. 'It's just it's scary, really scary.'

'I think all the time about the food running out and being stuck inside, you know?' His voice wobbles and I go to get up off the bed to hold him, to be held, but he steps back, perhaps embarrassed that we have both revealed too much of ourselves. 'I think I should go,' he says. 'Lie down in a darkened room or something.' He coughs out a laugh.

I hold up the towel. 'Do you want this back?'

He stares as though he can't comprehend what it is. 'God, no, you keep it. I've got loads more.' He goes towards the door. 'Seriously, though, I'm sorry. Let me know if you need anything and I'll see what I've got. Some paper, another notebook, whatever.' And then he's out of the room and across the corridor.

Dearest H,

The Principle Investigator, or PI, brought in a box of Krispy Kremes. The team stood about in his office eating them and drinking coffee. It was a big day. But I felt odd, like there was something none of us was admitting. I couldn't tell if the others felt it too. As though we'd been planning an act so terrible – mutilation, murder – that we couldn't look at it face-on. Instead, we pretended it was something else – science, research, for the good of humanity – in order to justify it to ourselves. Larry, the other assistant, took me aside and asked if I was okay. 'Are you?' I asked him, surprised that anyone could be okay.

To anaesthetize an octopus: immerse in ASW containing 2 per cent ethanol for five minutes until a clear change in body pattern can be observed. The tests for whether the octopus has properly 'gone under' have not themselves been rigorously tested.

Neffy

At the table at dinner time, Rachel says to me, 'Are you still going to leave?'

'I don't know,' I say. 'Not yet.'

Rachel's smile is wide with a relief that I don't feel my staying justifies, and I can see that Piper is pleased for her own strange reasons. Yahiko ducks his head, an acknowledgement that I need some time to think about going outside, finding them – us – some more food. The idea fills me with panic. Leon reaches out and squeezes my hand and I squeeze his back, smiling at him, and I'm sure we're both thinking about Revisiting – the places I can go and the data he can collect. But when Rachel sees Leon's hand on mine, her smile disappears, and she stares from him to me and back again.

I pull my hand out quickly and put it on my lap, but I'm worried I've read him wrong; maybe he has been flirting with me and I've been too stupid and wrapped up in Revisiting to see it.

'Really?' Rachel says to Leon. It's not a question.

'No –' he starts, but the sound of her chair scraping on the floor as she stands masks what he has to say.

'Really?' she says again, hands on hips. 'That is so wrong.' She says it slowly as though what she has witnessed has sickened her. Yahiko is looking away, embarrassed, but Piper is smiling, though when she sees me looking at her she stops, immediately. 'That is very, very wrong, Leon,' Rachel says.

And she picks up her dish and her fork and she leaves.

The third time I Revisit, I try once more, like Leon says, to think of a good thing, a happy cue. I am still desperate to see Baba but, guiltily, I think instead of Justin. I am deserting my father before I've even seen him, but I remember Justin at the dinner table the first time I met him in Clive's house when he passed me a bowl of salad. What was it? Whatever. I knew we both felt something. But as soon as I find myself sinking, down through the blue of my Revisit, as soon as I let go, I'm sitting on the pebbly beach below the Hotel Ammos, facing the sea and eating one of the pastries that the man in one-nineteen hadn't wanted. If I hadn't got to it first, Margot would have stashed it away – the next day sprinkling it with water, warming it in the oven and laying it out in front of the fresher ones on the hotel's buffet breakfast table. The taste and the smell of the *bougatsa* – filo, custard and icing sugar – is, was, exquisite, its memory almost a physical pain.

Mum always warned me, along with brushing my teeth *before* breakfast and making sure I form my first opinion about a person from their shoes, that I shouldn't swim straight after eating. But it was late afternoon, and hot, gloriously hot. The sea was cerulean, shining like glaze on tiles, too intense to be true. Standing in the water, up to my waist, I spat into the inside of my mask and rubbed the spit about with my fingers, dipped the mask into the water and pulled it over my head, sealing it tightly around my face until the suction tugged on my eyeballs. I put the snorkel in my mouth. Other people were in the water, guests from the hotel and other holidaymakers, and I swam away from them towards the edge of the cove, to the rocks. The light flickered over fields of green weed and there were damsel fish here, rainbow wrasse and saddled seabream, rocking with the current. I reached out a hand to touch them but the fish were always much further away than I thought. If I tried to swim with them, they were gone in an instant. I lay face down on the surface, letting the wavelets bob me up and down or break shallowly across my lower back. My breath was loud through the tube, something medical or industrial which threatens to lift me out and back into the unit for a moment. I let the noise float away and instead noticed how I was levitating above the gap between the two rocks where I had hovered this morning, and I waited for the animal which I knew was there to trust in my stillness, my lack of threat, and for its arms to feel their way out of the crevice it hid in.

'Neffy! Neffy!'

When I came upright and looked back to the beach, pulling my mask to my forehead, Baba was standing beside my towel, smiling. My twenty-seven-year-old self wants to look and look at him, here, on the beach in Greece, while my twelve-year-old self was cross at what his shouting had spoiled. I don't know how it is possible to know and feel both at once, the idea is disorientating, and it makes my father on the beach shimmer as though this golden image is passing across a corrugation. 'Come on!' he shouted, and the picture settled. From the water, Marmari beach was a narrow oyster-coloured scoop, the olive trees so close to the water that in the late afternoon their shadows dipped their heads into the sea. Behind the beach, more olives and fir trees climbed, dusty green, up the hillside to the hotel, which showed the top-floor windows framed by white, and a red-tiled roof. The other people on the beach were staring but Baba didn't notice, or if he did, he liked it. 'Got to see a woman about a cat!' He meowed and clawed at the air with his hands. His left hand was missing half of his ring finger after a moray eel bit it before I was born, or so he said. Mum, when she was annoyed with him, would say he lost it in a bar brawl. When I once asked Margot, she said, 'Who cares?' Baba was large, not fat, but barrel-chested, broad-shouldered; his arms, chest and back were dark with hair but now he was in a white T-shirt, trousers and his beach shoes which Margot threw away weekly and he retrieved weekly, from the bin. I swam and then waded towards him. Hurry, I try to tell myself, these moments won't last. Nothing lasts. I was disappointed not to have seen the octopus but, even at twelve, the draw of Baba was stronger. When I was dry and dressed, we linked arms on our walk to the village and he sang a song about a pussycat and refused to tell me why he was so excited, although I know. I know.

In the bar by the old soap factory my father was slapped on the back and hugged, kissed on both cheeks by half a dozen men. My cheek was tweaked, my head tousled although I was the same height as some of them. I liked it too, the way they swept me up, welcomed me, accepted me as Greek. 'Oliver!' the men cried and they talked as though they hadn't seen him for weeks rather than a couple of days. Their speech was too fast for me – I'd never learned

Greek properly – but I caught *gata* – cat – and then someone said *mouni* and they all laughed. Drinks were poured into tiny glasses, and I stuck my hand between the men and took one to sip at. It burned my tongue and all the way down my gullet, but I took a longer sip and the men laughed, and Baba said, 'Watch it,' but was smiling. My father was half Greek and he had lived on Paxos with his Greek father and English mother until he was ten, when his father died and he and his mother moved to London. He had lived between England and Greece until nine years ago, when he returned permanently to the place where he was born, bringing Margot with him and buying the hotel. Some of these men still remembered his father and they liked Baba more for that. More drinks were poured and little plates of food were brought out and we sat in the back of the bar where it was dark and the ceiling fan shifted warm air about. I ate the olives and the bread, and the little squares of feta with melon, but I would not even look at the fried octopus. I could not look at the octopus without tears coming.

Baba talked and drank, and I ate and drank until my head felt larger than it should and when I bit the inside skin of my cheeks it was numb. Then Baba was saying goodbye and he did more kissing and back-slapping and gave promises to return with the *gata*. When we went out into the sun I sneezed from the brightness and Baba sneezed too, the same sneeze, like a shout. 'Come on,' he said. 'That cat won't wait all day.'

'Are we really getting a cat?' We walked up between the houses, keeping to the shade close against the white walls, Baba behind me. 'A kitten?' I would have liked a tabby of my own, but the island was overrun with cats, feral and ugly creatures that sneaked into the hotel kitchen looking for food until Dimitra, the woman who came to clean and help with the cooking, chased them out with a broom.

'Bigger than a kitten,' he said and when I looked at him over my shoulder, he winked. 'Something that will make the tourists flock to the Hotel Ammos. Here.'

We turned right, up some steps and through an ironwork gate into the garden of a house I hadn't noticed before. I could tell the person who lived here was wealthy, because the grass, while coarser than English grass, was bright green. The sprinklers must come on at night or there would be a network of waterpipes under the earth. Exotic plants grew in large terracotta pots and the back of the house had a wall of glass. A woman came out to greet us and although Baba and she kissed on each cheek like everyone did, I saw him slip his arm around her waist and his hand squeeze her before she pulled away to say hello to me. I narrowed my eyes and hated her already. She laughed and went inside, and we waited in her green garden for five minutes while Baba wandered around, touching the plants and whistling. And when, finally, the woman returned she was carrying a tiger cub.

Baba sat and drank with the woman while I played with the cub in the garden, marvelling at its enormous paws, laughing at its attempts to bite me. Then she put a collar and lead on the animal, and Baba and I walked back to the bar. I insisted on carrying the tiger, but only got a few paces before it became too heavy and, anyway, wouldn't stay still. So I insisted instead on holding the lead even though I said a wild animal shouldn't have a collar and lead. Baba seemed to think it was cute that I was telling him off but, Revisiting at twenty-seven and even at twelve, I knew what would happen when he got it home.

Now, eavesdropping on my own twelve-year-old head, I can admit that I wanted to be the one to take it into the bar and get the admiring glances. Perhaps Baba knew this too. I wanted to know how much had it cost. Had he even bought it? What was his relationship with the woman? But these weren't the sorts of questions I could ask a man like my father.

In the bar, he put the tiger on a table and the men laughed and tried to feed it fried fish. They got the owner to bring out some raw lamb and the tiger cub chewed on it with its back teeth. There was more drinking, and I begin to drift off, leaning against the wall with the cub sleeping, draped over my shoulder.

The twenty-seven-year-old me knows that later that evening I will hear Margot and my father arguing, a low rumbling row for the sake of the guests, which will occasionally erupt into short bursts of anger. The fight will start in the kitchen under my room and then spill out on to the terrace, where Margot will curse him in English about the tiger, the hotel, the cost of everything, all the work she does while he goes to the bar. For five minutes his voice will be calming, apologetic, conciliatory, until she spits: 'And you brought Neffy back drunk! What the hell sort of father are you?'

'You're not her bloody mother,' he'll throw back. Now, I know the meaning of his unsaid words and that they are designed to hurt: *you're nobody's mother*.

In my bed upstairs I will pull the tiger closer, both of us floppy with sleep, and the smell of her warm fur will remind me of the upholstery of the buses I would take with Mum back in England.

And then I feel myself rising up through the blue. *Not yet, not yet!* I make myself heavy, battling the feeling, sinking down again.

I am back in Greece, a week or so later. I smell once more that humus-rich earth, and feel the sun heating my back where I lie on the wall of the kitchen terrace, arms propped on a cushion, reading, as a man arrives. I know now, of course, who he is – who he was – but at twelve I only thought he looked uncomfortable in a uniform that was too big for him, shiny shoes, and a cap with a badge which he held in his hands, along with an identification card which he showed to me when I sat up. It was in Greek but his picture was on it, looking startled as though he was surprised to find himself in this job, whatever job it was. I wondered if he was some kind of policeman and whether I should be worried. He spoke in Greek, and sensing that I didn't understand, he managed in heavily accented English to ask whether my father was home.

When the man showed Baba the card, the realization took less than a second, it was there and gone so fast that only a daughter or a girlfriend could have seen it. A smile that wasn't right, a blink which was a little too quick, and the man was invited to sit. Margot was called to bring a plate of *mezethes* and a bottle of Tsipouro. And although I went back to the wall and my book, I knew something was going on, because normally Margot would tell my father to fuck off and get his own snacks and drinks, but she smiled at the man and brought out a platter of *dolmades*, *taramasalata*, *pitta*, *yialantzi*, and the treats usually only served to the hotel guests at the public end of the terrace, beyond the line of little potted olive trees. Margot brought me a glass of Coke, placing it beside the wall where I could reach down for it. Had she ever let me have a Coke before without me begging? We drink it together, me and myself, but only the older one truly appreciates it. It took Baba several invitations in Greek to get the man to sit at the little table on the terrace and try the food I so long for. Finally, he did sit, and he put away the official-looking piece of paper he had pulled out of his jacket pocket.

Margot had named the tiger cub Sophia, although I'd argued that wild animals shouldn't be named or tamed, and she mostly slept in a large dog's cage which Baba had borrowed, or sometimes in my room when I could sneak her in at night. But night was when Sophia was now most awake and wanting to play. She peed on the bed – a smell like buttered popcorn – deposited her musky poops in the corner of my room and chewed everything she could get in her mouth. I had four red scratches across the front of my chest and imprints of sharp teeth up both arms; I was careful to wear long-sleeved tops when I was around Baba and Margot. I didn't want them to say that the tiger had to go, even while I knew it was wrong to keep her. I recognize that split in my younger self – between wanting wild things to be free, while craving something of them for myself. I just hadn't remembered that I'd felt it so early.

Baba kept refilling Nicos's glass – that was the man's name, he learned – offering him food, and Nicos drank and ate, and laughed at Baba's stories. He loosened his tie and, after another drink, took it off. I went in to eat in the kitchen and, when I came out again, Margot was watching my father slapping Nicos on the back and seeing him on his way. I knew we weren't allowed to keep the tiger but somehow, through some arrangement or bribe, Baba had saved himself a fine or perhaps imprisonment for not having a licence to keep a wild animal.

Sophia! I think now. What a name for a wild animal. I remember the sadness of having to let her go, tempered by my relief that she would be in a more suitable home than ours, or maybe even released into the wild. More her own self when not contained by the cage or my bedroom – free to hunt and swim and roar. In my fantasy I saw her in a Greek landscape of stone walls, olive groves and wild seas, a place without humans where she could hunt goats and find a mate. I wasn't naive enough to imagine it would actually be Paxos or any other Greek island, but I was satisfied that this Nicos, in his baggy uniform, had saved her.

When I rise properly from this Revisit, everything appears miraculous, as though I am seeing the world – even inside Leon's messy room – with fresh eyes, like everything has been washed clean. I remember when I was nineteen I did a skydive to raise money for a marine charity. My back was strapped to the chest of a soldier and we were in free-fall for about a minute before he deployed the parachute. For a month afterwards, whenever I looked up into the sky, I felt again those sixty seconds of ecstasy when I was something more than an earthly being. This is like that. For the next year I jumped again and again, trying to recreate that high.

I'm sleepy but I let Leon ask me his questions and I answer them as best I can. I know I've become a subject, a specimen to be documented, but I don't care if it means I can go back. *Be* observed. *Be* recorded. I look over his shoulder as he writes my answers down on a chart he's drawn in the back of his notebook – my notebook. I tell him that I was there for several hours, that I almost came out but was able to make myself sink back. He bounces in his chair at this news and then jumps up, too excited to remain seated. I admit, though, that thinking of a memory doesn't take me to it and I can't seem to control them. Neither of us can explain how or why this happens.

Subject: Nefeli. Age 27. Female. White British/Greek heritage

	Day 8 / Session 3
Length of actual time under	30m 7s
Length of reported time	12 hrs / 4 hrs (subject reported two time periods in one session)
Sense of sound during session (speaking and hearing) 1–10	10
Sense of proprioception during session 1–10	10
Sense of sight during session 1–10	10
Overall feeling of reality during session 1–10	10
Glitches (incl. jumps, déjà vu, intrusions, confusion, etc.)	Minor 'shimmering'
Desire to repeat 1–10	10
Post-session tiredness 1–10	8
Post-session disorientation @1 min	Mild
Post-session disorientation @5 mins	Insig
Post-session disorientation @30 mins	Insig

Dearest H,

It was my job to collect the parts of the severed octopus arms, tag each one to identify which octopus it had come from, and fix the arm part in formaldehyde before it would be embedded in paraffin wax and serially sectioned. Observe, record. Of course, it was how the octopus regenerated its severed arms that the study had been set up for, but since we had the arm parts, the PI decided to record how the parts would react when separated from the body.

I would have liked to email the fucking PI with an alternative list just to see his face:

Makes a thumbs-up

Makes a thumbs-down

Gives the finger

Gives two fingers

Gives the peace sign/victory sign

Other

Neffy

Day Nine

At breakfast Rachel is withdrawn and sulky even though the conversation runs through all the old social media platforms and who was on what and which was best. The fact that Leon is distracted doesn't help and as soon as she's left he starts talking about Revisiting and the success we had yesterday. I'm itching to do it again, to go back and see Baba, or Justin, or Mum.

'Would early evening be okay?' he says. 'I just want to do a few checks, tweak some settings. See if I can get you Revisiting the memory you're thinking of.'

Early evening, I think. That's hours away. 'Yes, that's great.' I sense that voicing my desperation would be inappropriate.

'Does it work on you, then, Neffy?' Piper says, and I don't quite believe the surprise in her voice. Leon would have told her, like they all talk about everything.

'It certainly works on Neffy.' Yahiko gets up.

'Later, then,' Leon says to me and the two men leave.

'Oh, Piper, it's incredible.' I take her arm, surprising us both. 'It was like I was there with my father in Greece. Not even like I *was* there, but that I *am* there.'

She laughs at my excitement. 'I let Leon try it on me but nothing happened. I was pleased, really, who wants to keep looking back, it's never going to do any good, is it? You can't change anything. We have to keep moving forward.'

'But don't you think we can learn from the past? See

things differently, or let it help us decide what we do in the future?'

'Humans are useless at learning from their mistakes. We just have to keep making new plans,' Piper says.

I spend most of the day sleeping or sometimes writing a few letters to H, but mostly attempting to ignore my growling stomach and my desire to Revisit, the need to see Baba again, the idea that I could give Mum a hug, kiss Justin. Since I'd last seen them in real life my memories of them were becoming more limited and increasingly vague, hardened and immutable. I was remembering what I'd already remembered and with each iteration a little more of their personalities and features were eroded like a statue touched so often by passers-by it starts to wear away. Now, amazingly, I have been given the opportunity to stop that process and even reverse it.

My pen is in my hand and moving but my head isn't writing, and too often I stop to check the time on my phone – I am now almost beyond checking it for messages and a signal – getting caught up in looking at pictures or the video Justin sent, and then trying to decide whether it is too early to walk down to Leon's. I told myself I could go at six but at five I can't wait any longer.

When I arrive at Leon's door, it's not completely closed. I hear music, although I didn't think we had any in the unit; none of us had downloaded any to our phones and Yahiko hadn't found any mobiles in any of the empty rooms. I stand on the threshold and look through the gap to see Leon and Rachel dancing. The room has been tidied and their arms are clasped about each other as they slowly turn to the sound of a jazz trumpet lamenting. As they rotate and Leon's face comes around towards me, I see and hear that the music is emerging from his clamped lips. It rises and falls, surprisingly loud, reverberating out of the room. I stay quiet and watch as Rachel unravels from his arms, their hands catch and he rolls her back in to his chest. They sway together for another moment and he lets the music fade away. I turn back from the door and face the corridor, not wanting to be caught spying as I listen to the ripple of their laughter and glasses chinking. They talk louder now and I think they must be coming to the door, so I move away, trying to make it look as though I'm just arriving. The door opens and Rachel appears, turning immediately right and not even seeing me, but Leon comes out, his expression already a question.

'Sorry,' I say. 'Am I too early?'

'No, no.' He opens the door wide.

I follow him in and he picks up two glasses and an empty bottle from the windowsill and heads towards the bathroom.

'Wow,' I say. 'Vodka?'

'Yup.' He stops trying to hide it.

'Yahiko?'

'Yahiko.' Leon bobs his head.

'A volunteer brought in a bottle of Russian Standard? How did they manage that?'

'It belonged to a nurse or a doctor. Yahiko found it in one of the lockers. Probably swigging it to get through a shift. Did you know, Yahiko's picked the lockers in the staffroom?' Leon holds the bottle out. 'There was only three fingers left.' Perhaps he thinks he should have left some for us to drink together.

'And Rachel?' I give her name a teasing ring. 'You've made up?'

'A misunderstanding.'

'About that stuff she said to you at dinner yesterday?'

He looks sheepish. 'All sorted.'

'That's good because I'm not, you know, looking for . . .' I pan my hand between us, palm up. 'I've got someone. Or I had someone –'

'No, no, yeah, right,' he says. 'So, you want to Revisit?' He puts the bottle and the glasses back down and picks up the solar recharger.

'I do,' I say. 'I've been thinking all day about my next Revisit. Is it virtual reality?' I sit in one of his chairs and start to unlace my trainers. It seems polite this time to take them off before I lie on Leon's bed.

'RR, not VR. Remembered Reality.' He takes the silver box out from under his bed and opens it.

'But how am I actually there?'

He stays squatting on the floor, connecting the charger to something in the box. 'Long-term potentiation. LTP. The essence of memory is representation and what we're interested in here is episodic memories as opposed to declarative memory or procedural or whatever. So –' His London accent has all but disappeared.

'What? Wait. Procedural. What's procedural?'

He looks round at me. 'What did you study, again? At uni?'

'Marine biology. In the end. At Plymouth.'

He sighs, although he tries to hide it.

'Why, what did you study?'

'Maths at Imperial. Procedural memory is like when you learn to ride a bike and you'll always remember how to ride a bike. Declarative is remembering facts. There are more types but they don't matter; this technology is concerned with episodic memory.'

'Episodes I remember?'

'Consciously remember, in time and place and with all the associated emotions.'

'So we retrieve these, play them back?'

'Sort of. Except that memories aren't stored in one place. Remembering is a process created on the fly by synapses firing and connecting neurons.' He's still crouching over the case and not unpacking any of it. I can tell this is his favourite subject and he's been waiting for me to ask. '*You* switch on the process by starting with a cue – hopefully a good memory. Your father, wasn't it? And the technology eavesdrops in on it, amplifies the LTP, and lowers your consciousness – the person you are now – inside it. Clever, eh?' He doesn't wait for an answer. 'And, in fact, the process doesn't just happen in the brain. We've identified five other body zones and we suspect maybe even some external influences, although that's going to take more work.' I notice he's talking in the present tense. 'We now understand mostly how memories are stored and retrieved but it's the last bit, how the present human consciousness interacts, that we haven't fully pinned down yet.' He gets up, puts the case on the bed and sits beside it. 'Once we get that worked out, we want to see whether it's possible to drop someone else's consciousness into another person's memory and let them experience it. Cool, eh?'

I let him talk some more about neuro plasticity, synaptic strength, the entorhinal cortex and glutamates. And when he finally winds down, I say, 'So why is it I've never heard about Revisitors?'

'Firstly, we never launched to the market. Not properly. The current version only works on about one person in five hundred.'

'That few?'

'I couldn't believe it when it worked on you. Such a fluke. We don't really know why it works on some people and not others. But I have to say, I haven't seen any subjects who have had as intense an experience as you seem to have had.'

'A *subject* now, am I?'

He holds his hands up in apology, puts them on his head. 'Sorry, but I have so many questions I want to ask.' He goes to his desk and picks up his notebook, flicks through it, showing me. It's nearly full.

'And the other reasons I've never heard of it?'

'Only that it wasn't always suitable for everyone even when we found a subject it worked on. It needed a few more tweaks, a bit more work.'

'Like what?'

'Oh, you know. Checking reactions, timings, how subjects disengage. Nothing to worry about. Anyway, you ready?'

Dearest H,

For half an hour after they were severed the octopuses' arms continued to move, to curl, to uncurl, to try to work out what had happened. How their connectedness was now unconnected. I don't need to tell you that octopuses taste as well as touch with their suction cups. They will stick themselves to human skin and when they are prised off the sound is like bubble wrap popping.

I let the pieces of severed arms stick themselves to me, against my wrist, up my arm, tasting, feeling. I hoped it might comfort them in their distress and confusion. Larry found me sitting on the floor of the cold room with part of an arm on my neck. When he removed it, the arm had given me a love bite.

At the meeting with the PI and a woman from HR I was given a verbal warning and told to take five days off.

An octopus can regrow a severed arm in one hundred days. This is not a pitiful arm like the replacement tails some lizards grow but one that is full length and with functioning suckers.

Larry covered my work while I was away. On the chart he wrote that the octopuses didn't appear to be affected by the amputations. They continued to eat and go about their normal activities. Their skin did not deteriorate. When I returned, I added to Larry's notes, 'But aren't we measuring their behaviours by our own?' I didn't try to disguise my handwriting. At the next meeting the PI accused me of putting make-up on my love bite so it would appear redder, he called me deranged, dangerously anthropomorphic. The woman from HR had to ask him twice to sit down. He was wrong in every instance.

Neffy

As I climbed into the hotel through the window with the loose catch, the Greek man, standing behind me, said, 'You don't have key?' I have forgotten this detail – how we got into the lounge. I'm disappointed to find myself here, in Greece again, and without Baba. I recognize my seventeen-year-old body, the newish breasts and hips, and I am also familiar with the internal mixture of lethargy, irritability and sudden zeal. I know this Greek man too, of course, with my benefit of hindsight. But to my younger self he's a stranger, a bit older than me, who I'd brought back from a party in one of the villas the other side of the bay. I had a key. It was tucked into the front pocket of the cut-off shorts that I'd pinched from Margot's bedroom. 'Nah,' I said to the man, whose name I don't yet know; I wanted him to think I was wilder than I really was, more rebellious and older. I was on Paxos for the summer again, and I'd promised both my parents that I would spend it revising after poor AS results. But I was bored of my books and studying and bored of my virginity. I went to the party, to which I wasn't invited, to lose it. I'd drunk a lot but not enough to not know what I was doing, and I wanted to get it over with. I felt it like a stone inside me, a boulder blocking a gateway to something, although I didn't know what. Enlightenment? Acceptance? I wasn't sure, but I believed I'd see the world differently when it was rolled away, and this man seemed nice enough. Me, the twenty-seven-year-old Neffy, laughs inside, is embarrassed and would like to look away, but cannot stop the projector from projecting, cannot resist the smell of the old hotel. I landed clumsily in the residents' lounge and the man stepped up on to the sill behind me and filled the window frame for a moment before he came down into the room. Moonlight was scattered across the empty sofas, the rugs and the occasional tables, a pearly sheen too beautiful to be true. I want to pause and look about but the other Neffy stopped instead at the bottles huddled together on the sideboard – the hotel's honesty bar. I picked one up and, without even looking to see what it was, I said, 'Do you want a drink?' Coolness was everything. I hoped he'd say no because the bottle was nearly empty; they were all nearly empty.

'You have *fagitó*?' the man said.

I tried to read the bottle's label in the dark.

'No.' He stopped to think and then said, 'Food.' He

gestured towards his mouth as though I didn't know the English.

'No food,' I said. 'A drink?' I shook the bottle at him and realized I was being too loud. A guest might wake and come down, although only one couple was staying at the moment. The place was run-down, with broken tiles to replace, walls to paint, warped window frames to repair, and house centipedes down the plug holes, but the taxes were too high, Baba said. He complained about how the little guys couldn't make money in the hotel business any more. No one wanted to come to Greece with its riots and corruption and its stinking, uncollected rubbish. Certainly, I thought, no one seemed to want to come to a hotel that had a leaking roof and broken windows and views of the chunky hotel skeleton next door, which had grown as high as the second storey before the unpaid workers left. 'You want a drink?' I hissed at the man.

'*Fagitó kai potó.*' He shook his head sadly. He had no hope for me. I knew what he meant: that he didn't understand how the English could drink without eating – some little morsel, a titbit to soak up the alcohol. In Greece, amongst Greeks, drinking without eating never happened. He thought I was drunk enough already but still I found a glass and poured whatever liquid was in the bottle into it. It smelled sweet but when I gulped it down it burned. I put the bottle back and scrawled an illegible line in the honesty book.

I remember now that in a week's time, when the family in room 115 check out, they will argue with Margot about this signature, saying they didn't write it, they didn't drink anything from the honesty bar. They'll leave a review on Tripadvisor which is so scathing and brilliantly written that it will briefly flare on Twitter, only snuffed out by tweets about 700 Zakynthos residents who claimed blindness in order to receive government money (including amongst them taxi drivers and a hairdresser), but not before the hotel review ensures that the few remaining summer bookings, including the regular from 119, are cancelled.

'Wait,' the Greek man said, looking around as though he recognized something. I took hold of his hand and tugged him along, through the dark reception area, and for a minute he resisted and let go of my hand to turn, looking upwards. In English I said, 'It's probably going to be repossessed soon.'

'Repossessed?' He rolled the word around in his mouth. His English was better than my Greek but he didn't know this word.

'Taken by the bank.' I shrugged, although he most likely didn't see it in the dark. I hoped to sound nonchalant, unemotional, grown up. I had worked out that Baba and Margot were living off her money, or rather Margot's mother's money. They still had their apartment upstairs but now – tonight – they were both away. A long weekend in Crete, they told me, but I suspected something else was going on. I try to tell my younger self to pay attention – this is what you should be worrying about, not this man and this night and your virginity.

I feel the younger me twitch, a tiny spark illuminated and then extinguished. I was already on the turn of the stairs, impatient. I took the man's hand again and tugged him upstairs to the best room in the hotel. Room 127, the suite Baba called it, but really this was because it was the only room with an en-suite bathroom, and it was big enough to have a sofa at the end of the double bed. I put the light on without thinking and the shabbiness of the room became clear. We'd had to let Dimitra go and the room hadn't been cleaned all summer. Dead flies sprinkled the windowsills, cobwebs dusted the corners. I turned it off quickly.

'Wait,' he said. 'How old are you?'

'Eighteen.'

Even in the dingy light I could sense that he didn't believe me.

'Okay, seventeen. But the age of consent is fifteen in Greece.'

'Seventeen! You are too young.'

'I'm not.'

The man got undressed and into bed, shuffled around a bit and immediately began to snore. I also undressed, slowly, and crept under the covers. I lay awake, too aware of the body beside me to sleep, and when daylight came, I got up with my head banging and waited for the water in the bathroom tap to run clear before dipping my head to drink. In the bedroom the man was sitting up with his knees raised under the sheet. I saw his shoulder-length hair, the way his eyes turned down at the edges, and I recognized him as Nicos, the man who had come to see my father about the tiger cub, and I saw on his face his surprise as he remembered the girl on the wall reading a book.

I sat on the edge of the bed, still naked. 'What did my father do with the tiger?'

Nicos thought and then said, *'Exafanístike.'*

I tried to repeat the word, but it had too many syllables. Nicos smiled. *'Exafanístike,'* he said again more slowly. He extended an arm above our heads, clenched his fist and then opened it gently with a puff of air from his mouth. A magic vanishing.

'Disappeared?' I asked.

'I don't know how. We agree for the tiger to be gone . . . disposed.' He seemed pleased to have remembered this word.

'What? Disposed of!' I looked at him and he stared back, wide-eyed. Was Sophia buried somewhere on Paxos? For five years I had imagined her wild and free, making her own cat decisions, living her own big cat life, when really she was dead and had probably been killed the day she'd been taken. Rocks and sandy soil over bones and striped fur. My knickers were on the floor and I got off the bed to yank them on.

'Did you do it?' I shouted. 'Was it you who killed her?'

'No!' He was outraged that I should accuse him.

'My father?'

'A man. Someone he knew. Friend of friend.'

'And I suppose you didn't report him?' I turned from Nicos, found my bra, attached the hooks at the front and swivelled it round so fast it scratched my skin. 'All those mezes and brandy, eh?' One strap snapped against my shoulder, then the other. It was not possible to be naked and angry. 'Or did he pay you to keep quiet?' I rubbed my thumb and index finger together. 'A backhander?'

Nicos rolled on to his front across the bed, out from under the sheet, reached for one of my hands, but I pulled away and he rolled back, head on a pillow, eyes closed.

'Did he?' I demanded.

'No money, no,' Nicos said. The full length of my first almost-lover was laid out before me: the dark hair sweeping upwards from his groin to his throat as though a tide had surged in and out, leaving behind his cock, a piece of soft flotsam marooned on a mat of seaweed.

'What, then?' I spoke softly like he had and when I sat again on the bed he opened his eyes.

'I met a woman in the town. My first time.'

I shook my head slowly back and forth. 'What house?'

'Big house.'

'A house with glass walls? A green lawn? He took you to her?'

The Neffy I am now knows the answer, and although it is banal, it reminds me of how much one person will do for another, to save them.

'Zylina.' Nicos scrubbed his palms across his eyes, embarrassed perhaps or just tired, but he said her name with gratitude. 'But not your father. Your stepmother – Margot? – she take me.'

After this night Nicos and I will leave the hotel and go down to the beach and we'll swim, and he'll buy me breakfast, and we'll swap numbers, and although we phone each other and meet every time I'm on Paxos and he'll become a good friend, we'll never speak of the tiger again.

Leon lets me rest in his bed and gets me up before it's time to go and eat.

'Does it work on you?' I call out. He's in his bathroom and I can hear the sound of his pee hitting the side of the toilet and then the water, and then the side. Justin used to do that; some kind of target game. Justin in our shared bathroom at his dad's house, the mess he left – if I can go back to see him,

I wouldn't mind about the tidemark in the bath, the damp towels on the floor, his stupid pissing game.

'What?' Leon calls back.

'Can you Revisit?' I hear the zip of his fly and he comes into his bedroom. 'Can you do it on yourself?' I'm sitting on one of his chairs, putting my trainers back on, tired and hot from my Revisit, and the air con blowing down on me is good.

Leon shoves his hands in his pockets. 'Yeah. I used to do it quite a bit. It was never very clear, not like yours. But I try not to do it much now.'

'Why not?'

'Too much difficult shit, stuff with my mum I'd rather not see again. It was just her and me when I was growing up. She was the one who got me to uni. Anyway, did it work? Did you go where you wanted to?'

'No. I wanted to see my mum or Justin, but I went back to Greece.'

He cocks his head. 'Boyfriend?'

I nod. 'I didn't see my dad this time but it was chronological.'

He stares up at the ceiling, thinking. 'That is weird. I don't know how that's happening. Except that memories are like threads, you know, in that way when you think of one memory and suddenly you'll be thinking of something else. They seem totally unrelated but one leads you to another and another and another. Maybe when *you* Revisit, yours are doing something similar but they're stuck in one timeline? Actually, I really have no fucking idea.' He laughs. 'As long as it's working, yeah?'

'Yeah,' I say. 'It's working. It's incredible.'

'Come on, it must be time to eat.' He flicks on his phone

to check the time. It's dark outside and my stomach – the best clock in the unit – is telling me it's almost eight.

Dearest H,

Everyone in that lab loved the octopuses. I'm not saying anyone was deliberately cruel. Not to the animals, although they were fed defrosted prawns and squid because they were cheaper and easier to manage, even though everyone knows octopuses prefer live crabs. One octopus that I would feed would wait until I was watching and then deposit the prawns and the squid in the out-flow pipe to show he didn't approve of that day's menu. You two would have got on well.

As well as squid and prawns, octopuses in the wild will also eat small fish, clams and of course crabs – when they can catch them. Denied this chase in lab conditions, octopuses often go into decline. The defrosted squid and prawns we fed our octopuses were already dead, therefore when it was feeding time the best Larry or I could do was to swirl the food in the water and, if the octopus did not come, drop it into the tank. I emailed the PI and suggested we put the prawns and squid into jars to give the octopuses the challenge of removing the lids. The PI took five days to reply to say no. Observe, record and question.

Neffy

'Thanks for coming, everyone,' Piper says as though we might be there for some other reason than because it's dinner time. She claps her little hands, calling a meeting to

138

order. We're all in the staffroom, and even my stomach is waiting for the beep of the microwave from the kitchen. We stop talking and look at her. 'Let's sit,' she says. And I'm glad to sit, in fact I would like to fold my arms on the table and put my head on them and sleep – my Revisit is catching up with me. There are enough chairs but, when each of us has settled, Piper remains standing. 'It's come to my attention that we're getting low on certain items and I thought we should discuss how we're going to share them out, assuming you are all happy to share them out.'

'What items were you after, exactly?' Yahiko says. The expression on his face is eager like he's anticipating a good transaction. I can almost see him rubbing his hands together.

'Condoms?' Leon says and Rachel rolls her eyes but I see pleasure.

'Toothpaste, coffee, chocolate,' Piper says as though checking off a list.

'You've forgotten alcohol,' Yahiko says.

'Wait, wait. You've got more booze?' Leon reaches across the table, his arms out and his palms upwards, begging. Yahiko only smiles.

'And teabags,' Piper says. She looks straight at me.

'What?' I say. It is true I have five mint teabags in my room. I found them in the pocket of my suitcase when I was looking for my mooncup. I didn't know they were there. But they are mine and I'm not going to share them; they would be gone in a day if I did. I had made myself a cup of mint tea in the kitchen when no one was in here, just to test whether I could taste or smell it – I couldn't. I put the bag straight down the waste chute, hoping I wouldn't be found out.

'What else do you have?' Leon asks Yahiko. 'Beer?' Yahiko raises his eyebrows, turns down his mouth. 'Wine?' Leon guesses again. Yahiko smiles.

'He has every-fucking-thing,' Rachel says.

'You've got more vodka?' Leon asks. 'You sneaky bastard. I didn't think it was true when you said that was the end of the bottle.'

'I thought it was a diode you were longing for,' Yahiko says. 'For your little radio project.'

Leon snorts.

'Haven't you seen the other rooms?' Rachel says moodily. 'We all know he's emptied them. And the lockers.' She flaps an arm behind her. 'You're such a wheeler-dealer.' I can't tell if she's joking or being bitchy.

Yahiko blinks, accepts the description as praise.

'Please, everyone.' Piper raises her voice, and we ignore her. 'Let's discuss this calmly and reasonably.'

'What about chocolate?' Leon continues. 'Do you have chocolate?' Leon told me that Mike was going to confiscate the two tubes of Starbursts he'd brought into the unit, but Leon charmed him and he was allowed to keep them. Leon told me he finished them on his first afternoon but, rather like my teabags, I think he might have some left which he isn't telling anyone about. 'What kind of chocolate?' Leon says.

'Everyone!' Piper claps her hands again.

'A Mars bar, two fingers of a four-fingered KitKat,' Rachel drawls as though bored. 'And fifteen M&M's.'

I don't look at Yahiko while I think about the two halves of Matchmaker in their pot, pushed to the back of my bed-side drawer. He tips his chair on its rear legs, leaning against the counter, and puts his hands behind his head.

'I only know,' Rachel says, 'because he's been swapping one M&M at a time for five pages of some business book I found: *Seven Ways to Crap on the People You're Supposed to be Helping*.' She kicks at a leg of Yahiko's chair and he yelps as the chair moves, eyes wild as he fumbles for the edge of the table to tug himself forward.

'You've been trading?' I say, pulled into the argument.

'Piper will trade with you,' Rachel says to me. 'Won't you, Pipe? Another veggie dinner for a good outcome of her grand plan.'

'Stop it, Rachel,' Leon says.

'Stop what?' She's all innocence and big eyes.

'Stirring.'

'What's the grand plan?' I ask. Is this the thing I've been sensing them conspiring about, something more than trying to persuade me to go outside to get them food? Leon won't look at me, but he glares at Rachel.

'Please, please.' Piper backs away from the table.

'No one's bothered to tell Neffy?' Rachel's tone is snide. 'What a surprise.'

Leon stands, kicking his chair out of the way. 'You know what, looks like you're as much of a fucking dick as your father.'

And Rachel whips upright too and her fist comes out, springing straight from her body and catching him in the throat. He coughs and staggers and Rachel's face crumples: her bottom lip turning out, her features folding in on themselves and her eyes filling with tears. Leon, with one hand on his neck, reaches out for her, an apology I think, but Rachel turns and runs from the room.

'Another little meltdown from Rachel that we can do without,' Yahiko says, as he and I quickly stand. We speak over each other while Piper is motionless with both hands pressed against her cheeks.

'What was that all about? Rachel's father?' I say to Leon. 'What's the grand plan? What the fuck is the grand plan?' I say to the room. 'Will someone just tell me!'

'Shit, man,' Yahiko is saying to Leon. 'I don't think you should have said that.'

The microwave beeps, and we fall silent and stop moving.

'Her father's in prison,' Piper says, heading for the kitchen. 'He went in a year ago today. His sentence finished the day before yesterday. She's been waiting for him to turn up, to come and fetch her.'

'Oh no,' I say. And I remember our conversation about the zoo animals, the astronauts stuck on the space station. I'd only been thinking of Justin in his own tin box and the octopuses going unfed in their glass ones.

'He broke her boyfriend's nose,' Leon says. 'With one of those telescopic poles with a net on the end for cleaning swimming pools.'

'Ouch,' I say, raising my fingers to my own nose. 'Her swimming coach? He's still her boyfriend?'

'Was,' Yahiko says and makes a sawing action with his fingers under his jaw. Leon shakes his head – at Yahiko or the boyfriend, I'm not sure.

'What about her mother?' I ask.

'Long gone,' Yahiko says.

Piper comes out from the kitchen with four microwave containers on a tray. We sit at the table, and she sits too, and we watch her dividing the food up between five, like siblings making sure their mother doesn't favour one child above the others.

'Do you think they'd have let prisoners out?' I ask.

142

'Of course not,' Piper says.

'Of course not,' Yahiko says, mimicking her. 'Have murderers and kiddie-fiddlers roaming the streets? I don't think so. Better to let them rot inside.'

The door to the staffroom opens and I realize it was never fully closed. Rachel comes in, her make-up reapplied. She sits at the table and pulls her dish towards her. 'I know they were let out,' she says. 'No one would be so cruel.'

Dearest H,

The live crabs at the fish stall were too big and too expensive. On one Saturday I caught a bus to a cove further along the coast and turned over rocks until I caught a middle-sized edible crab. I kept it at home in the bath (3.5 teaspoons of salt for every 1000ml of tap water) and took it into work on Monday in one of the plastic boxes I used for my sandwiches.

That evening I dropped it into a tank. The octopus let the crab scuttle into a corner, but I knew the cephalopod was aware of the change in the water, either from the ripples or a particular crabby flavour. I watched him nudge it like a cat will play with a mouse, until Larry called out to me that he was locking up. I smiled all the way home. But giving the octopus the crab was unwise because I hadn't considered that the shell would be left in the tank for Larry to find in the morning.

He reported me.

Neffy

Day Ten

'So, what is the grand plan?' I ask Leon. I'm lying on his bed with my eyes closed and I can feel his hands skimming my body, touching down at certain points – the tops of my humeri, the centre of my forehead, my suprasternal notch, my belly button. My palms are open waiting for the pebbles – I know they're not pebbles but that's how I think of them.

'What?'

'You know. The grand plan that nobody's told me about.'

'Do you want to do this Revisit or not?'

'I want to know what this fucking grand plan is. Should I be worried? Are you going to lock me in my room again and leave me to die so you can eat all the chocolate and drink all the vodka by yourselves?'

'What?'

My eyes fly open. Leon looks uncomfortable and now I really am interested. I'd saved up this question until we were alone, knowing he would tell me when the others weren't here. He sighs and sits on the bed beside me. 'It isn't my plan, it's Piper's.' I look at his profile, drawing around the edges of him – the spiralled hair, the straight nose, the lips that are closed over slightly forward-pressing teeth, the tufts of beard on his cheeks and chin.

I wait and when he doesn't continue, I say, 'And?'

'You know she thinks you're immune?'

'Okay.'

'And you know she thinks we have a duty to continue the trial?'

'However irrational that is.'

'It's more than that, though. She believes this is about the continuation of the human race – keeping it going. So she thought –'

I half sit up on my elbows and realize I have already worked out the answer to my question. 'She thought you should have sex with me, make a baby or two and tah-dah, the human race continues. Meanwhile you get in a few extra shags.'

'No,' he says. 'No.'

'Because you're shagging Rachel?'

'I'm not shagging Rachel.'

'Not yet.' I hold my hands up. 'But you can of course shag Rachel. That's no concern of mine. But then neither of you are immune and all those little babies Rachel pops out in the future won't be either.'

'Neffy.' Leon sounds appalled but I'm not stopping now.

'And Yahiko only wants to shag you so he's no use. Jesus Christ. Do you think Piper's even heard of consent? You know she stole my mooncup? Presumably so she'd know when I had my period because I'd have to ask Yahiko for some tampons and then she could tell you when I was ovulating.' I shout 'ovulating' and he puts his hands on top of his head and shrinks from me. 'It really is a pathetic grand plan.' He still says nothing. 'Whatever.' I flop back on the pillows. 'Can we just get on with my Revisit, now. Please.'

I have forgotten that Baba didn't meet me off the hydrofoil this time like he'd always done in the past. It was something I'd looked forward to, enjoying the feeling of being the one the loud handsome man was waving his hat at, as though we both might have been almost famous. The older Neffy knows that Baba will never meet me off the boat again, and I think about trying to return to the previous time to revel in it, but no, I will let this play out; it has to be done. This time I wanted him to meet me so we could drive across the island for a drink in a bar we would often go to, and maybe another drink or more until I'd swallowed enough courage to tell him I'd decided to give up studying medicine. It had taken me a year to realize I didn't want to be a doctor and now I didn't know why I'd ever thought I had. I never imagined it would be so much about human bodies, their insides and their outsides. And then there was the smell of hospitals, of human bodies in hospitals, which, during clinical practice, I had discovered I could not stand.

But, Baba wasn't amongst the throng of people waiting on the quay for the boat to come in and he wasn't sitting at one of the little tables outside the cafe with a coffee in front of him. The sky was low, as heavy and dark as an old oil painting, and the cicadas were warning of rain as I put my suitcase into a taxi and directed the driver to the address in the town that Margot had texted me.

'Your dad's in bed,' she whispered at the door. She looked thinner, tired. It wasn't late but inside their rented apartment above the supermarket the sofa bed in the main room was already pulled out and made up for me. 'He said to say hi.' She took my suitcase from me and looked around for somewhere to put it, eventually taking it into the kitchen and packing it in behind the door. The kitchen was windowless and tiny, the countertops full of ingredients, packets and jars. She shooed me out, saying, 'I saved you some food.' And she brought me a bowl of *stifado*, still warm. 'Vegetarian,' she said. I looked around but the apartment didn't have a table, so I sat on the edge of the bed.

Although I'd known they were no longer living in the hotel because the bank had taken it, I had still, naively, imagined us sitting down to eat one of Margot's dinners at the table on the terrace, opening a bottle of wine and talking with the sound of the sea below. For the first time that I could remember I was homesick for England, although Mum had moved out of the rented flat in the ordinary town we'd been living in because she had fallen in love again, this time not with a man but with a non-religious community in the south of England where she now lived – the latest in a long line of husbands, lovers or obsessions.

I spooned up some of the mushrooms in red wine gravy – a large dollop of mashed potato on the side. For me, now, the taste is sublime, it fills my senses so I have to concentrate to listen to what Margot is saying: 'I managed to get some dried porcini from the supermarket.' She seemed to be searching for my approval in a way that she'd never bothered with before.

'It's delicious,' I said, and although I kept it to myself, I was surprised she hadn't made a lamb version for her and my father. The stew was rich and flavourful, and I would have liked some wine to go with it but she didn't offer anything.

'Have you had yours?'

'Oh, yeah,' she said. 'A while back.' She stood at the glass door which led to a narrow balcony and I saw the rain had started. Margot's face was reflected, ghostly and gaunt amongst the drops on the pane. 'It won't last long,' she said, and she turned and asked about my journey, how my mother was. I didn't tell her about the community. Margot had never been good at idle chat, she was either silent or else the conversation was intense – digging right to the bone. I knew we were both aware that these questions and my perfunctory answers were filler for something that was coming: why my father hadn't met me off the hydrofoil, why he was in bed this early. Finally, she removed a pile of clothes and books, and sat on a chair which was so close to the sofa bed our knees were almost touching.

'Tomorrow,' she said, 'Oliver has an appointment with the doctor.'

'The doctor?' My mouth was full of creamy potato and mushroom.

'His legs are swollen.' She was still whispering. 'And he can't catch his breath. Any little thing tires him out.'

I must have pulled a face because she said, 'It's not just the stress of the hotel closing, although that's been bad enough. Something else. He isn't eating.' In my next mouthful I could taste the flavours of kalamata, parsley, bay. 'And you know how Oliver likes to eat. He says he isn't hungry.' Her words were quiet as though this were the most terrible thing that could befall Baba and, right now, eating this food, I could imagine it was. 'And he is so proud of you, studying medicine. He tells everyone who will listen – about his brilliant daughter, the doctor.'

'I'm not –' I started.

'I love Oliver so much, Neffy.'

'I don't think . . .' I licked my lips and wondered if she was expecting me to diagnose him. Before I could find the words a noise came from behind one of the doors off the sitting room – a cough. And she touched my knee with her hand and said quickly, 'So I thought you could go with him, to the doctor.'

I heard the door open behind me. I swallowed a tiny onion and felt it travel, whole, down my oesophagus as I turned from Margot to my father in his pyjamas and robe, and back again. 'What?' I said to her, but she was already standing.

'Oliver. What are you doing up?' She was gentle with him, softly spoken, as though she were talking to a child who had got out of bed because he'd heard the adults chatting.

'Neffy,' Baba boomed, his arms outstretched, and I thought Margot must be mistaken, there was nothing wrong with him at all.

When I'd finished eating, Margot hustled Baba back to bed and wished me goodnight. As the younger Neffy undresses, my older self is concerned about staying in this Revisit and going to sleep: what if I don't wake? I might never get back to the unit, although maybe this might not be such a terrible thing, but I know how this time with Baba and Margot will go; I know how it ends and I don't want to sit through it. I try to rise but it doesn't work and eventually I fall asleep.

In the morning Baba and I didn't mention his doctor's appointment while he helped me pack away the sofa bed, but Margot chivvied us over our breakfast and while Baba was in the bathroom she turned on me, saying didn't I realize how serious this was, and making me promise that not only would I go with him to the clinic but that I would sit in the doctor's consulting room with him.

'If he goes in alone nothing will happen, he won't

mention how he has to go to bed early, how often he has to go to the bathroom while nothing comes out. Promise me.'

I promised, but no way was I going to tell the doctor about how many times my father pissed or didn't piss in the night. I didn't want to go. *Stop whining*, I try to tell my younger self, who never listens. *This is Baba; look after him.*

The island's medical clinic had tiled floors and blank walls except for a single poster encouraging vaccinations. The window was barred and the dark smells of blood, disease and disinfectant made me hunch on my chair and pick at the skin around my fingernails. Baba dragged his chair across the floor and sat beside the receptionist, pretending to look over her shoulder at what was on her computer screen while she covered it with her hands and laughed, exposing the metal train tracks across her teeth. As far as I knew, Baba had never used a computer; he had a mobile phone but rarely turned it on. He would get Margot to call me on hers and then pass it over. I thought he looked more Greek than ever – he'd let his beard grow and he was no thinner. If he wasn't eating, it didn't show. He crossed his legs and one trouser leg rose to expose a glimpse of ankle, hairy but thick, with skin that looked stretched to bursting point like a frying sausage. Baba saw me looking and gave his trousers a sharp tug to make the ankle disappear. The doctor came out of his room and Baba and he talked in Greek, greeting each other like old friends. Perhaps they were. I'd never had to come to the clinic before. During all my times on the island I'd only ever had stomach aches, cut knees, a bee sting – problems that could be treated at home. I stood up too and Baba introduced me in English.

'Neffy is studying to be a doctor,' he said. 'Just finished her first year.'

I still hadn't found the opportunity to tell him.

'Congratulations,' the doctor said in perfect English. 'Where are you studying?'

'Plymouth.' My eyes slid to Baba's glowing face and away.

'Plymouth,' the doctor said, sounding as though he didn't know where it was. 'Very good. And how are you getting on? Any thoughts of a specialism yet?'

'It's far too early to think of that, isn't it?' Baba said at exactly the same time as I said, 'Cephalopods.'

'Sorry?' the doctor asked.

Baba stared at me and I replied, 'I really don't have any idea yet. It's too early.'

Baba made a *hmm* sound and then they were back to Greek and gone into the consulting room and the door was shut. The receptionist smiled at me with a closed mouth, nodded to my chair, indicating that I should sit again. A printer began churning out pages and she picked each one up and glanced over it. The sheet then either went face down on a pile or she fed it to the shredder behind her which made a terrific effort of eating each page. The side of my index finger was bleeding and I sucked at it, tasting iron, and I thought perhaps I could tell Margot that the receptionist had made me stay in the waiting room.

I knew that Baba only agreed to me coming because otherwise Margot would have come herself. They'd been arguing about it when I was in the bathroom trying to go as quietly as I could. The bathroom opened straight into the living room and I had heard every noise Baba had made when he'd used it before me.

'Please, sorry,' the receptionist said, indicating the shredder. I got out my phone and brought up Nicos's number.

I'm on Paxos! Are you about? A minute later I got a reply.

Nicos: *Neffy! I didn't know you coming*
Me: *Stuff going on with my Dad, had to come and help*
Nicos: *Everything okay?*
Me: *Fancy a drink?*
Nicos: *Yes, but . . . I'm in Australia*
Me: *What?!*
Nicos: *I told you I was thinking about it*
Me: *But I didn't know you were actually going*
Nicos: *No jobs in Greece*

I knew this was the truth and I knew it had been hard for him but I was sorry for myself; not even Nicos was here to go out with after this doctor's visit was over.

Nicos: *You never guess where I work here*
Me: *Where are you working?*
Nicos: *You guess*
Me: *I don't know. Tell me.* I didn't want to play this game.
Nicos: *Guess*
Me: *I really don't know Nicos. In a surf shack?*

A couple of minutes went by. Maybe he was on Google Translate.

Nicos: *No! Kalýva gia sérfin'nk! No!*
Me: *Please, just tell me*
Nicos: *I work in Sydney Aquarium*

What? How did he manage that? I was pleased for him but envious.

Me: *Really?! Which animals are you working with?*
Nicos: *I clean*

I tried to think of what to say. Nicos had a BSc and an MSc in Animal Welfare. He had two or three years of experience working as an animal inspector.

Me: *Well, it's a start*
Nicos: *We have octopus predicting the election!*

Me: *I'm getting on the next plane . . .*
Nicos: *I see you in 19 hours and 19 minutes*
I couldn't believe I wouldn't be seeing him. Nothing here was the same. I wondered what Mum was doing – pulling up muddy carrots, cooking lentils for a houseful of non-religious freaks. I was cross with her that I didn't have a home to return to.

Baba came out of the doctor's room after ten minutes. The two of them did some more back-slapping and hand-shaking, and as far as I could tell promised to meet for a drink sometime without any firm arrangements being made.

The overnight rain had gone, and it was hot and clear as we walked back to the apartment. Baba offered to buy me a waffle-cone ice cream, like he used to do when I was younger, from one of the shops by the harbour but when we reached the counter he discovered he didn't have any money on him and I paid. We strolled along beside the boats and by the time we turned inland I'd eaten all the ice cream and had bitten the cone down to the end.

'Would you like some?' I said, like I used to say when I was a child. He was supposed to reply, 'Okay, just a lick,' and when I handed him the tip with its bit of melted vanilla in the bottom he was meant to play surprised that this was all that was left. But this time he shook his head. 'No thanks.' Had he forgotten the routine or, as Margot said, maybe he didn't want to eat? I couldn't bring myself to put that tiny end of cone in my mouth although the ice cream was melt-ing into my palm and dribbling down my wrist. I tried not to think about what it was Baba might have, but I couldn't help myself. Something from that year of medicine must have stuck: swollen ankles, lack of appetite, lots of peeing.

Urinary tract infection? Heart disease? Trying to work it out reminded me of those awful moments in seminars when the lecturer would cast around the room for someone to answer the question she had just posed, and I wasn't sure whether avoiding her eye or looking at her directly would stop her from picking on me. I had tried it both ways. She'd always seemed to ask me and I'd never known the answer. And I didn't know it now.

'I'm thinking of changing course,' I said as I dropped the tip of the cone into a bin.

'What direction? North, south, east or west?'

'Baba.' I drew out the final vowel, turning the word into a moan.

He smiled sadly. 'No more medicine for Neffy?'

'It's not for me.'

'I could have told you that a year ago.'

'Why didn't you, then?'

'Because you wouldn't have listened.'

'True.' I was relieved that he wasn't angry but now it seemed foolish that I thought he might have been and I'd put off telling him for so long.

'What's it to be, then?'

'Marine biology.' I glanced at him, but his face didn't give anything away.

'I'd like to be able to help, with the fees, the cost, but . . .'

'I wasn't asking for that.'

'Things are tight at the moment. Margot's speaking to her mother, seeing if she can help. We just need to save a little more. Get someone to build a better website, get some reviews or whatever it is those marketing people do. I reckon we should be back up and running in a couple of months.'

'What? The hotel?' I didn't believe it. He couldn't afford an ice cream.

'Yes, the hotel. Did you think I was going to give it up just like that?' I had disappointed him, not because I was giving up medicine but because I didn't believe in him.

'Okay.' In the past I might have argued but not now. Now I was thinking about his heart or his liver or his stomach.

'We can go and look at it later. I'll tell you what I'm planning.'

'All right,' I said, not wanting to encourage him but not knowing how to tell him this was just a dream.

We were at the apartment door when he hugged me to him. 'It's going to be octopuses for Neffy, is it?'

'It is.'

'That sounds much more like your thing.'

Still with his arm around my shoulders, not looking at each other, I finally found the courage to ask, 'What did the doctor say?'

Baba dropped his arm from my shoulder. 'The doctor?' he said in a surprised tone, the one I recognized from our old ice-cream routine. He fished in his trouser pocket for his door keys. 'He told me about his daughter, Ariadne. She's getting married next year to some young man from Athens. I persuaded Dr Papakosta to have the reception at the Hotel Ammos.' Baba's smile was wide and innocent, delusional. His key was in the door. 'So it was worth going after all.'

As Leon lifts the pieces off my forehead and chest, and places them back in their little boxes and then into their places in the silver box, he says, 'I'm sorry about Piper.'

I'm drifting off on a feeling of absent contentment and it takes me a moment to work out what he means, and then I realize he's continuing the conversation we had before I went under about Piper's grand plan. Fifteen or so hours had gone by in Greece, while here in the unit it must have been only – what, an hour?

'I would have turned you down, anyway.' I notice that my speech is slightly slurred.

'But you'd have been missing all this.' Leon strikes a pose, arms up like a bodybuilder. He knows he looks idiotic in his BioPharm robe and now he hops backwards and forwards on the balls of his feet, uppercutting like a boxer.

'Nifty footwork but it won't cut it.'

He moves faster, making little exaggerated puffs with his cheeks.

'You don't have any books.'

He stops moving, drops his arms.

'You know what they say,' I continue. 'If you go home with somebody and they don't have any books, don't fuck 'em.'

'I have books!' Leon says, throwing his arms in the air. 'I just didn't bring them with me.'

Dearest H,

In my final meeting with the woman from HR and the PI, he claimed I'd compromised the whole experiment. He said they'd had to give all of the seven other octopuses a live crab to mitigate my action. That made me very happy. He and his colleagues had decided they could and would continue the study. The PI talked again about my response to the amputated arms, how I'd cried and stuck them to myself. What had you been expecting? he asked. When I tried to answer, it seemed his question was rhetorical. He said he didn't think I was cut out to be a scientist. The woman from HR said I had to collect my things and leave. She said they would give me a reference since the study was continuing. I knew that giving me a bad one would have called the whole project into question.

Neffy

Leon was right when he said I wouldn't be able to live in a state of shock for long. My racing pulse, sweating palms and pounding head have left me. Now time ticks slowly by while I think about going outside. I move from bed to window, to the mirror in my bathroom and back to window. A caged animal following the same path round and round its enclosure. I once heard about a *National Geographic* report of a captive tiger refusing to leave the perimeters of its cage when released into a nature reserve, even when the cage was removed. From my window I watch a piece of litter blow slowly from one end of the alley to the other. Its meandering journey is a tale of doubling back and indecisiveness, while all the time having no choice but to be pushed forward because the invisible wind says to go back is only an illusion.

Last night I woke unsure if I was in Baba's hotel, my stepfather's house, or somewhere else. Was it the past or the

future? Time continues to loop and fold, making a single fit-
ful night take days, while the sun rises and sets in a couple of
hours. I sat up in bed and pressed a hand on to the wall of
the adjoining room, wondering where Orla and Stephan
had gone and whether they'd made it.

I wait for Leon to call me, twitchy with the possibility of
seeing Mum and Justin. I wonder whether trying to not
think of them would help make me Revisit them. And I
worry about going outside; I want to find the courage to get
food, or even to leave, but I am desperate to stay.

I'm sitting at the staffroom table rereading a magazine about
houses and gardens since I can't focus on the two psycho-
logical thrillers I brought with me – I don't feel able to read
someone else's drama when I'm living my own. If I spend
too long in my room, I find myself flicking through picture
after picture on my phone until they blur together, or zoom-
ing in on one – Justin reading beside the pond, Mum and
Clive holding hands on a walk, Baba raising a glass to the
camera – and examining every detail for something I've forgotten. Those photo sessions never end well, and every
activity is only to make the time pass until I can Revisit
again. The magazine is from the table in reception. Rachel
took the fashion magazines and Yahiko got the one about
fancy food and wine. This one, with features on how the
owners of an apartment in Venice used blues and yellows to
create an elegant simplicity and how to choose the best kitchen worktop, has been hanging around the staffroom for

days, its corners curling. It is distracting and I prefer it to the newspaper which was in here for a while, with its headline: SCIENTISTS CLAIM KILLER VIRUS CAUSES FORGETFULNESS. Forgetfulness! They made it sound as though a few people were going to mislay their door keys for a couple of hours, discover them in the fruit bowl on the hall table amongst the old postcards and dusty nutcrackers still left from Christmas, and everything would be all right. I find pleasure and pain in looking at a world where macramé hanging baskets were worth making and could be used to 'brighten up a gloomy corner'.

'You're not reading that again, are you?' Yahiko says, coming in.

'No worse than you rereading that list of the best bars to visit when you're next in New York.'

'I can dream, can't I?' He takes the lid off the black marker pen that lies in the whiteboard's gutter and I go back to how to create a natural look with roses, and sip my tea. It's what was left in the pot after breakfast, topped up with boiling water. There is no tea-ness about it and only a slight discolouration.

'Have you thought any more about what I asked, about going outside?' Yahiko says this with his back to me, as though it isn't me he's asking. Mum would employ this technique when I was helping her with the cooking, taking the opportunity when we were busy with other things to bring up subjects like what I was doing with my life. Her voice would be calm, light and, under the surface, roiling.

Piper comes in. 'What are you doing?' she says. I close the magazine with a huff and I'm just about to confront her about her grand plan and the fact that she went into my room and stole my mooncup, when I look up and see her question is directed at Yahiko, and Yahiko is replacing the lid on the black marker.

He widens his eyes at her. 'What does it look like?'

'That's my job,' Piper says.

'What is?'

'Marking off the days. I've been doing it. That's my writing.' She goes up to the board and taps her finger under one of the four-bar gates that I've only just realized weren't there before.

'They're lines, not writing,' Yahiko says.

'Whatever, they're mine.'

'What? Like, you own them?' Yahiko laughs.

'Like,' she says, pointedly, 'you've been duplicating days.'

'No, *you've* been duplicating days.' He's still smiling and it's infuriating Piper and he knows it. She moves away from him towards the table.

'Why don't I get my phone and see what the date is?' I ask, although it doesn't really bother me. 'We can easily work it out.' Yahiko and Piper ignore me.

'It's meant to be Rachel's birthday on Tuesday,' Piper says.

'Well, it still can be.'

Piper folds her arms. 'And what about the end of the trial date?'

'What, when we're going to be rescued?'

'Now, we have no idea what day it is or how long we've been in here.'

'But it's on our phones,' I try to interrupt. They aren't interested; this is about more than what the actual date is.

'That's right. No idea!' Yahiko yanks the lid off the pen again and makes another four strokes with a bar through them and then some more, much bigger and wilder than the others.

'For God's sake.' Piper tries to grab the pen, but Yahiko flourishes it around her head while she tries to catch his hand. The pen makes contact with her cheek and a long black line appears from her eye to her chin like a poorly drawn fake scar, and she cries out, her hand pressed to her cheek as she backs into the table as though Yahiko is going to come after her. He pauses, his eyes wide and his mouth open as though he has actually cut her. And then Piper grabs my mug, still half full of lukewarm tea, and throws it at him. The liquid arcs out sideways and splatters against the whiteboard. Her throw is poor and would probably have missed except that Yahiko ducks and swerves, and the mug hits him full in the face in the middle of his glasses and he goes down to his knees, clutching his nose. The mug smashes on the floor and his glasses fall.

'Piper!' I shout, stretching the whole of my upper body across the table to them both.

'They're my lines.' Her lips are drawn back from her teeth as she wags her finger at Yahiko. He's still crouching on the floor and when he doesn't respond she wags her finger at me. 'I mark down the days!' She moves to the other side of the table and the door slams behind her.

'She's broken my nose! If she's broken my nose I'll fucking kill her,' Yahiko says, one hand on his face, the other patting the floor around him. 'Shit, shit, shit,' he says.

'Wait,' I say. 'You'll cut your hand.'

'I can't see without my glasses.'

I go to him, take hold of his hands. 'Stand up. You're bleeding.' Two small trickles of blood flow from a cut on the bridge of his nose.

'Bleeding?' he says in horror and he stands, both his hands to his face. He takes one step forward and we hear the

crunch and snap of his glasses breaking. 'Oh fuck, oh fuck.'
He goes to crouch again but I get there first, pick up the two
halves of his glasses, snapped in the middle. Both of the
lenses are in pieces.

'Maybe we can fix them,' I say and hand him the halves. I
collect the bits of lens. It's some sort of plastic, not glass. I
put them in his hand.

'I'm going to fucking kill her.'

'I didn't realize that you needed them to see.'

'Of course I need them to see.'

'I thought they were, you know, a fashion accessory.
Maybe we can find some glue. Maybe we can tape them
together.' I pull him up by the elbow and sit him on a chair.
'Wait here.' I go into the kitchen – aluminium shelving and
the industrial microwave – and find the freezer with the food
in it – it looks even less than I thought – and at the top a tray
of ice cubes. I tap some out on to the counter and find a tea
towel to wrap them in and hurry back to the staffroom
where I make Yahiko hold the tea towel to his face.

'It's cold,' he complains.

'Exactly. Come on, come with me.'

In the treatment room I sit him on another chair, snap on
some gloves and pull his fingers away from his nose where
he's prodding and wiping at the blood. He's already dumped
the tea towel with the ice cubes on the counter. I've only
poked my head into this room before. It's small with a
couple of chairs, a desk with a computer, and a metal cupboard. Inside are drawers of medical equipment. I find packets
of the same clamp I had to put on my nose after I was given
the virus, the bags we used for tissues, and scissors. I take a pair
out of their sterile packet but then discover that the plasters

and other items are behind a glass-fronted cabinet, which is locked.

'Does Piper have the key?' I say to myself, but Yahiko jumps up.

'For fuck's sake.' He fumbles for the scissors and shoves them between the cupboard's door and its frame. I cry out at the violence but the door springs open. 'There,' he says, slamming the scissors back down on the desk and sitting in the chair, pressing the tea towel to his face again. I take out a packet of antiseptic wipes, tear it open and tilt back Yahiko's head, pulling the tea towel away.

'At least it was only a mug, not one of those poles for cleaning swimming pools.' He doesn't laugh, just winces and jerks his head as I wipe gently at the cut. He looks different without his glasses, naked and startled, an innocent. 'I don't think you need stitches, but you might get a couple of shiners.' I try to sound confident even though I was never taught how to sew up lacerations.

'For fuck's sake,' he says again under his breath.

'You know that girl and man we saw from Rachel's window,' I say, more to distract him from what I'm doing than anything else. I go back to the cupboard and rummage around until I find a plaster of the right size. Yahiko puts the bits of broken lens on the desk, peers in and begins sliding them about with a fingertip. He glances up at me and back to his puzzle. 'Why did we hide from them?'

'What?' He isn't really listening. I move so I'm in his eyeline.

'Why didn't we bring them inside?'

Yahiko stops what he's doing, stares at me and blinks myopically. 'Because they were probably infectious. Because only you have had the vaccine. The man certainly had the virus. Because, as you know, we don't have food for more people.' He shakes his head at my naivety, goes back to his jigsaw.

'But I could have put on PPE and brought them in without them touching anything, made them stay in a room, brought them whatever food we had.'

'And what then? Are you offering to go outside and get some more?'

'That girl,' I persist. 'She couldn't have been more than ten.'

'So what do you want to do? Go and find her?'

He isn't being serious. He lifts his hand to his nose as though to push up his glasses but his finger finds the wound and he dabs around it again, testing the bruising.

'No, no. But what about the next person we see?'

'I see them all the time from Rachel's window.'

'Really?'

He straightens up and I can see he's realized that what he's said might put me off going outside. 'Well, not that many. A few. I've stopped telling you lot who goes past. That girl was the first normal one to walk by since a couple of days after Day Zero. The few others behave like, I don't know, crazies. I saw one woman on all fours, coming down the street on her hands and feet. I couldn't look at her. We couldn't have let her in. And that guy we saw with the girl, he could have been anyone, could have done anything. Smashed someone's face in with a mug of tea or a swimming pool pole.'

'But why should we be the ones to decide who survives and who doesn't? Maybe if we fed him, looked after him, he'd have got better too.'

'No. He was infectious and we would have all died.'

I take the backing off the plaster. 'Come here.' He leans and I stick it over the bridge of his nose. The plaster is too pink for the colour of Yahiko's skin. 'Keep the ice pack on it.' I gather up the tea towel and give it to him. 'It'll keep the swelling down. Get more ice when you need to.'

'You want to let people like Rachel's father into the unit?' he says.

'Who knows what any of us have done in the past. I might be a murderer for all you know, just too clever to have been caught or put it down on my application form.' Yahiko stares at me, eyebrows raised, but it's not his usual mocking face. It's an expression I can't work out. It might even be horror. 'I'm not, though.' He continues to stare. 'What?' I ask, and finally he looks back to his bits of lens.

'You can't save everyone, Neffy.' He nudges them around again, and then slams his hand down on the desk. 'There's a fucking piece missing.'

Dearest H,

I was perhaps lucky with my timing and with the reference from the lab. I saw a vacancy for an aquarist at the local aquarium. Rather like with the lab job or keeping the tiger cub, I wasn't sure about it – confining animals in tanks, even if they did have breeding programmes for rarer species. The irony of that hasn't passed me by. But, I needed the money, and I got the job. Part of the role was to help the public Meet the Creatures! I was hired to look after their octopuses but when I started they only had two so they would get me to fill in wherever someone was needed. No one ever wanted the starfish gig and therefore it went to the newest recruit.

The tank I had to stand in front of was a wide and shallow basin with a pile of fibreglass rocks and some 'sunken treasure' half submerged in the saline water. I would sign in on the rota sheet and check the number of starfish in the tank against the number on the sheet: three. A story was circulating that a starfish had once gone missing. Whether it had inched its way out of the tank without anyone noticing or it had been taken, no one was sure.

'Would you like to stroke a starfish?' I said to a boy hesitating near the tank, who stared with incredulity as though I'd invited him to put his hand in a bucket of sharks. 'They're perfectly safe.' I smiled and nodded. The boy's parents stood behind him – the mother in a flowery dress and the father a little apart and wearing jeans which were too blue and a T-shirt that was tucked in tight so that a small belly overhung his belt and I could make out the hollow of his navel. Then I thought, he might not be the boy's father but a mystery shopper checking up on me, or a supervisor in disguise. They were supposed to pretend to be litter-pickers, holding a grabber and a bin bag, but how much litter is dropped in an aquarium?

I checked the list to see which starfish had been stroked last. A strict rotation operated so that none of the animals became stressed through over-stroking, but I suspected the other attendants weren't as rigorous as me. 'Pull your sleeve back so it doesn't get wet,' I said to the boy. I couldn't care less if his sleeve got wet but I didn't want the water contaminated with wool or ice cream or anything worse. I would have preferred that guests – that's what we had to call the punters – had to wash their hands first or, even better, that they didn't get to stroke the starfish at all, but then I suppose I wouldn't have had a job.

The red starfish with the black horns was next on the list. 'Here,' I said to the boy. 'You can stroke Ringo. Just use one

finger.' I straightened my index finger and the boy copied me.
Ringo, for fuck's sake. *Protoreaster nodosus,* or the horned sea
star, eats microorganisms and dead creatures. I would have liked
it if they ate small boys' fingers. The animals stand on the tips of
their arms when they spawn and release both eggs and sperm at
the same time.

'These are chocolate chip starfish,' I said, and the boy with his
finger on Ringo stared at me while his mother laughed as though
sharing the joke. It's no joke, I wanted to say. That's their
common name. But instead I smiled and said, 'Can you feel their
bumps? Phantasmagorical, aren't they?' I glanced at the man
who might or might not be the boy's father. The man didn't smile.
'Phantasmagorical' was the word I and the guest-facing staff
had been given at that morning's briefing. If a supervisor heard
me using it, I'd get a credit. After ten credits, I'd get a voucher to
spend at Magic HQ – the staff canteen – for a meal and a
pudding, worth £3.

'I expect Ringo is a bit tired now,' I said.

The boy continued to stroke the starfish. 'No, he isn't,' he said.

I looked at the chart. 'How about stroking Freddie? Don't you
think he seems lonely?'

'I like Ringo best.' The boy twisted his head and looked up at
his mother. His mother frowned while the father/supervisor
continued to stare at me. The boy's finger was rubbing harder
now, faster.

The father/supervisor folded his arms.

'Or what about Lucky?' I tried to keep my voice even. 'He
loves being stroked.' Lucky – pale with reddish bumps – was half
inside the fibreglass treasure chest.

'Ringo,' the boy said, two fingers on the starfish.

Out of sight, I gripped both my hands into fists and forced my
voice into a singsong intonation. 'You might rub his bumps off

and then he wouldn't be a chocolate chip starfish any more. Don't you think he would be sad?'

With a sharp movement the mother grabbed the boy by his wrist, yanking his hand out of the water. 'What have I said about not doing the same thing for too long?' The boy whined and let his feet drag as his mother pulled him away.

The man, still beside the tank, tilted towards me and said in a whisper, 'Do they have brains?'

'No,' I said, maybe too sharply. 'While a starfish lacks a centralized brain, it has a complex nervous system with a nerve ring around the mouth and a radial nerve running along the ambulacral region of each arm parallel to the radial canal.' The man backed off and turned towards the seahorses.

I thought about Ringo as I left the aquarium that evening and whether he knew in any sense where he was and whether he would prefer to be in the open sea. I was one of the last to leave. The security guard – the one I was friendly with – called out, 'All right, Neffy?'

'Phantasma-fucking-gorical!' I shouted back.

The next day I was on the rota for Meet the Rays! with their funny little faces looking as though they're hiding behind a sheet, with holes cut out for their eyes and their mouths.

Neffy

In the afternoon I knock on Leon's door and go in. The tap is running in his bathroom and I hear a scrubbing sound.

'Hi, it's Neffy?' I call out as casually as possible. 'You okay?'

I stand at his desk where the radio junk – the wires and the pencils and now-dismantled lighters – have been pushed to the side to make room for the open silver case and all the parts, which are laid out beside the lit screen. Leon comes out of his bathroom carrying his white trainers. He holds them up. 'Can't get the black marks off. My mum used to do it but I don't know how.'

'Tipp-ex?' I say.

He licks a finger and rubs at the end. 'Maybe.'

I lean over the desk. 'So, this is the piece that goes on my forehead?' I pick up the small circular box and jiggle it around. Suspended in the liquid is a disc about the size of my little fingernail but black with what look like silver filaments across the surface. This sensor, marked 'B', is the one which goes on my chest but I know poor Leon will be drawn in too easily and he won't be able to resist coming over and explaining what goes where and how he's been tweaking the settings again based on the feedback I've been giving him and the questions I've been answering. I listen and make the appropriate sounds of interest at the correct moments.

'Do you want to see whether what you've done has made a difference?' He looks at me sceptically and I think maybe I'm being too obvious. 'I thought perhaps if I tried *not* to remember a particular memory, like Justin in the swimming pond at his dad's house, while also . . . remembering it?' I scrunch up my face, knowing this doesn't make sense. 'Maybe that would work? Maybe that would take me there?'

He huffs and sighs and mutters that one Revisit a day is enough, but I know it's for show and he's going to let me try.

169

I am almost angry to find myself in the reception area of the Athens clinic waiting for Margot. I know what's coming, and I don't want it. I want Justin, but I also don't want nothing. I tell myself to sink, to be calm, to go with it. Eventually, in the next Revisit or the one after, Justin surely will appear.

From outside, the car horns of the traffic and the wail of sirens penetrated through the glazing. I closed my eyes and tried to convince myself that I was in a hotel in the city centre but the smell of disinfectant, flowers and illness, and the squeak of rubber-soled shoes on plastic floors stopped it from working. I picked at the skin around my nails. I was worried about Baba's health cover in Greece – did he have insurance? Would he get treatment as an expat? I wasn't even sure if he was an expat or a Greek citizen. How could I not know such basic information? I hadn't ever thought about which people should have to pay for their healthcare and who could; all I knew was he didn't have any money.

Just as I worked it out and realized it must be Margot's mother who was paying, like she must have paid for the flat on Paxos, Margot was suddenly flinging herself down beside me, leaning in for a hug. I was not much of a hugger but I was pleased to see her.

When she let me go, she kept hold of my hands. 'Thanks for coming. Thanks for doing this. It's a big thing you're doing, Neffy, a massive thing, and I –' She waved her hand in front of her face as though to wash away the tears that were coming.

I shook my head. 'I want to help. It's only a kidney!' I laughed.

'I know, I know.' And she drew me to her again for her own sake, so she could be held. And I held her.

Baba was sitting up in bed with a machine whirring next to him. I tried not to look at the tubes going in and the tubes coming out. Margot got me a chair and left us. Perhaps she couldn't stand to see the look on my face, which I did my best to hide. *It's Baba!* I tell myself, but so changed. He was shrunken, unbelievably, too small for his hospital bed. He had grey at his temples and his beard was gone. Perhaps it was this that made him seem diminished. He smiled.

'I don't know what lousy hotel they think this is,' he said.

I smiled back, waiting for the joke. He must have been thinking of this one all morning, saving it up for me.

'Where's the honesty bar?' he continued. 'Do they not think I'm honest? I've made a complaint on one of those little cards and posted it into the box in reception.'

The dialysis machine whirred and clicked, sounding as though it was also complaining about the lack of Baba's gin and tonic. We ignored it.

'I'm sure they'd bring you anything you want,' I said.

'Except for the wine, women and song.'

'No singing in the clinic. Didn't you see the big sign in reception?'

'Just the women and the wine, then.'

'I don't know what Margot would have to say about that.'

'Just the women, then, is it?'

We could go on like this for hours. Margot couldn't stand it. It was avoidance but it had always been our way. I didn't ask him about his kidneys, and he didn't ask me about the ultrasound and the tests I would be having shortly or the forms I'd have to sign to agree that I still wanted to give him a kidney and that there had been no monetary gain or pressure to persuade me.

I had been practising avoidance with him for the longest time. Even when it showed in my face, in the boxes of tablets in their bathroom, in his thrice-weekly trip to Corfu for dialysis, we denied it, would not talk about it or what was happening. My father continued to pretend that he was eating and drinking whatever he wanted when in fact Margot was cooking dishes without egg yolks, with turkey mince instead of lamb, stocking the fridge with almond milk rather than cow's. Margot was fierce and if she couldn't be fierce in my father's presence, she was in mine. She bought multivitamins and a juicer, recipe books for vegan diets, an exercise DVD that didn't make it out of its cellophane wrapping. My father was put on the list for a kidney transplant, and as his nearest blood relative – the only blood relative he knew about – I agreed to be tested.

He never said 'Why me?' If he were asked, I knew he would have laughed and said he'd lived a good and full life, and Margot would have got up and left the room. And I indulged him, encouraging the stories, laughing and staying up long after Margot had gone to bed. And then we had bypassed the clinic on the small island and a date was booked without me ever remembering booking it, for some tests and a scan at a bigger clinic, a hospital in Athens.

I got up to leave his room after an hour and I was at the door when he said, 'Thank you.' I shook my head.

'I'll be back in a mo with a whisky and a packet of honey-roasted peanuts from the mini-bar.'

He closed his eyes and this time the machine glugged. Baba had been on the kidney transplant list for two years:

in Greece, 1,535 patients were waiting for a kidney transplant – I'd looked it up, and it had been rising each year. Greece's rate of organ donation was the worst in Europe. Back in England I'd left the internet page open on my laptop in the studio room Mum was renting after her time with the non-religious community hadn't worked out. I gave it a sly nudge when the screen timed out and went black, in the hope that she would see it, and understand why I had to do this for my father.

It is disconcerting to experience a memory within a memory, as though I have fallen backwards and I'm falling with nothing to stop me.

Mum was standing in the kitchen area with her back to my computer and a cup in her hands when she sighed and said, 'Oh, darling.'

'I'd do it for you too,' I said. She must have been waiting for this conversation to start for a long time.

'That's not the point. I'd do it for you but that's because parents would do anything for their children, give up any part of their body or their life, but it isn't right the other way round. You're too young to understand the implications of what you're doing.'

'I'm twenty-four. I'm an adult. I know exactly what I'm doing.'

Twenty-four already feels like so long ago to me now, aged twenty-seven. I know I had no idea what I was doing then and maybe I never will.

'Your other kidney will have to last the rest of your life,' Mum said. 'Perhaps another seventy, eighty years, who knows, maybe more.' She was her usual calm self. She'd thought it through. 'Sometimes, your father . . . I don't know. Sometimes I don't understand him. I'm not sure he should have asked you.' She stared at me in that intense way that she always did.

I put a teabag in a mug and held it out to her so she could fill it with boiling water. 'Dad didn't ask me to give him one of my kidneys, Margot did.' The stream of water had wavered but didn't spill.

In the Athens clinic I was unnecessarily made to sit in a wheelchair, wheeled to the ultrasound room and asked to lie on the raised couch. Margot sat by my side, holding my hand, while a nurse smeared jelly on my stomach.

'Do you want to know what sex it is?' I asked Margot but my joke fell flat and she laughed a little too late. I was my father's daughter, I thought, with my poor jokes.

With a probe the technician pressed hard on one side of my abdomen and then the other. She turned the monitor fractionally away so that neither Margot nor I could see it, even obliquely, and I felt Margot remove her hand from mine as though still holding it would betray what we were both thinking: this wasn't good. The technician was practised, professional. She wiped the jelly from my stomach and the probe with a piece of blue paper, turned her screen black and said in perfect English, 'I'm sure it's nothing to worry about but I'd just like to get a second opinion.' Margot and I waited without speaking, without looking at each other. The technician returned with a woman with bouffant hair, backcombed and sprayed. They went through the process again – the jelly, the wand, the turned-away screen. They talked to each other in Greek, the conversation too low for me to make out, medical words which I didn't understand anyway, and I suspected Margot didn't either, although her Greek was better than mine.

Finally, after the technician had removed the second lot of jelly, the older woman turned to me and smiled without showing her teeth. She spoke to me in Greek and Margot and I looked at each other. The technician translated from the end of the couch: 'We should do a CT scan to double-check but I'm afraid to tell you that it appears you have only one kidney.'

Dearest H,

The octopus was caught in a net by a fisherman off a beach on Büyükada in Turkey. It was identified as a fully grown Callistoctopus macropus or white-spotted octopus. It was weighed and measured and transported in a firmly lidded bucket on the hundred-minute journey by ferry to Eminönü ferry docks. There, an official placed some seawater in a large plastic bag and sealed it shut with an elastic band. He put the bag in a crate with a selection of other invertebrates and spent an hour filling out the Transportation of Animals forms, and the crate was loaded on to a truck. The octopus travelled fifty-eight minutes to Istanbul airport where the crate was unloaded and the paperwork was checked and stamped. Five hours later it was loaded into the hold of a plane flying to London Heathrow. All the connections were made, all paperwork was signed off. The crate was collected by a courier arranged by the aquarium. Near junction 9 of the M3, the van's steering started pulling to the right and the driver was forced to stop and wait for assistance. The van sat on the hard shoulder for three hours in the heat. When the aquarium took delivery of the plastic bag the octopus was only just alive, or so I was told. This octopus was you, dearest H.

Neffy

It's Yahiko's turn to be late for dinner, and Rachel, Leon and I are subdued while Piper carries on as normal, cooking the food, dividing it up between five. The lines Yahiko drew on the board this morning have been wiped away and the shards of china and the spilled liquid have been cleared up. Yahiko's meal sits on the table and I wonder if I should take it to his room, checking again that the missing person is all right. I decide that I will eat first. Only Piper talks while we eat, about keeping our rooms tidy, bagging up rubbish, cleaning our bathrooms. She's disappointed, she says, that someone has broken the lock on one of the cabinets in the treatment room, and she's having to check through everything and make an inventory of the contents. Mid-flow, Yahiko bursts in.

Rachel is up first, her hand on her mouth. 'Oh my goodness,' she says, looking at his face. Leon is up too and backing away. The skin under both of Yahiko's eyes is smeared with dark purple.

'It's not what you think,' I say loudly to Leon and Rachel. 'They're just black eyes.'

Yahiko shouts something and I think I can make out 'bitch' and 'glasses', but Piper, who has hardly looked at him, continues to talk about the cabinet in the treatment room and how we must check items off the sheet she's going to draw up if we use anything.

'Fucking shut up!' Yahiko shouts at Piper with his hands on his hips, and in a gap in her monologue he says, 'I think Boo is downstairs. Out on the street.'

Piper shuts up.

'Of course, I can't actually see if it's her because I don't have my fucking glasses, but I spoke to someone on the intercom.'

We're all talking now, asking Yahiko questions: Was it Boo's voice? Is she alone? How did she sound?

'Is she sick?' Piper says as we jostle out of the room to the lift where the laptop is still jammed between the doors.

The intercom buzzer goes and as a group we flinch.

I'm the nearest. I press the button and on the screen we see a head in that grey monotone I already know. It's a shock to see a face, tilted up, looking into the camera, a reminder that there is some kind of life going on outside of our own little world. The light illuminates a forehead and combed hair.

Yahiko peers closer. 'Is it her?'

It's someone who might be Boo since they're female, shortish and have mid-toned skin with Boo's round face. I speak into the grille. 'Hello? Are you okay?'

The woman makes some sounds, words maybe, fast and garbled and unidentifiable. Maybe the intercom isn't working correctly.

'Ask if it's Boo,' Rachel says.

'It's her,' Leon says.

'Whoever it is doesn't sound well.' Piper folds her arms.

I'm not going to wait for a consensus, I'm not even going to wait to see if it is Boo. 'I'm coming down to get you,' I say.

'No!' Piper pulls my hand off the button. The screen goes blank. 'They can't come up. Obviously.'

'If it even is Boo,' Yahiko says. He moves around on his feet. 'Did the neck look almost . . . It was hard for me to see. And the eyes. I didn't like how the eyes seemed.'

177

'It's definitely Boo,' Leon says.

Piper still has her hand on my wrist and I shake her off. 'If it's not Boo it's someone who knows we're here and needs our help.'

'Well, they certainly know we're here now, thanks to you and Yahiko,' Piper says.

'It might have been Boo,' Rachel says. I can see from her face that she's remembering things about her, as I am. Rachel told me that Boo brought her a phone charger when she thought hers wasn't working and swapped her dinner for one she preferred. Little things. She looks as though she's calculating if these are enough to save someone's life by risking your own. But isn't this what Boo did for me? Came back into my room to bring me toast, tea, water and medicine. 'But her skin,' Rachel says. She catches my eye and adds, 'Or it might be the quality of the camera.'

'The person was talking gibberish,' Piper says. 'Whoever it was cannot come up. We've agreed, right?' She appeals to us. 'We need to look after ourselves. We can't save anyone else before we save ourselves.'

'It was Thai. She was talking Thai,' Leon says.

'I thought we were already saved,' I say to Piper.

Leon moves past me and presses the button. 'Boo?' He has his mouth up to the grille. We don't see a face on the screen this time but, instead, a strappy high-heeled shoe and a section of leg.

'I don't think that's Boo,' Rachel says. 'She wouldn't wear those kinds of shoes. Not to work.' The foot and the leg don't move.

'What shoes is she wearing?' Yahiko asks.

'She hasn't come to work,' Leon says. 'She's come for

help or to see how we are. She can wear whatever shoes she likes. Have you decided what shoes you're going to wear to the end of the world?'

'Well, not some dirty old trainers like you,' Rachel says.

'Stop bickering,' I say to them both and, surprised, they stop.

'She left us, remember,' Piper says. 'She walked out on her job, which she had a moral and legal obligation to complete, and she left us here alone. It's gross misconduct if nothing else. If we can't agree we should vote on it.'

Yahiko and Leon pause and stare at Piper, but Rachel's hand turns into a fist and she punches Piper in the face. Her knuckles find the other woman's cheek and Piper's head flips back while her hands fly up and she staggers, almost falls, catches herself, and tips forward to grab a handful of Rachel's hair. She doesn't let go and, with Rachel yowling, both women bend forward, shoulders locking in a wrestling hold. Rachel's clawing hand must find skin because now there is screaming – Rachel and Piper, and Yahiko. 'Woah!' Leon shouts, moving between them and taking hold of Piper's wrist, squeezing to make her let go.

There is a moment then when I step out of myself and this place and these people and see us for what we are. Insular and territorial, guarding it against all-comers, and it's not who I want to be. These people saved me; now I need to save in turn. While they're busy, I move around them and tug the laptop out from between the lift doors, shoving my foot into the gap. I force the doors apart and squeeze inside the lift. I press the button for the ground floor. 'Doors closing,' a woman's voice says from another era. And then I am in the dark, my stomach dropping.

'Doors opening,' the woman's voice says and I step into the ground-floor lobby. The certainty I had upstairs suddenly falls away and I wonder what I think I'm doing. I consider getting back in the lift, and then I make myself step forward. The air conditioning is off down here but it is still cool – the small overhang outside stopping the sun from reaching this far back. On the corner, through the plate-glass windows, I see the bashed-in car, the ambulance and the bus, which is much bigger, more real than when we had looked down on it from Rachel's room: a red two-storey mausoleum still urging me to wash my hands. There is litter too, stray flotsam which the wind has carried and items that people dropped as they fled the city. Straight across the lobby, also outside, I see Boo. Even from a distance it is clearly her, from her size and the way she's standing; a stance I recognize even though I'd forgotten it. She's wearing the strappy heels we saw on the monitor and a pink woollen skirt which comes to just above her knees, and a collarless matching jacket with square shoulders. A handbag on a gold chain hangs from one shoulder. She sees me too and her face transforms with delight as she mouths my name and, although she cared for me for only a short time, I have an overwhelming rush of familiarity and comfort as though it might be Mum outside, come to collect me from a horrible school trip. I want to be removed from all of this, to be taken home and looked after by someone who knows what they're doing. We come towards the door at the same speed and meet with the pane of glass between us. My hand goes to the exit button but

Boo slams her palm against the door. 'No,' she says and this time I hear her. 'Do not open.'

Up close I can see that her face is rounder than it was before, slightly discoloured, and her eyes bulging. Last year at the aquarium the fish in the small exotics tank caught a disease that made their eyes swell. The aquarist put them in isolation tanks and treated them with droplets in the water but one morning I found him crying with his head pressed to the tank where the fish floated like vegetable ribbons in a clear broth. Had I looked like Boo does now when I was ill? I blink and have a memory of pressure behind my eyes.

'Neffy,' she says. I've forgotten her accent too, the way she says my name, lengthening the 'y' until it rises and falls. 'You made it.' Her words come slowly, her tongue thick in her mouth. 'I came to see. And the other two who were given the vaccine and the virus, what were their names? Are they well too?'

'I don't know. They left.'

Her face falls. 'But you made it?' She seems to want to confirm I'm actually here on the other side of the glass.

'I did,' I say, although I don't feel the joy she appears to want me to express. My survival seems too unlikely without Orla and Stephan to compare symptoms with. 'How are you?'

She moves the chain of her handbag higher up her shoulder, opens the clip and closes it. 'Oh, well, I'm not so good.' Her voice shakes.

'Will you let me take you upstairs? We can look after you.'

'No.' She puts her hand on the glass again near the button on my side which opens the door and I hear the clink of her wedding ring. 'Do not open the door. Look, I can come in if

I want to.' She shows me the lanyard around her neck with VACCINE BIOPHARM: YOUR DREAMS OUR REALITY printed along it and holds out the clear pocket with her identity card inside, showing its barcode. 'I would have come upstairs if no one answered.'

'Please. You're right, I did get better,' I say, but I don't open the door and my words sound hollow, and only now after all my impetuousness in coming downstairs to see Boo do I think about the people upstairs, none of them sick. Could I, should I, bring this woman and the virus inside? Could I even persuade her or somehow force her given that she appears to have capacity and doesn't want to come? I think about the medicines and equipment I saw in the treatment room when I was searching for Yahiko's plaster: pain relief, antiseptic cream, catheter, saline. Basic supplies. Would I open this door for my family, for Justin, if they were ill? Would they even let me?

'No,' Boo says, and she untucks the silky blouse from the pink skirt, half unzipped already, I see, and shows me her stomach, and I put both hands on the glass, dip my head at the colour of her skin and how stretched it seems. 'And look.' She holds up her hand, fanning out her fingers, her wedding ring embedded in the flesh. 'It won't turn.' She demonstrates.

'I'm sorry,' I say.

'Oh no,' she shakes her head. 'I'm sorry. I knew you were very sick but I had to leave. I'm sorry I had to leave. I had to go home to my –' She looks around as though she might find the missing word behind her and then, as she starts to cry, she opens her bag again and rummages around, finally taking out a tissue and dabbing at her eyes.

I could find eyedrops in the treatment room, something

that would help. 'Please,' I say. 'It doesn't matter. You did what you needed to do. And look!' I try to sound upbeat. 'You're right, I was given the vaccine and the virus and I survived!' She shakes her head, but I carry on. 'In fact, I was wondering where the rest of the vaccine is now? If it was only given to three people they must have stored more somewhere.'

'No, no,' she says, and I wonder if she has the new variant and her brain has swollen as well as her body and she isn't following me.

'Where's the rest of the vaccine?' I ask again.

Her tears drip from her bottom lip. 'The doctor took it. She took it and she left. I don't know where she went.'

I close my eyes and tilt my head, breathe deeply. Even if we'd found it, how would we know what to do with it, whether to dilute it and what with?

I open my eyes. 'How are you managing? Did you walk here?' I wonder at the fact that Boo has made it here alone when we've seen so few people from the windows of the unit. Perhaps she is one of the last.

'I almost forgot how to get here. I went round and round.' She laughs at her foolishness. 'And my feet are . . .' she thinks. 'Killing me.'

Holding on to the window, Boo lifts a foot and fiddles with the tiny buckle of her strappy shoes, and I see that her flesh is squeezing out from between the bands of leather. She lowers herself with difficulty to the pavement – her skirt tight around her thighs – and I sit beside her, just the glass between us.

She undoes one shoe and sighs with relief, and then works at the buckle of the other until her foot is released from its stranglehold. 'Better!' she says, resting against the window with her short legs straight out in front. 'Do you like my style?' She strokes her hands down the pink jacket. It has three gold buttons on the front and more on the cuffs. She lifts her hand to her head and fingers the gauzy fascinator pinned in her hair. 'Wait.' She opens her handbag and takes out a photograph, pressing it to the glass and holding it with her fingertips. I get closer.

The photograph is of a wedding group standing in front of a fountain, the water jet high behind them. The bride and groom are in the middle with their parents either side, and the husband is leaning down to his wife saying something funny so that she is caught in a moment of bending for-wards, hands to her mouth and eyes creased in laughter. I remember Boo talking about her daughter, the one who was pregnant and liked the rain. The photograph is a second out of time, already anachronistic. Boo is one of the six – the mother of the bride in the same pink suit and heels, beside a man who towers over her. 'My daughter, my what's-his-name,' she says. 'They died.' She looks at the picture and kisses it twice before replacing it in her bag.

'Husband?' I say.

'Husband,' she repeats.

'I'm sorry.' The words are wholly inadequate. 'Please come inside.' We both know by then that I don't mean it. She shakes her head. 'Do you have a temperature? Are you thirsty?' I think about going back upstairs to see whether Yahiko has any bottles of water.

'I am the nurse.' Boo ticks a finger at me. I smile and won-der if that's how she's kept herself alive.

She presses her forehead on the glass, her eyes close slowly, open again. Our heads are a few inches apart.

'How did you meet your husband?'

'My husband?' she says and for a long time says nothing else so that I think she might have forgotten the question. 'Have I told you that I worked in a hospital A&E? It was a long time ago when I first came to England. A man came in, a tall man. I had to tip up my head to see his face.' She demonstrates, smiling at the memory. 'He'd run three marathons. Do you know this silly thing? Up mountain and down mountain, up and down, up and down. For fun! All day and all night, thump, thump, thump on his bones. He had a hairline fracture in his heel. I knew it. I'm a good nurse. It hurt him when I pressed it but he wanted an MRI. He made a fuss. I spoke to the consultant and she was tired and cross. Always tired and cross. She said patients cannot decide their own treatment, especially when they cause it. It was his choice to run, she said. Send him home and tell him to rest, ice pack, elevate, all that stuff. So I told him, and the tall white man wasn't happy. He wanted his MRI, but I said, sorry, sorry, Consultant said no MRI. And he left. Ten minutes later the consultant came to find me. Where's that man, she said, with the hairline fracture? Maybe he should have an MRI just to be sure it's not a worse break.' Boo folds her arms. I think I can hear her tut. 'I telephoned him. I said, we'd like you to come back in, the consultant thinks you should have an MRI. When he came back he was charming, smiling, happy to get his MRI. I found a wheelchair for a porter to take him, and it was quiet in the department by then and I had time to talk. He told me more about running and mountains. And he said that he ran marathons for charity and that he'd raised thousands of pounds. You know what for? For a tsunami charity in Thailand. I thought maybe we should give him ten MRIs.' Her laugh is a gurgle and her shoulders move up and down, and then she is crying again with her eyes streaming stickily. She lays her head on the glass and I want to open the door and go out to hold her as though I am the mother and she is the child. She's saying more under her breath and I lean in to catch it but it must be Thai.

Eventually she asks me who is upstairs looking after me. I don't say that it isn't quite like that; that they want me to go out to get food but I'm too afraid to go and that part of me wants to leave to see if Mum and Justin are in Dorset but that I'd rather stay in the unit in the hope that I'll see their recollected versions.

'Yahiko,' I tell her. 'In the room opposite me. Do you remember him? With the big glasses?'

'Yahiko,' she says, the 'o' extending and wavering like the 'y' of Neffy.

'And Rachel. Pretty with long hair?'

'Rachel,' she says.

I'm not sure she does remember, but I keep going. 'Piper, about your height? Feisty.'

'Piper,' she murmurs.

'And Leon.'

'Oh, Leon! I remember Leon.' Boo smiles. 'He's a lovely young man. It's good that you're all together. You can look after each other. You won't get sick. I made sure there was a lot of food. Are you all well?'

'I've lost my sense of smell and taste, and we're cold. We can't turn the air conditioning down. That's why I'm wearing the robe and all these clothes.'

'The controls are –' she waves a hand – 'in there.'

'Yahiko's tried to turn it down but it's stuck.'

'They're in the whatsit.'

'I'll find them,' I say, to try to stop her worrying about the forgotten word.

Boo gathers her bag to her and looks at her shoes with disgust and discards them. With a grunt she uses the window to lever herself to standing and I rise with her.

'Where will you go now?' I ask.

'Home,' she says. 'To be with you-know-who.' I don't want to think about what that means.

'Will you find your way back?'

'Oh yes,' she says confidently.

I want to keep her here, talking, give her water, something to help. She doesn't need me, though, I can see this. She decided to walk here to check we were okay, and now she will walk home to her dead husband. I'm envious of her resolution, her plan, her determination, and I can't think of anything to say. Nothing will make this better.

'You keep well, Neffy.' She's already turning and walking away, each step slow and deliberate, painful.

'Wait, Boo!' I rap on the glass. I heel off my trainers, pull off my two pairs of socks. I slam my palm on the button to open the door and the catch releases. The temperature of the outside hits me: the end of a warm day, and the minute noises and the breath of the real world. No hum of the air conditioner, just the sound of leaves moving, a bird, the tick of something metallic cooling as the shadows of a late summer evening steal across it. And a smell. I inhale a subtle scent, something floral, sweet – grass and earth, perhaps – and then it's gone. I could step out. I could step out and have no ceiling above me or walls to keep out the things I'm afraid of. I could step out and find some grass to dig my toes into, lie under a London plane tree and gaze into its leaves and beyond to an empty sky. But as I glance up, the sun catches on one of the windows in the flats above the row of shops opposite, glares at me and dazzles. And then the air seems full of an unseen menace, and the silence is malevolent as though someone is behind those net curtains, watching. Boo has stopped in the road and turned towards me. I cradle my trainers with the socks inside as though now I am unwilling to let them go. I teeter on the edge of the doorway, I am almost through, when Boo says, 'Throw them.' She puts her arms out ready to receive. I'm a poor thrower, never had been any good at sport. I toss each of the trainers low to the ground and, surprisingly, they land near her. She looks at them and sighs. 'Not good for my style.' She sits again with difficulty, sideways on the kerb, and puts on the socks and the shoes, tying the laces tight.

Dearest H,

You were known as a troublemaker: an octopus that liked to squirt the aquarists and refused to be handled. They said you were a fussy eater and too easily bored. They had paid a lot of money for you a year ago – their adult white-spotted – but I took one look at you and knew you were a curled octopus, Eledone cirrhosa, found, as well as off the coast of Turkey, around the shores of England. You must have been a juvenile when you arrived and when I started working at the aquarium you were maybe already eighteen months old. The aquarium was not happy that you weren't the species they'd been sold and they spent many hours and much money trying to find out where their white-spotted had gone. They had to change the information plate in front of your tank but they kept your name: Hydna. I would have preferred you to have no name but it could have been worse. I have known an Octy, a Squidge, a Squirt and an Octoman. Hydna was a diver from Ancient Greece who, together with her father, contributed to the destruction of the

Persian navy in 480 BC by cutting the boats free from their anchors.

I changed the light cycle on your tank and fed you live crabs. Every day I put my hand in the water so that you might be able to taste me, and on the fourth day you reached out to touch me. Do you remember? Your arms with their single row of suckers were slender and finely tapered so that at rest they curled neatly like seahorse tails. Soon you began to come out from your den when I approached your tank but you still drenched the other aquarists on my days off. Then finally a day came when you reached over the lip to wrap your arms around my wrist. It is possible to fall in love with an octopus.

Neffy

'Doors closing.'

Only in the ascending dark do I think I should have taken the stairs. I was too buoyed up to think about it on the way down but now, as the yellow numbers rise to floors one and two, I have a terror about the power failing and the lift stopping between floors. I know there won't be anyone at the end of the emergency button.

'Doors opening.'

The reception area is silent but they're all there, waiting for me in the frigid air. I breathe in, but can't catch any smell. Yahiko, sitting on the receptionist's chair, is slowly turning one way and back while the others stand. Leon steps forward and hugs me while Rachel rubs my back. 'It was the right thing to do,' Piper says. She has a plaster on her cheek covering the place where Rachel must have scratched her. I let them take me into their fold but I'm unsure whether they understand my confliction of guilt and relief.

'Would you like some shoes?' Yahiko says. 'I'll get you some shoes.'

'You did the right thing,' Leon says, releasing me.

'I didn't not let her in,' I say. But I also didn't insist she came upstairs. I didn't open the door except to toss her some second-hand shoes. Could I, should I, have tried harder? 'She wouldn't come.' My words sound like self-justification.

'Would you like some tea?' Rachel says.

'I want to Revisit,' I say.

'Maybe you should rest,' Piper says.

'No. I want to Revisit. That is resting.'

The others glance at each other, some collective understanding to keep me from running back outside and dragging Boo in. 'Okay,' Leon says. 'Just a quick go.' I hear in his voice a mixture of anticipation of getting notes from another session and the knowledge that this will be three times today I've gone under and he's allowing it.

I lie on his bed with the pebbles in my palms and try not to think too hard about Justin in the swimming pond. But, naturally, my Revisit doesn't ever take me where I plan on going.

Mum put her arms around me – my twenty-five-year-old self – and my twenty-seven-year-old self sinks into them, inhaling her scent, feeling the softness of her skin, over-whelmed by the joy of it and that I'm finally with her, and I know, with any luck, who else I will see now. But there is also pain from the knowledge that, again, I know what's coming and can do nothing to stop it. She held me at arm's length to look at me and then hugged me again. I want to say, *It's me. I'm here.*

But the younger Neffy knows nothing about the future and that this is one of the last times she will get to touch our mother, smell her, see how she's rubbed away half an eye-linered line without realizing, or that her hair is frizzy at the back where she didn't brush it after she got up. 'You're so brown,' Mum said, looking at me. 'It always suits you. How are you doing?'

I hadn't wanted to tell her about the single kidney but Mar-got had guilted me into it, saying that it's the sort of thing a mother has a right to know about her child. I'd phoned Mum from Greece and she had cried.

'How's your father?'

'I'm fine. He's fine,' I said, wanting to shrug off her embrace. I was twenty-five but I still reverted to teenage-hood – not wanting her to make a fuss, or for me to have to speak to each parent about the other as though in doing so I was acknow-ledging that they once loved each other, had sex, made me.

We were standing outside Clive's house in Dorset – interlocking glass cubes which reflected trees and sky. It had a miniature moat around it – water trickling between cut stone – so small you could step across without extending your stride. My older self remembers that later, Mum will call it *the rill*, and I will see that she loves Clive and every-thing about him, including his sharp-lined architecture, and I will genuinely hope that this one will stick.

'Margot's fine too.' I make my pathetic point, and my perceptive and generous mum doesn't rise to the bait. I'd received a text from Margot just as the taxi was pulling up outside the house but I hadn't read it, even though she rarely texted me.

The taxi turned on the front paving and I went towards it, getting my purse out of my bag. 'There's no need,' Mum said. 'Clive has an account. Come on, come in and see the house. How was the train? I'll put the kettle on. Clive and Justin are in London but they'll be back soon. We're going to have an early dinner. Clive and I are going out later, I'm really sorry but it was arranged before we knew you were coming. I'm sure you'll be okay spending an evening with Justin, won't you? Give you a chance to get to know each other.' My older heart leaps at the mention of Justin's name, a secret excitement low in my stomach and at the ends of my fingers. Clive was an architect with his own practice designing eco houses which had won awards and been featured on the telly. And Justin? I didn't know anything about Justin yet.

'Is this all you've got?' Mum tried to take my bag, but I held on to it. 'Did you leave some things in Greece? You know you have your own room here. Shall I show you it now or do you want something to eat first? We've put you next to Justin's room. You must be starving. Are you starving?' Mum always chattered when she was nervous, and I knew she was nervous about it all – the house, another new husband for her, a stepbrother for me. I followed her through a hallway with smooth stone walls, or maybe it was concrete, and polished floors. The light came down at crisp angles from high windows and the end of the corridor revealed a double-height glass room that looked over a garden with stands of silver birch, blue grasses and more stone. A view opened through the trees and down across fields and then up again to a hill, where a solitary house tucked itself into a fold in the landscape.

We stood there and I said, 'Wow,' and she said, 'I know,' and then we turned together to gaze back into the room past the L-shaped sofas positioned around a woodburning stove, and a table which could seat a dozen people or more, towards the far end and the kitchen area, as big as some of the houses we'd lived in. Every surface was empty, no toaster, kettle, dirty teaspoon or plate left out from lunch cluttered the surface, and I wondered what she'd done with her stuff, all the things she'd saved from her time in India and dragged – with me – from one house to another, until I remembered that she'd given them away when she took up with the non-religious community. Lightening the load, she'd called it. This house was like none of the places we'd lived in together. This was starkly beautiful, and Mum, as she moved to the kitchen area in her maxi dress, lit it up like a blue bird fluttering from one place to another, unable to settle. I saw her glancing at me, embarrassed and excited, trying to gauge what I thought, whether it would get my approval, and I felt ashamed that what I thought meant so much to her when really I had only come back to England because I'd got – thank God – an interview for a job as an aquarist. 'Tea?' she asked and pressed open one white cupboard after another looking for the tea or the cups or the pot, laughing because she couldn't remember where they were.

'It still doesn't feel like my house yet,' she said. 'It's so big,' she whispered, her mouth next to my ear.

'Just some water,' I said. 'Honestly.'

She took me along a glass-walled corridor that looked out to the same grassy garden, and into a bright bedroom, cupboards cleverly recessed into the walls, and a double bed, the covers tightly tucked. 'It's wonderful. Like something off *Grand Designs*,' I said.

'It's your home too,' she said, as though we could share the responsibility for landing here. She showed me the bathroom, letting me stick my head in to see a walk-in shower and bath, and I caught a glimpse of towels on the floor, a scummy tideline around the bath. 'Justin,' Mum said rather too chirpily. 'It's a Jack and Jill bathroom. I hope you don't mind sharing.' My heart that knows, leaps again. She slid open the glass door in my bedroom and we stepped outside on to a path which snaked between the clumps of blue grass.

'There's a swimming pond at the end. Lilies and frogs and everything.' She said it breathlessly, as though she were here on holiday and had discovered something that wasn't mentioned on the website and she couldn't believe her luck. 'Anyway, come and help me find those bloody teabags.'

Mum laid four places at one end of the dining table with napkins and glasses and sets of cutlery. I wondered how she knew how to do it because most of the time I was growing up we'd eaten from plates balanced on our laps, sitting in front of the telly on whosever sofa we were sleeping on temporarily, between husbands and houses. The kitchen roll would be wedged between us while we watched a romantic comedy, tearing a strip off the roll to wipe our mouths and fingers when we'd finished eating.

I helped make salads while a chicken roasted, and inside I'm as excited as her. When they come in I want to shout in my own ear, *It's Justin!*

He looked younger and, my God, so full of life and joy. He smirked at me as though he too could anticipate the future. We stood in the kitchen with glasses of champagne, and oh, the taste of champagne. Mum said how unbelievable it was that Justin and I never managed to meet before we'd sat at either ends of the top table at the wedding. Actually, I don't remember much about him from that day – we shook hands I think, laughed when Clive said that we each now had a sibling, as though my mother and his father had been arranging a playdate for their kids. My older self wants to linger on Justin's ruddy cheeks, his blondish hair, but the younger Neffy's eyes skittered across his face, looking away and then coming back to look again. I can feel the bubble which was forming inside and not because I'd swallowed my champagne too fast.

At the table Clive talked about the house, using words like symmetry, altered perception, shadow gap and linear sequence. Mum sat and soaked it up, looking at him with doe eyes although she must have heard it before. In two months' time Justin was starting two years of practical architectural experience with his father.

We passed dishes of food, Justin forking chicken on to his plate, and I shook my head when he offered the dish to me. 'Vegetarian,' I said. Mum asked me about the lab and the octopuses, and I lied and said it was fine and changed the subject to the wedding and what a beautiful day it had been.

When Mum and Clive were involved in their own

conversation about a dress that one of their guests had worn – so low cut – and as Justin passed me the lentil and feta salad, he said, 'Your hair smells nice. Mustardy.'

'Mustardy?'

'Lemony, then.'

'Well, which is it?' I laughed.

'Lemony?'

'Okay, we can go with lemony.'

'I lost my sense of smell a few years ago.'

Oh, Justin, my present-day self thinks. You and me and nearly the rest of the world.

'I got it fixed, though, mostly.'

I was aware that he hadn't let go of the dish although I already had hold of the other side.

'But sometimes you mistake lemon for mustard? They're both yellow, I suppose.' I gave the dish a gentle tug and Justin let it go. When I passed the lentils to Clive he picked up on our conversation: 'Cost me an arm and a leg to get his nose sorted.'

'Sounds like a pretty poor deal,' I said.

Justin snorted, and Mum laughed and covered her mouth with her hand.

'Very good, very good,' Clive said.

When I took the tomatoes with basil from Justin, our little fingers touched. I tipped my head to look at his profile. 'Pretty straight, though.'

He stroked the bridge of his nose with a finger. 'Completely straight, I think you'll find.'

Clive shook his head at our joking and said to Mum, 'It was only a bad sinus cold. He was in bed for a couple of days.'

'A week at least,' Justin said.

'A week, then. Nothing serious. But when it cleared up he couldn't smell a thing. He stopped eating, had no interest in food. Lost a stone.'

'As svelte as a greyhound.' Justin sucked in his cheeks, caressed his hands down both sides of his body.

'I can't see it,' I said.

'Hey, watch it,' Justin said. And while Clive continued to talk over us, Justin held my gaze a little too long and I felt my insides contract. That tiny electrical squeeze low in my belly. It was me who broke away.

'I got my man in London to take a look,' Clive said. 'And he passed us on to one of the best ENTs in the country. Most of his sense of smell seems to have come back, but they aren't always the right smells at the right times.'

Mum was nodding and putting a chicken drumstick on to Clive's plate with her fingers.

'Phantosmia.' Justin wiggled both hands over his head and made a ghostly noise. I feel an echo of something, a glitch, but the memory continues.

'One day he'll smell bread baking when there isn't any, and the next –'

'New carpets.' Justin closed his eyes and swooned. 'The fur on a cat's back after it's been sitting in the sun.' He put the back of his hand to his forehead.

'Epilepsy drugs seem to have sorted it, mostly. There are a few side effects, as expected.'

'An increased libido,' Justin said, and now it was my turn to snort.

Mum passed the coleslaw around again.

After dinner, Justin loaded the dishwasher and I washed up the bigger bowls. Although we didn't really speak, I was intensely aware of his body and the movements of his limbs as though a pocket of air between us was compressing and expanding as we tidied up. Clive and Mum got ready to see some local band playing in a barn at a farm down the road. 'Not your thing, Neffy,' she said, meaning not her thing either. 'Dad rock,' she whispered on their way out. Justin and I stood in the doorway and waved.

'Don't be back too late,' he called, tapping his wrist.

'Or you won't be allowed out for a month,' I shouted but they were already in the car.

'Phew,' Justin said and closed the door. 'Another glass of wine?'

'Wine, yes,' I said but neither of us moved towards the kitchen. Maybe he leaned forward, or perhaps I did, but then we were kissing, ferocious, fierce kissing, as though we might have been denying these feelings for months or weeks rather than an hour. I put my hands under his shirt, flat against his chest, and he took the shirt off over his head, and I took mine off too and he lifted up my bra and kissed my breasts. I stopped him to take his hand and pulled him towards the bedrooms, only pausing to decide which one and then choosing his.

'Is this okay with you?' he asked, and in answer I turned my back to him and said, 'Unhook me,' and he undid my bra and cupped my breasts and bit the back of my neck, hard. On the bed he kissed his way down my stomach and my hips rose to his face.

When we were both naked, he fished in his bedside drawer, opened my legs and knelt up between them to put the condom on.

'You're well prepared,' I said.

'Nothing to do with me. My libido put it there.'

And before I could think of anything to say back, he was inside me.

Afterwards we lay together, joking and laughing, and we didn't hear the car on the drive, only the front door closing.

'Fuck,' I say.

It wasn't late. Justin stood up on the bed, straddling me, wobbling on the mattress. His legs were wide, arms outstretched, penis dangling stickily. 'Giant man,' I said, smothering my laughter. He made himself swing before he jumped off the bed. 'How was the gig?' he called out to our parents.

'You in bed already?' I heard Clive say.

Justin opened the door and put his head out. 'Early night.'

He had a nice bum.

'Neffy too?' Mum said, surprised.

'Yeah. I guess she was tired. Or I just wasn't good enough company.'

'You bastard,' I whispered as I gathered up my clothes.

'Night, then,' Clive said, and my mum echoed him. She sounded disappointed that I hadn't stayed up.

'Night, Dad.' Justin closed the door and saw me heading for the shared bathroom. 'Me first,' he hissed. He grabbed me by the wrist and we grappled silently, laughing and pulling each other back from the bathroom door, until finally he let me go first.

In the bathroom, sitting on the toilet, I remembered to read the text from Margot: *I think I've found a clinic in the US for your dad. Cutting edge stuff. Call me asap.*

As I rise out of the Revisit, I remember that in the morning during breakfast, Clive and Mum will laugh, telling stories about older men mosh-pitting at the front of the stage, and how from where they were standing at the back of the barn next to the generator, they couldn't hear the music, which was just as well. 'You look rested,' she will say to me. 'Clearly the country air agrees with you.' And I will agree with her, making sure I don't catch Justin's eye. For the next few nights and often in the daytime when we think we can get away with it – until I have to leave for my job interview – Justin and I will fuck like animals in the shower in our shared bathroom, in each other's bedrooms, on a sun lounger beside the swimming pond. I cannot get enough of him. I will get the aquarist job but will tell them I can't start for another month so that I can come back to the house. Justin will leave teeth marks on my body which I have to cover with make-up and I will scratch his back until he bleeds. He will make me laugh until I wet myself and he will listen intently when I tell him about my father's illness and Margot's plans. I'm certain our parents have no idea about what's going on.

When I finally have to leave and I'm sitting in the back of another taxi to take me to the station to catch a train to Plymouth and my new job, despairing about going, Mum will put her head through the open window and say, 'Don't look so sad, love, Justin will be waiting for you when you get back.' Before I can even ask her how she knows, she will withdraw her head and pat the top of the taxi for it to move off.

Dearest H,

You had sea urchins and starfish in your tank but no fish and, of course, no other octopuses. I brought you ping-pong balls and put your food in lidded jars but as soon as you had worked out the

*puzzle you were bored. Enrichment, it's called, or in this case,
ways to keep your octopus artificially entertained. There are no
stories about octopuses chewing off their own arms in the wild;
in the wild, octopuses hunt, tidy their dens, and mate. I knew the
aquarium would never allow you to mate because there was every
chance you would eat your partner.*

*The male octopus has an adapted arm, a hectocotylus, which
he inserts into the female's mantle in order to deliver packets of
sperm, usually at arm's length. Wise, or at least well modified.
Wary of mating and then being devoured, some male octopuses
will make dens near the females so that they can simply reach
with their hectocotylus around the rocks and mate with their
neighbour without ever leaving home.*

Neffy

Day Eleven

In the morning, in my bed, I lie still, staring at the ceiling, full up from seeing Justin and Mum but also longing to go back, right now – to run down the corridor to Leon and demand that he let me Revisit. I know I can't. I have a feeling that the more I demand, the more Leon will restrict my use of the thing. Instead I try to be content for now with remembering Mum in her blue dress, the smell of her, the softness of her cheeks. And Justin: the shape of his shoulders above me, the feel of his body pressed into mine, the conversations we'd had after sex and the laughter I eventually gave up supressing:

'What's a lady-orgasm actually like?'

'Like starting a fire that spreads outwards until it gets to my hands and the soles of my feet and sets them alight.'

'Nice.'

'What's yours like?'

'Like really needing to go to the loo and then suddenly being able to. But a bit more magical.'

I have a physical pain in my chest at the lack of him as though a part of me, a limb or an organ, has been ripped away, and it's when I feel the tears trickling down the sides of my neck I realize I am crying. I turn into the pillow and sob, wishing I was brave enough to go outside. I'd had a cat as a child. It was a tabby with a white bib and paws, and it came with Mum and me on each move to a new house or flat, new boyfriend, new husband. Eventually, that cat refused to leave its box, preferring the safety and familiarity of confinement.

I wipe my eyes and turn on to my back and my vision comes into focus and I take note of the camera in the centre of my room's ceiling – a small protrusion, white like the walls but with a dark centre. I'd seen it before but not registered it. An octopus eye. I stare into the lens and the lens stares back, and then I scramble out from under the covers, kneel on the bed and look up. 'Hello?' I clear my throat, embarrassed by the sound of my own voice. 'If you're there, if you're watching, we need help. Some more food, information, rescue, something.' I don't know who I'm addressing and I don't believe anyone is watching but maybe the cameras are still recording, filing away time, creating their own partisan memories of my life from one angle, filling up space on some hard-drive or internet database. 'We need help. Come and help us, you fuckers!' This last comes out as a pathetic squark. And now the unblinking eye makes me furious, looking down on me, judging my choices, my weaknesses, my indecision.

Outside, the corridor is empty. I sniff the air and wonder if I can smell the stink of the waste chute in the staffroom. Yahiko never came yesterday with the shoes nor Rachel with the tea, although Leon would probably have told them not to disturb me after my Revisit. I've put on socks, but the floor is cold.

In the treatment room, I pull open the cupboard and grab the plasters. The same as I used to patch up Yahiko's nose. I take two and scribble out 20 and wickedly write 19 next to *Plasters* on Piper's sheet.

Back in my room, I release the brakes on the bed and pull it until its end bar, where medical notes might once have hung, is beneath the camera. I peel the backing off the plasters and stick them to my thumb and then I climb on the bed, balancing on the mattress. The bar is a shiny tube of curved metal. I put one foot on it and launch myself upwards, my other foot on the bar, fingertips touching the ceiling to steady myself, body swaying – like a new and too enthusiastic yoga student, all excessive, unrealistic stretch. I stick one plaster over the lens and have the other up before I fall, landing with a full-length bounce on my back on the mattress, winded. The second plaster dangles absurdly from the ceiling.

'It doesn't work,' Rachel says from the doorway. I scramble up, embarrassed to have been caught. 'Yahiko got one down when you were sick and took it apart. He said it was a pretty basic model. And even if someone was watching once, they're not there any more, are they? They're dead.' She says this matter-of-factly, different from how she said it when I first met her, and I notice that she doesn't have any make-up on this morning, maybe only a little eyeliner. 'But anyway,' she says, 'Yahiko has some shoes for you to try.'

In Yahiko's room – with no outside window – the lights are on and he's sitting on the side of his bed when I knock and go in, shoulders arched and head drooping. It's musty in here, I can definitely smell it. When he looks up I see he has his glasses on, the frames and the lenses held in place by strips of white tape, but there are so many pieces, they look like crazy paving. He takes them off quickly and slots them behind his jug of water, embarrassed. The colour under his eyes is darker now, a deep aubergine, and his eyes themselves are puffy. I'd like to check them if he'll let me but my gaze is drawn by the items in his room. It's the first time I've been in here and although I knew that Yahiko had been collecting things from the other rooms I had no idea of the extent. A narrow path from the door weaves between waist-high stacks of items: bedding and pillows, rolls of toilet paper, clothes, books, suitcases and rucksacks. The space under the bed is stuffed full and in the bathroom I can see more piles.

'My God, look at all this.' I go further in. It reminds me in a horrific way of the pictures I'd seen of the piles of shoes and glasses and clothes at Auschwitz. All the personal information, the individual who wore them or cared for them, utterly removed when they are piled with so many identical others. Although these things were left, not forcibly taken.

'Anything you need, Yahiko's your man.' I turn to see Rachel, who has followed me.

'Whatever you want,' he says morosely.

'What shoe size are you?' Rachel says. 'I guessed eight.' Footwear is tumbled on the bed: sandals, boots, trainers, Vans and a pair of slippers with lions' faces.

'This is so much stuff,' I say, pulling on a bag that looks like it contains hospital linen.

Yahiko picks up one of the lion slippers, puts it on his lap and begins to stroke its mane, sweeping the matted brown fur backwards and forwards.

'He has it all organized,' Rachel says. 'Don't you, Yahiko?' She pulls her hair across one shoulder and combs her finger-nails through its shiny sleekness.

'I think I have it.' Yahiko is hugging the slipper to his chest now and bowing over it so he appears to have a long orange goatee.

'Yes, but what's he going to do with it all?'

'No one's going to come back for any of it, are they? And it makes him feel safe. Doesn't it, Yahiko?' She's talking to him as though he can't hear her properly. 'We all need something, don't we?'

'I really think I have it,' Yahiko says again and makes a small groaning sound as he presses the furry slipper to his lips.

'Piper says there's no harm in Yahiko's hoarding. We're all more worried about you, Revisiting so often. That's not healthy.' Now she sounds like she's speaking Piper's words. 'And Leon told me –'

I interrupt her, irritated that how often I Revisit should be any concern of theirs. 'What did Leon tell you?'

'I think I've got the virus,' Yahiko says.

'What?' Rachel snaps.

He rubs at an ankle. Yahiko wears smart shoes, dress shoes I think they're called, black and shiny, with thin socks. Like a car salesman. His feet must be freezing.

'You can't have,' Rachel says. 'Where would you have caught it from?'

He raises his eyes and glances myopically first at Rachel and then longer at me, and I see her shrink back from the doorway.

'From me?' I say. 'I didn't go anywhere near Boo. I opened the door and threw her my trainers. What symptoms do you have?' I'm aware that the pitch of my voice is rising and I consciously lower it. 'Do you have any swelling around your torso? Do you feel nauseous?'

'My eyes,' he whispers. 'And –'

'Rachel,' I say, 'pass me some gloves.' A wall-mounted dispenser is just outside Yahiko's room. 'No, wait. I'll get them.' She moves across the corridor when I come out to pluck the gloves from the box. I pull them on and, standing beside Yahiko, gently tilt back his head and move so that the overhead light is shining fully on his face. At medical school I'd learned some mnemonic for taking a medical history but I can't remember it now. His nose is swollen around the plaster and I pull up one eyelid and pull down the lower lid, repeating with the other eye. He submits willingly, and I get the sense that he is relieved by the examination, comforted by the fact that someone – even someone who had only one year of medical training – is taking control. And I find an equivalent strength growing inside me as I take on the persona of the knowledgeable doctor, in the way that acting the part will often make the role become real.

'You have two black eyes and some contusion and inflammation on the bridge of your nose.' He relaxes into the medical terms. 'You should get another ice pack and apply it. This is definitely not symptomatic of the virus. I'd like to see your stomach now?' I sound efficient and clear, as I apply pressure on Yahiko's shoulder and he lies back on the bed, swinging his feet in his polished shoes up on to the duvet on top of the shoes they've selected for me. I wait for him to open his robe, pull up his jumper and untuck his shirt. His stomach is shockingly concave, loose skin falling away from the cliff edge of his ribcage and the outline of each rib showing like strata. His torso reminds me of a dead goat we would pass every few days by the side of the road on Paxos one summer, its flesh gradually collapsing until there was only skin draped over bone. To hide my shock and the flash of guilt that accompanies it, I palpate his stomach in several places and ask him if it hurts. He shakes his head each time. I pull his shirt down for him. 'You can sit up now,' I say and tug off the gloves, turning them inside out as I do. Yahiko doesn't look at me, just sits on the side of the bed with his shirt untucked and his head hanging again.

'You don't have the virus. No swelling, no tenderness, no discolouration. There's nothing wrong with you apart from two black eyes and an abrasion on your nose.' I don't mention that he looks as though he's starving.

'But I think I'm forgetting things,' he says in a whisper.

'Really?'

'Like what?' Rachel says. I hadn't remembered she was watching. If I'd done the examination correctly I should have asked her to leave.

Yahiko begins to rock. 'I couldn't remember the Prime Minister's name when I woke up.'

Rachel bays out a laugh. 'Is that it?'

'He is, or was, pretty forgettable,' I say. 'Or at least, worth forgetting.' I sit on the bed next to Yahiko. 'Listen,' I say. 'I'm certain Rachel or I would have noticed if you'd been forgetting things, but you've been fine. Angry, about that stuff with Piper, but not forgetful.'

'Neffy's right,' Rachel says. 'I haven't noticed anything and I'd be the first to let you know if you were going batshit crazy.'

Yahiko gives a weak smile and mouths *Fuck off*.

'You know that I can lose my shit too, right?' Rachel says, gently.

Yahiko looks down in acknowledgement.

'I had a bit of a meltdown after I got to the unit,' she says to me in explanation. 'I started reading stuff about anti-vaxxers, on Instagram?' She says it like it's a question, as though I might have seen it too. 'And I wasn't sure I wanted to go through with the trial, so it all got delayed, like, the vaccinations? Didn't it, Yahiko?'

He gives the slightest of nods.

'And then I changed my mind back again but it was too late. We didn't get the vaccine, none of us did.'

'You were just scared,' I say. 'We're all scared.'

'Bloody terrified,' Rachel says.

'And hungry,' Yahiko says.

'And hungry.' I know what that means but the thought of going outside makes me crave those pebbles in my palms. I take the slipper from him. 'However, I don't think these are quite my style.' I see Boo in my trainers and her pink mother-of-the-bride suit, walking away from me. 'What do you have in a seven?'

Dearest H,

Your arm is a muscular hydrostat. A muscle that can work without needing to be attached to a bone. Like an elephant's trunk. That's what I'd tell the older kids standing around the Meet the Octopus! tank, where you waited. The volume of an octopus's arm is always constant. If it lengthens it gets thinner, if it shortens it gets thicker. I would pick a particularly cheeky child; one who had an answer for everything and thought that octopuses were disgusting and slimy. I would say, 'You have something like an octopus's arm, all stretchy and bendy.' The boy – usually a boy, but not always – would scoff and make a flippant remark for his classmates to laugh at. 'Don't you believe me?' I'd ask. 'Open your mouth and stick out your tongue.' The kid would never do it, he'd keep his mouth closed, which was fine by me. I'd get the rest of the class to stick out their tongues instead.

Neffy

'Boo remembered you,' I say to Leon. I'm propped against the wall in his bathroom, watching him in the mirror as he brushes his teeth with his electric toothbrush. My toothbrush is manual. 'She said you were a *lovely* young man.'

He smiles and white suds foam from his mouth. 'I am a *very* lovely man,' he says. Or I think he does. 'If we weren't here, you'd have let her in, wouldn't you?'

'Yes! No, I don't know.' I tilt my head back and look up at his bathroom ceiling while he continues brushing. 'I just wanted to make things better for her. Or make her better, even though that's probably impossible. Maybe I should have forced her into a room somehow. Kept her in isolation?' I chew the inside of my lip. 'In my first year at uni I took an extra philosophy module. It was about positive and negative freedom. I've forgotten most of it but there might have been something about self-mastery, I think, and how the opposite is about interference from other people or the state. You know, telling us what to do, controlling us. I wish I could remember.'

He says something with his mouth closed and the toothbrush still going.

'What?'

He stops the toothbrush but keeps it in his mouth and talks around it. 'Isaiah Berlin.'

'Yes, that's it! Isaiah Berlin.' He starts to brush again but the motor is winding down. 'One side of freedom is being able to make good choices for ourselves, and the other is the government or someone making us do things, or not do things.'

Leon makes a positive noise.

'Well, I don't think I'm making good choices. I don't think I've ever made good choices. Jobs, letting Justin go to Denmark, signing up for the trial. Fuck.' I knock the back of my head against the wall. 'And I still don't know what to do. Leave or stay?' Leon rinses, spits into the sink. 'Everything I've ever done or might do in the future inter-feres with someone else's freedom, doesn't it?'

'Freedom for the pike is death for the minnows,' he says, wiping his mouth on a towel.

'Exactly. And freedom for the minnows is death for the flies, or whatever it is that minnows eat.'

'We just have to make the best choice we can and try to think about the consequences for other people when we do it.'

'You make it sound so simple.'

'Sometimes it's not simple at all, like maybe when the majority make a decision and you don't agree with it.'

'What, like whether I should go outside or not to get food? I know you all think I should.'

'It's a personal choice about whether you agree with consensus.'

'And you do?'

'I do,' he says.

I slide my back down the wall and squat on Leon's bath-room floor.

He starts to hum a song like it's a message.

'What's that?' I ask.

'You don't know it?' I shake my head. ' "I Wish I Knew How it Would Feel to be Free",' he says. 'Nina Simone.' He sings a few lines and I tilt my head and close my eyes to listen. He has a beautiful voice. 'For what it's worth,' he says. 'I think you're doing okay. Rachel told me about how you calmed Yahiko earlier.'

'I did,' I say.

'Come on.' He takes my hands and pulls me up to standing.

'Can I Revisit now? Please? I need it.'

He closes his eyes for a moment and sighs. I go into his bedroom and lie on my back on his bed with my palms open. Justin, I think. Justin.

From the windows of Baba's room in this third medical clinic I could see the Pacific smashing itself against tumbled rock, and beyond, scrub scratching across khaki hills. Somewhere down there, out of sight, was Highway One, winding up to San Francisco. Justin is not here. I don't want to be here, I think. Please, not this, even though I know that the gods of the Revisit never listen to what the now-Neffy wants. Near by, the sprinklers started up over the summer lawns, but I couldn't hear any of it, only the huffing of the dialysis machine behind me. I refocused on the glass and saw Baba lying fully dressed on his hospital bed with a red blanket folded across his calves. His cheeks were sunken and dark rings circled his eyes. I remember now that he took drugs for nausea which gave him constipation, laxatives for his constipation, and something else for the diarrhoea. Three times a week he had to come to this Californian clinic for his dialysis which was fifty miles from Margot's mother's house where we were all staying.

Baba's chest rattled and I turned quickly towards the room at the same time as Margot sat upright from her slumped position on the sofa where she was staring at the lunch menu with her feet on the coffee table. *Margot!* I'm so pleased to see her, even here in this place. I want to ask her what she would have liked me to do differently but it's not possible.

She was wearing platform sandals with white leather straps that wrapped around her ankles like she was tied into a low-level stilt. We didn't catch each other's eye, both of us thinking the same thought although we knew Baba wasn't quite out of options yet, because for the second time I had agreed to help try to slow his march towards death. For now, he was only clearing his throat.

'I overheard two nurses talking, earlier,' he said. 'An Arabian prince and his entourage have taken over the clinic's penthouse. Why does he get all that and I just get this crappy room?'

'Crappy room?' Margot said, lowering her feet to the floor and flinging the menu on the coffee table.

I interrupted before she could continue. 'Christ, I know what you mean,' I said. 'Look at all this shit. Call this a sea view – you'd think the ocean might be a bit calmer so we could actually swim in it.' I went over to Margot and stuck my face in the flowers on the coffee table. 'And these . . . these smell of nothing.' I sliced my hand through the air as though summoning someone to come and take them away. With a dark humour, my older self laughs silently at this lack of odour. The flowers were in fact barely scented, it was all about show for this place. Now I notice that the clinic smells of face cream and lotions as though it is a spa, but under those, now and again I get a whiff of the familiar antiseptic, illness, blood. I went to the sofa and sat down next to Margot and squeezed her hand. My phone buzzed in my jeans pocket but I didn't look at it. The message would be from Justin, and it would say, *Don't do it.*

'And don't get me started on the food,' Baba said.

I picked up the menu and flicked at it with my other hand. 'Who wants wild mushroom risotto with heirloom tomatoes followed by plaice in lemon butter sauce? I ask you?'

We laughed while Margot rested her head on the sofa. 'There's no Arabian prince upstairs,' she said. 'This isn't that sort of place. They only do proper research here.'

'We're kidding, Margot,' Baba said.

'Kidding,' she replied, wearily. 'I know.'

'And it's single storey,' he said, and I sniggered even though I knew it would exasperate her.

After the nurse had come and turned off the dialysis machine, removed the tubes and stuck a plaster on Baba's arm, a food operative brought Earl Grey tea, slices of freshly cut lemon on a saucer, a jug of milk and a plate of cookies. There was a knock on the door and Dr Adeyeye came in.

Margot helped Baba to an armchair, the doctor took another, and Margot and I sat on the sofa. It might have been a social call, a visit from a friend, except that Baba was asleep. Dialysis wore him out. The doctor had on a suit and tie, and his hair was pure white against his black skin. His philtrum was pronounced – the crease between the nose and the top lip and one of the few, useless, anatomic pieces of information I remembered from medical school – as though two tectonic plates had come together and formed a pair of steep and parallel mountain ranges. And when he smiled, which he did often, his mouth widened and his top lip became a thin burgundy line, while his philtrum disappeared completely. I catch my younger self trying to assess his face to see whether I could trust him. *It's not the doctor you should be worried about*, I think hard, but she doesn't notice.

'I know, Oliver, that you met with our transplant surgeon

yesterday,' the doctor said. 'And that I explained much of this on our video call, Neffy – can I call you Neffy? – but it's always best to meet face to face so I can answer any questions you may have. Is that okay?' He looked carefully from one to the other of us, practising the technique he probably learned on a training course about the link between good patient outcomes and maintaining eye contact. He stared at me the longest. He'd already seen pictures of my insides on X-rays, ultrasounds and CT scans, parts of my body that no one else had seen, not even me. Now, he was looking inside my head to see whether I was still up for this. I slipped my hands under my thighs to hide their shake.

'No doubt you'll have been doing lots of internet searches, someone of your age,' he said to me. 'And I want to make sure you understand it is organ primordia we're working with here, not stem cells as many online articles about organogenesis say. There is a big difference. Stem cells can develop into any organ; primordia are already locked, if you like, into developing into a specific organ, in our case, a kidney.'

My phone buzzed repeatedly and everyone looked at me. I dug it out of my pocket and turned it off. The call was from Justin. Surely it was the middle of the night in England.

Baba's eyes were closed. I want to stop a while and look at him, take him in, but I turn back to Dr Adeyeye, who is talking only to me and Margot now and managing to smile at the same time. 'Kidneys are challenging and complex organs and you and your father will be in the vanguard of this technological advancement. You will be pioneers, leading the way to allow the possibility of changing thousands of future lives for the better.' He sounded like the videos I'd watched which had been made by the clinic about what they did here. The same soft, reassuring tones. Maybe he had a side hustle with the voice-overs. 'And, naturally, to prolong your father's. The procedure is, as you know, not without risk. In this trial our focus will be on safety first. We will be monitoring and evaluating every stage. Obviously, we're all also hoping for success but that is secondary to safety. We need to make sure you are both well looked after. If any of the procedures we're planning appear to be too great a risk to either you or your father, we will stop. I just need to make that clear.'

Dr Adeyeye paused to take a breath and his philtrum reappeared for a moment. As he got going again, I remembered, also from my one year of medical school, why we had them. The philtrum was the place where everything finally pinched together in an embryo's developing face: the palate, the top lip, the nose and the cheeks squeezed like the seal on a dim sum dumpling. I wondered whether a kidney had an equivalent.

'. . . extremely positive results with porcine embryonic tissue implanted into primates . . .' Dr Adeyeye was saying. 'At the optimum time in the next month we'll implant the primordia in your uterine wall. The immune suppressant drug regime will be started immediately, and you can come in when your father visits for his dialysis, to have regular ultrasounds to see how things are progressing. But we estimate functional maturation should be around one hundred and twenty to one hundred and fifty days. Then . . .'

Perhaps it was as a countermeasure against the clinic's smell, the doctor's smooth American voice or the idea of what I had potentially agreed to, but a preposterous image arrived in my head and I interrupted Dr Adeyeye's flow with a question: 'Will I have to give birth to it?' His philtrum reappeared for a few seconds as he frowned. He and Margot were silent while they took in my question. 'Really. Will I?' I looked from Margot to the doctor and had to press my lips together to keep the bubble inside me from escaping, as I imagined a woman on her back, wearing a Victorian nightgown, with her legs in stirrups, straining and moaning. *Push*, Dr Adeyeye said, and out popped a kidney.

And I laughed. I've forgotten this. I actually laughed, covering my mouth with both hands and bending over.

'Perhaps we should meet tomorrow,' Dr Adeyeye said after a pause. 'Go over any outstanding questions then.'

'Sorry,' I said, still laughing. 'Sorry.'

None of it was funny.

'She won't be doing it,' Baba said. He was awake.

Beside me, Margot bristled.

'Oh, Dad. Of course I'm going to do it. Of course I am.'

'I'll leave the three of you to discuss it.' Dr Adeyeye stood. I felt I should tug on the bottom of his jacket and get him to sit down again. He clasped my father's shoulder, gave it a squeeze. 'Tomorrow, then. I'll get our nurse coordinator to come and sort out a time.' He was gone, closing the door gently behind him.

'I've decided I don't want you to do it,' Baba said. 'You're only twenty-five. It's not right.'

'You've decided now?' Margot said. 'When we're here already?'

'I'm twenty-six,' I said to Baba. 'It's my body. This isn't up to you.' I rested back on the sofa, crossed my arms. The laughter had gone so completely that I felt emptied out.

Margot raised her hands at him, despairing, angry. 'You couldn't have said this earlier? When we were still in Greece?' Her voice is layered with a sarcasm I'd not heard before.

'I can refuse it.' Baba folded his arms too.

'For God's sake, Oliver,' she said. 'Don't be so childish. If Neffy is happy to do it, if the physicians are happy, then let her do it.'

'And what about the long term? What if it means she can't have a child? Dr Adeyeye doesn't know about that. He didn't say anything about that.'

'That's because it's never been done before,' I said.

'We can ask him tomorrow,' Margot said. 'It's Neffy's choice and she's okay with it. Aren't you, Neffy?'

I nod, although was I okay with it? I wasn't sure. It was bizarre. Too like science fiction to imagine it really happening inside my body. And the thought of having to come into this clinic so often was not an easy one.

'I don't like it,' Baba said. 'I think this is a bad idea.'

'And what's the alternative?' Margot put her feet back on the edge of the table.

He shook his head. 'I am the father. She is the daughter. It's unnatural.'

The same argument I'd had with Mum over the kidney donation, before that became impossible.

'No more unnatural than if they'd transplanted her kidney.'

'We – Neffy and I – are the guinea pigs here. We are the lab rats, we are the fucking pigs and the monkeys.' His face was sweating, too red.

'Someone always has to go first,' Margot said. 'Someone had the first ever kidney transplant, the first ever skin graft, the first open-heart surgery.'

'And do we hear about the outcomes of those people? No, because they didn't last five minutes. I will not have my daughter mucked about with; her insides mucked about with. It isn't right.'

'You're just going to give up, are you? Just give up and die.' Margot threw her arms in the air. 'When your daughter has made this offer, this incredibly generous offer.'

'This offer, from my daughter and your mother.'

'Ah – so that's what this is really about.'

'Okay, yes, the whacking great donation that you persuaded your mother to give this damn hospital.'

Donation. Now, I know about the donation, but then, in the Californian clinic, no one had told me about any donation. I'd thought this experimental procedure was being performed by the hospital for the advancement of medicine. If we'd paid, I thought, does that mean they'll try harder to make it work? And what about the people who couldn't afford a donation? If it was technically a trial, shouldn't the hospital be paying us – me? I hadn't told Baba that in order to come to California, the aquarium had made me take unpaid leave, that I'd started a month later than I could have done, that I was behind on my rent, that my credit card was maxed out and I didn't know how I was going to pay the interest.

'Mom *wants* to help me,' Margot said. 'Like your daughter wants to help you.'

'Except that your mother is paying with money and my daughter is paying with her body.'

'How else did you think we got to this stage so fast?'

He talked over her. 'Being able to pay for all this. It's obscene. It's wrong. Fucking wild mushroom risotto, ocean views. Red blanket.' He gestured towards the bed where the blanket that had covered his legs still lay.

'Here it comes,' she said. 'The proletariat, blue-collar, working-class man, wanting everyone to get the same treatment.'

'I know what that blanket means. That I should have special service.'

'You're none of those things, Oliver. You ran a hotel on a Greek island.'

'Like I'm a fucking VIP.'

'Do you think you'd have even been offered this in England? Let alone Greece?' She scoffed, shook her head.

'If one person pays, then down the line, we'll all be paying.'

Margot pushed the coffee table with her skyscraper shoes. The vase of flowers tottered and rebalanced. 'My mother is paying to save your life, Oliver. And you're being an ungrateful bastard.'

They were facing each other, heads jutting, getting ready to charge.

'This is Neffy's womb, Margot. Her womb.'

I wasn't sure I approved of my dad considering or mentioning my womb. Like I didn't want to think about his testes, his kidneys, any of his insides.

'I know, Oliver. The place in a woman's body that is specifically designed to grow things.'

When I stood, they didn't notice.

Stay, stay! I'm shouting at myself from offstage. I don't listen; I can't hear.

'But babies. Babies! Our grandchildren, not kidneys.'

I picked up my bag carefully. 'I just need to use the bathroom,' I murmured. When I closed the door behind me like the doctor had, they were still going at it. A nurse walked by wheeling a trolley. 'Hey,' he said to me with a trained smile. He didn't acknowledge what we could both hear.

In reception I asked the woman behind the desk if I could borrow a pen and a piece of paper. *Going away for a couple of days to have a proper think*, I wrote. *Please look after yourself and don't worry. I'll text Margot.* I asked the woman to give it to Oliver in the Rose Suite in half an hour.

I turned my phone on again and saw three missed calls from Justin and several messages. I hated that he might be right, that I should think about it more. I didn't want him telling me what to do. Still, I texted him back: *Going to San Francisco to think it through.*

When I checked my purse, I saw I had about fifty dollars. If I could get to the city, I was sure I could find a hostel. I didn't want to go back to Margot's mother's house; I needed some space.

The Californian air outside was warm and a salt breeze blew in off the ocean. Giant Pacific octopuses lived in these waters; maybe a few were down there now. During some work experience a while ago, I'd had the pleasure of knowing a giant Pacific octopus called Giovanni. He'd been huge – maybe twenty feet in length – but gentle enough to let him touch my face.

I walked down the winding drive to the road where I found a parking area, stuck out my thumb and within half an hour I had a lift all the way to San Francisco.

As I come upwards out of the Revisit, I remember an exercise I had to do in English at school: write a letter to your younger self. What warnings might you give, our teacher said. What things would you tell yourself not to worry about, what would you say you should do differently? Oh, so many things.

Dearest H,

*Institutionalized. Isn't that the adjective? I'd google its proper
definition if I had the internet. Living under someone else's rules
and regulations for so long, or perhaps so intensely, the person
becomes unable to act independently. It's seen too with zoo
animals: the crowd-pleasers bred in captivity – the tigers and the
orcas – often don't do well when they're released into the wild.
And what about sea creatures? Small fish don't seem to have any
problem, but octopuses? No one knows. They're routinely released
into the wild from aquaria but only when they've been captured
as adults and kept in captivity for just a few months. And
humans? I think we know how that generally goes.*

Neffy

Two days ago on my way from Leon's to my own room I
went into one of the rooms a volunteer had deserted along
Leon's stretch of corridor. Out of curiosity. The blinds were
down on the corridor window as they are in every room –
someone must have lowered them before I got better. The
name on the door said *Robin*. I stood in the doorway and saw
that the layout was the same as Leon's: bathroom on the right,
big picture window straight ahead. I stepped inside and closed
the door behind me, not wanting to be seen, feeling as though
I were trespassing. At the window I saw that the room over-
looked the same backyard as Leon's with the bin still turned
on its side. To stop myself from thinking about what Leon
had described – the woman on the road, the swollen-faced

man and the sound of the dogs in the night – I turned back to examine the interior. Robin had certainly left in a hurry, but Yahiko had maybe been here, scavenging: drawers were hanging out of the desk, and the duvet and pillow were on the floor. But whoever had left it like this, whether Yahiko or Robin, had missed the denim jacket hanging on the back of the door. In an inside pocket was a wallet with some cash and a debit card, as well as a campus card showing that Robin Willis was an undergraduate at the University of Reading. I guessed from his photo – wide rugby-player neck, acne – that he was eighteen or nineteen. Stuffed into another pocket was a well-thumbed self-help paperback. I worried that of all the things Robin should have with him – if he were alive – it should be this. *How to Stop Feeling Overwhelmed: When the World Gets You Down.* I was flicking through it when I heard Leon's door open and him call for me. I jumped, feeling guilty that I was in Robin's room, snooping through his personal items just like Yahiko. I stuffed the wallet and the book back into the pockets of Robin's jacket and hurried out into the corridor.

Robin's room had felt so poignant in the way it had been abandoned that it left me with a feeling of despair for hours and I didn't subsequently try any of the other doors even though I passed the room next to mine – Orla's room – and then the empty room, and then Stephan's room, and all the others every time I walked down the corridor to Leon's.

This afternoon, though, without being aware of the decision even before I do it, I press down on Orla's door handle. It is, as expected, locked. I try to peer past the slats of her blind to see if she might have left anything behind, but they fit the frame of the interior window too well and the lights are off. I move on to Stephan's room and that, too, is locked.

I'm on my way to Revisit – surely I will see Justin again soon – but instead of walking on to Leon's, I return to the empty room between Orla's and Stephan's. There's no name on this door and it's unlocked. Inside, it's clear that, as Leon once told me, no volunteer was given this room. Apparently, Boo told him that they'd had to send one of the volunteers away as soon as they arrived because something was wrong with the shower, and indeed when I stick my head into the en suite, the shower head is missing. The bed is stripped to its mattress, the room completely empty. I've remembered not to put on the light, but I go to the window. Here is the same alleyway I look down on, almost the same view of the red-brick building opposite and, at a more oblique angle, Sophia's flat. From here I can see into what might be her kitchen. I press my forehead against the glass and wonder how many days it is since I've seen her. Her front door, which must be shared with the other flats in her block, is recessed; I can only see a plate with three buzzers. But the big squares of paper are still across her sitting-room windows where Sophia wrote her reply to me. One word per pane: YES, I'M HEAR in block capitals filled in with black pen. I should write another message, I think, what harm could it do? And I wonder what our building, this room, Stephan's room, Orla's room, my room, look like from Sophia's windows.

Dearest H,

The lid of your tank was ajar – the catch undone. Had I left it like that or had you opened it? You weren't in your den; I was sure of that when the bright light from my torch didn't make you grumpily emerge. In a panic I looked for you in the exotic fish tank, and around it, hoping I'd find you before you could

hook an arm inside. You weren't stuck to the glass looking in,
and I knew if I didn't find you soon I'd have to raise the alarm
no matter what trouble I'd get in. In the end, I found you near
the seahorses – you hadn't gone far. Perhaps a tiled floor is not
easy to walk across for an octopus. You let me pick you up but
clung to me when I tried to put you back in your tank – as I
removed one arm, another stuck to me. But I got you in, I had
to get you in, and I didn't tell anyone. Later I looked around
the area where you had been headed – towards a drain in the
floor. I got on my hands and knees and sniffed. Could I smell
the sea?

Neffy

Leon is sitting at his desk using a pair of scissors to dig into
a small wedge of wood, something that might have been
used to keep a door open.

'What are you doing?' I ask.

'Trying to drill a hole. It's hopeless.' He chucks the scissors and the wood across the desk. 'Fucking radio. Probably
no one's broadcasting anyway.'

And I suddenly remember what I'd seen previously in
Sophia's apartment, on her windowsill. Was it still there
when I'd just looked? 'There was a radio . . .' I stop mid-
sentence, but Leon isn't listening anyway.

'I've been wondering about the number of times you're
Revisiting,' he's saying. 'And I'm thinking we should maybe
cut it down a little. Limit it to once a day, yeah?'

I don't want to tell him about the radio because I know then he will make me go outside, of course I would have to go outside. Going outside would be the right thing to do. 'No problem,' I say. 'Absolutely.'

He sighs. We both know I'm going to Revisit.

By the time the car crossed the Golden Gate Bridge, Justin had booked me a room in a small B&B in a district of San Francisco called Cow Hollow, and himself a seat on the next flight over.

This time I'm surprised that the Revisit has returned me to the next second in time after the last one ended. Maybe, I think – and I try to remember to tell Leon this later – it's to do with intensity of emotion, since I'm rarely taken back to moments of mundanity.

I messaged Justin to tell him that he didn't have to come, that I only needed some space and a little thinking time, but the truth was I wanted to see his face and have his body next to mine even if I knew he would try to persuade me not to go ahead with the procedure.

The two guys, Marcus and Gary, with matching curled moustaches, who stopped their Subaru for me, were going on a three-day weekend to a hotel in the Russian River Valley, north of San Francisco. I sat in the back and let my jet lag catch up with me while they enthused about the hotel's awesome pool, the free bikes and the cool way the restaurant served Brussels sprouts. Their excitement about their trip and the way their eyes found each other's even while

Marcus was driving meant they didn't ask much about where I had come from and why I was hitching on Route One, and so I was able to give them the briefest of information about my father and the clinic, and it meant that for a few hours at least I didn't have to consider what I should do. A little way north of Monterey, I told them that Justin had booked a room and was flying over to meet me and they thought this was so romantic they insisted on driving me to the door of the B&B.

I ate a pizza at a place down the street, texted Margot to say I'd arrived safely and that I loved them both and I was thinking carefully. Whereas, in fact, I went to bed early under chintzy covers and fell straight asleep. My older self isn't used to this yet: existing within a sleeping body. I worry again that if I sleep too, I'll miss the moment of waking and sleep on forever. I would rather come out of the Revisit and sink again into the morning, but that doesn't happen. Eventually I sleep, knowing that the next evening I'll see Justin.

In the morning after breakfast I walked through the city without paying attention to where I was going, and when I got tired I sat on a park bench and looked between the houses to the water. I couldn't make my thoughts settle, couldn't focus, and after a while I searched on my phone to see whether there were any octopuses in San Francisco. Google told me the city had two aquariums, neither of which I'd heard of. The only Californian one I knew from my work was back in Monterey. I picked the Steinhart Aquarium housed in the California Academy of Sciences. If I'd brought my aquarist pass with me they might have let me in for free but I'd left it back in England.

I bought a full-price ticket to the aquarium. Inside, they had a tidepool, a swamp with an albino alligator and the obligatory penguin exhibit. The Twilight Zone was a 25-foot-deep tank with coral reefs flickering with thousands of fish. Longnose hawkfish with their pattern of loose crocheted stitches swam with a newly discovered species of rainbow fish, while fluorescent comb jellies cast out their tentacles alongside brittlestars. But walking through this stage set of dark ceilings and brightly lit displays without being able to slip through some invisible door to the backstage area of concrete floors, strip lighting and wheeled tanks made me miserable, so I hurried on to the California Coast exhibit. A massive eye-shaped window showed kelp swaying in an artificial swell, a school of jacksmelt flashing their silver sides as they turned in unison, a bright-orange wolf eel curled in the bottom sand, and sea urchins and different types of anemone clinging to a huge central rock. I sat in front of the window for an hour or more while children and a few adults surged and flowed around me. A school group of nine- or ten-year-olds in navy blazers and checked skirts rushed as one towards the glass to press their faces up against it, making exaggerated hoots of disgust at what they saw. And then just as quickly they decided to move on; some subtle twitch of a ponytail from an unobserved leader and they were gone. I continued to sit and wait but the giant Pacific octopus that the sign said was in the tank next door didn't show. Probably, I eventually thought, it had been removed for feeding.

On the back of my aquarium ticket, using a pen I found in the bottom of my bag, I wrote a list of reasons why I shouldn't grow a kidney for my father:

1. *It is a risky experimental procedure which hasn't been done on humans before*
2. *No one knows the long-term effects*
3. *It is weird*
4. *I will have to go into the clinic many times*

I crossed the last one out. It was a pathetic thing to worry about. And then I wrote a list of why I *should* grow a kidney for my father:

1. *It might save his life*

I took my phone out of my bag to call Margot and let her know my decision but I didn't have a signal so I put it back in the side pocket with the folded aquarium ticket.

When I returned to the B&B Justin was asleep in bed, lying on his back. My older self is thrilled that this time I stand and look at him. He once took a picture of me asleep, showing my mouth slackly open and crust in the corners of my half-closed eyes, but Justin looks serene when he's sleeping, neatly laid out like a stone knight on top of a tomb. I stripped off, sat on the side of the bed and took my phone out of my bag. From behind me Justin stirred and I felt him turn and wriggle towards me. His hand crept around and over my thigh. It walked, spider-like, up my stomach and across my ribs, where it stopped to blindly squeeze a breast as though working out what it could be. I laughed outwardly, and inwardly. The fingers crawled along my arm to my hand where it discovered my mobile phone. 'No, no, no,' Justin said with mock authority and I let him take it from me. 'Come here.' I lay down, moving backwards until my shoulder blades were touching his chest. His body radiated heat. He put an arm over me, cupping a breast, and pulled me closer, inhaling, breathing in the smell of my hair, my neck. I wondered if I should have washed before I got in.

'You smell like the earth after rain,' he said as his cock nudged my bum and the small of my back. He pressed it down with his hand, pushing it between my legs. There was dull buzzing and I realized it was my mobile which he must have put under his pillow. We rocked like that for a while until I couldn't wait any longer and I rolled on to my front, knees under me, on all fours, and then he was behind me and inside. He pushed my knees apart and took my hips and held me still. And then he reached around to my front with fingers that I could tell he'd wetted, to rub me in time with the movements of our bodies. His noises made me move faster until I was slamming back against his pelvis, raising my tailbone to take more of him in. And still those fingers slid in circles until the heat grew from my centre, unstoppable. I couldn't hear myself, I could only hear Justin, saying, 'Yes, yes,' and I was thinking *don't stop, don't stop*, and I lifted a hand to press his fingers hard against me.

We dropped forward until I was prone with his weight heavy on me, my face squashed sideways on the pillow. I could feel him contracting, and then the exquisite slippery pop of his cock leaving my body. We both laughed. 'Evening,' he said, like some English policeman from an old comedy.

When he was lying on his back and I was beside him, one leg hooked over his and his arm around me, I could feel him begin to fall asleep. I gave him a prod.

'Aren't you hungry?' I said. 'You must be hungry. I'm starving.'

'You're always hungry after sex,' he said sleepily.

I lifted my head. 'I am not!' I let my head drop. 'Am I?'

'I didn't get any sleep on the plane,' he said. 'If you don't have any money, I've got some dollars, go and get some food, let me sleep. Tomorrow, I'm going to talk you out of it.' His words were mumbled like he couldn't open his mouth properly.

'It won't work. I've decided.' My stomach was rumbling. Justin knew I'd had to take unpaid leave to come to California and since I was still paying for my flat in Plymouth, things were tight. I wondered if it *would* be wrong to use his money to buy some food. Taking cash from his wallet seemed worse than him paying for the B&B on a card.

'Go and get yourself a pizza.'

'I had pizza last night.'

'So?'

'I don't want to move.'

'I don't want you to move.' He gave me a squeeze.

'Fiorentina, with an egg on top, soft enough for the yolk to ooze into the spinach and mozzarella. Extra artichokes. Garlic mushrooms.'

Get the pizza, I try to tell myself. *At least get the fucking pizza.*

I hauled myself out of the bed and went into the bathroom, sat on the loo and wiped myself. The toilet paper was full of his stuff. 'Jesus, Justin,' I called, laughing.

'What?' he said, pretending defensiveness. 'It's been at least two weeks.'

'And you haven't had a wank in two weeks?'

'I've been saving it all for you.'

'Thanks.'

I lay back down on the bed even though I wanted that pizza.

'I told your mum what you're planning,' Justin said in his dreamy, sleepy voice.

'What?' I half sat up to look at him. His eyes were closed and a day's worth of stubble was showing across his top lip and his skin was dry on the bridge of his nose from the air con on the plane. 'You told her? Christ, Justin. She was cross enough when I was going to give my father a kidney. Why the hell did you tell her?'

'Because I said I was flying over and that I was going to change your mind.' Anger flared for a moment in my chest at his presumption which was immediately extinguished by the knowledge that I wouldn't be persuaded.

I moved away from him and on to my back. 'I wrote a list of pros and cons and I'm going back to the clinic tomorrow.'

He propped himself on one elbow. 'Neffy, no.'

'Yes. I am. I was calling Margot when you took my bloody phone away.'

'Do you even have the money to get back to the clinic?'

'I thought I could borrow it from you.'

He shook his head. 'Not for that.'

'So it's okay for pizza but not to save my father's life?'

'This is completely different and you know it.'

'I'll get Margot to send me some, then, or I'll hitch again. I am going back.'

'I've come to save you from yourself.' He smiled, trying to win me over.

'I don't need saving. I know exactly what I'm doing.' I was serious.

'You don't, though.'

'It's my choice, it's my body.' I rolled over and scrabbled in my bag on the floor for my phone. 'I'm going to text

Margot now. She'll send the money. I'll get a taxi to the clinic if I have to. Her mother will pay.' My phone wasn't in my bag. I dived for it under Justin's pillow as he went for it too; I got there first: four missed calls from Margot and a voice message. I swung my legs off the bed and sat up. The chintz covers had fallen on to the flowered carpet. 'I'll call her. Look, she's called me.'

Don't call, don't call, don't fucking call! I shout at myself. I don't listen.

I dialled Margot's number, staring over my shoulder at Justin. She answered after one ring. 'Neffy,' she said, and I knew from her voice that Baba was dead. 'I tried to call you.' She started to cry. 'I tried to call you but you didn't answer. He had a heart attack. Where were you? What were you doing?'

Justin knelt up behind me where I sat on the edge of the bed and as I slid backwards on to his chest, he took the phone from my hand. 'No, no,' was all I could say. He spoke to Margot, gripped me with his other arm to stop me slipping to the floor.

'This is Justin. Yes, her stepbrother. Yes, I'm here with Neffy. I'm so sorry. I'm so so sorry.'

I feel it again, his death ripping through me, slicing me into bloody strips, and the thought that my father had died without knowing that I'd resolved to return is still intolerable.

Dearest H,

*Did you sense that something was wrong? I flew back to England
with Justin a few days later, leaving Margot to arrange moving the
body – Baba's body! – from California to Paxos. It would take her
more than two months to sort it out. The aquarium gave me three
days' compassionate leave on top of the couple of weeks of unpaid
leave, and two of those days were spent travelling, so I had to go
back to work immediately. I went straight to your tank. You formed
your eyes into craggy peaks and then flashed your colours through
deep red to mottled orange to white, a Turkish carpet lifting and
rolling as it flapped. Were you cross with me for being gone so long?
'Baba's dead,' I think I said, hanging over the tank. 'I didn't save
him.' I put my head on my hands, grasping the top of the glass and
letting my tears drop into the water. I've read since that emotional
tears, psychic tears, have a different chemical composition to tears
created to lubricate. Could you taste that? Did you know? Because
you came to me then, your pupils dilated, and you touched my
cheek with the tip of an arm, and then you climbed out of the tank
and I held you while I cried.*

Neffy

Leon and I are in the staffroom, rinsing out the sixteen water
jugs and boiling the kettle over and over. We should have
done this task this morning because now we won't have any
cold water to drink with dinner. Piper is in the kitchen, and
my saliva glands, my stomach, my intestines, my very
blood – against my will and against the Revisiting of my

father's death – are minutely tuned into the hum of the microwave as the food cooks.

Leon is concerned. He'd been worried when I came up from the last Revisit crying and gasping. I'd told him about my dad. 'We're definitely going to have to cut down the time you spend under,' he'd said. 'And you're only supposed to be Revisiting good memories, remember? I know that's hard but it's important to keep trying.'

Now, in the kitchen, he holds a jug steady while I fill it from the kettle. 'I Revisited my mum again this morning,' he says.

I don't look at him, I just take the jug and put it in the sink which is full of tap water to try to cool the drinking water down faster, and I wait for him to speak.

'It's always hazy for me, disjointed, like I'm dreaming. And it's not always easy getting a Revisit going for yourself, you have to set an alarm so you'll come out of it.' He picks up a tea towel from the back of a chair. 'My mum died too. In the early days of the pandemic. Did I tell you that?'

'Was she in hospital?'

'She never made it to the ICU. She died in A&E on a trolley. They said they didn't have a bed available. Well, that was a fucking lie. I was with her at home just before the ambulance arrived. I was sure I could have done more and I wanted to see, to know. So I went back to that moment. In our lounge. She was lying on the sofa and her eyes were nearly coming out of her head.' He closes his own. 'Her colour was all wrong.'

'Was she swollen?' I ask gently.

'No!' His eyes flick open, accusatory. 'I don't know. She was a big woman. Overweight, you know. I was always on at her to cut down but she wouldn't listen. She enjoyed her food, that's what she said, always cooking and snacking. I hadn't noticed the expression on the faces of the paramedics when they came in the room in my memory.'

'You can control where you go?'

'Yes, that always works for me. But anyway, I saw them looking at the size of her and I knew they were thinking about how they were going to get her down the stairs cos the lift wasn't working again. I should have said something to them or made her listen to me about the food. The Revisit was all just blame and shame and guilt. It didn't help. It won't help, going back, seeing their pain and yours. You can't change anything. My mum was obese and they chose someone else more deserving, someone thinner, to take to the ICU, and they left my mum to die on a trolley in A&E.' Leon has curled the tea towel into a tight twisted rope and now he flings out the end of it against a metal locker, making it clank.

'That's shit,' I say. 'All of this is shit.'

From the kitchen doorway Piper says, 'I remember hearing that death rates were higher for Black people even accounting for social and economic factors.'

'What?' Leon says.

'And taking geography into account.'

'My mum wasn't Black.'

Piper's mouth opens but for once she has nothing to say.

'My mum was white.' He says the word as though he has scored the line across the 't'.

The microwave pings and Piper turns back into the kitchen, embarrassed.

Leon shakes his head. 'Some people,' he says. 'So many fucking assumptions.'

'I'm sorry,' I say, even though I have no reason to apologize on Piper's behalf.

'It's my dad who was Black. He died before I was born.'

Rachel bursts into the room with Yahiko and complains about the warm water as she pours a mug for everyone, and while Leon is passing around the forks, I mouth to Yahiko to ask whether he's okay, but I'm not sure how well he can see without his glasses and his eyes still look awful. The swelling has gone down a bit but a dirty yellow colour has spread out from the purple. He'd joined us for breakfast but had been quiet, and I try to assess him now to see if he seems any thinner, weaker. I know that I'm looking for a reason not to feel bad about not going outside, and I don't find it. When we're all sitting, Piper comes in with the tray and divides up the food. She and Leon don't look at each other.

'Can any of you smell the waste chute?' I say. 'I'm sure it's beginning to stink.'

'Is your sense of smell returning?' Piper asks.

'I think it must be. Maybe we could go down to the basement and bag up the rubbish or something.'

'Let's discuss it at the next meeting.'

I find myself rolling my eyes at Rachel and she smiles weakly.

Yahiko is eyeing my plate as though he's assessing whether it's bigger than everyone else's, and I wonder if giving me more food was also part of Piper's plan – to make sure I continued ovulating. She should have asked me, though, because in cephalopods, at least, the nutrition of the male is almost as critical as that of the female. Anyway, I have rice and a curry which seems to consist mostly of an orange-coloured sauce. I put a guilty forkful of food in my mouth and I tell myself to save some for Yahiko. I move a grain of rice to the front of my mouth, take it out with my fingers and examine it. I swallow the rest and from the corner of my eye see Piper watching. I run my fork through the curry. It *is* only sauce, without vegetables.

'What is this?' I ask her.

'Curry and rice,' she says. It looks like she's eating a little bit of all four dishes, one tube of cannelloni with meat inside, a bit of my curry, a spoonful of meat stew and a small potato.

I bring another forkful to my nose and sniff.

'Just eat it,' Piper says. 'Before Yahiko gets it.'

'What did the label say?'

'Curry.' Piper starts chewing a mouthful of food. Her jaw is working up and down and with a slight sideways rotation, like a cow or a camel. She doesn't swallow and still her jaw moves. She closes her eyes. The muscles bulge in her cheeks as they work. We're all watching now.

'What the hell is she doing?' Yahiko says.

'She's chewing,' Rachel says. 'Are you all right?' she asks Piper.

I eat some of my rice while I watch too. We can hear her jaw clicking.

'There can't be any food left in her mouth by now,' Yahiko says.

Piper opens her eyes and swallows. 'I remembered an article I read online ages ago,' she says. 'If you chew your food one hundred times you get ten per cent more calories. I think. Or maybe twenty.'

'I don't know how you can do that,' Rachel says, and everyone tries to do it too. I manage to chew several times before I swallow but my stomach demands the food and it is impossible to keep it in my mouth for long, and anyway, I'm sure it's only sauce. I eye the other plates to see who might have got my vegetables.

238

Leon starts a conversation about learning to drive. It's a distraction tactic to stop us thinking about the lack of food and trying to eat slowly to make it last; the feeling when your plate is empty and you can see the hours stretching ahead to breakfast is the worst. But I know Leon's also doing it for my sake, so that no one will ask me when I'm going to go outside to find some more. The distraction works. Rachel and Yahiko say they've never had a driving lesson, Piper has failed twice and Leon reckons he knows how to drive although he's never passed a test. I learned as soon as I could and passed my test at seventeen. Leon moves the discussion on to tattoos. We all have one, apart from Piper. Yahiko has a giant blue koi swimming up his thigh – he has to take his shoes and jeans off to show us. Leon has a butterfly across a shoulder. Rachel points out that the name of a previous girl-friend is woven across the wings. She has a tiny rocket on her ankle, firing off into a cluster of stars. She tells us that her dad got the same one. I show them the small ammonite I have on my back, the animal's tentacles wriggling from its shell.

We go back to eating and discussing food, and whether beef or lamb makes the best meat in a roast dinner, and I put in a vote for stuffing and vegetarian gravy when I feel something thin and sharp in my mouth. I work it forward to my lips and remove it with my fingers. It's as fine as a cat's whisker and as white. It is a fish bone. Everyone stops talking and eating, and they stare at me and at the bone.

'I'm sorry. I took out as much of the haddock as I could,' Piper says.

I look down at my plate and it's empty. I forgot to save any for Yahiko. Three or four grains of rice are scattered around the edge where my fork chased them. My brain roils but my stomach hangs on to the food; no way is it going to let anything go.

A haddock is similar to a cod, only smaller, and a fussier eater. It has a blotch on its side called the devil's thumbprint. The aquarium had several haddock.

'You have to eat,' Leon says. I can feel the tears coming and I continue to look down at my plate. Rachel puts her hand on mine.

'We don't have any vegetarian meals left,' Piper says. 'I didn't want to tell you.'

They let me sit at the table as they tidy up around me. I see Yahiko gather together the four grains of rice from my plate with his fingers as he clears it away and slip them into his mouth. I can see he wants to ask, 'Now will you go outside?' but he is gracious enough to hold the words in.

When all but Leon have crept away, I ask him for a Revisit.

'It's not good,' he says, 'to use the Revisitor for comfort, for a prop when things are going wrong.'

'Are you telling me you wouldn't do that?' I say quietly. 'If it worked well for you, wouldn't you spend your days Revisiting your mum rather than just existing, here, where she isn't?'

He knows I'm right.

'That's why you brought it with you, isn't it?'

He looks away from me and then back. His expression doesn't change.

'Not just to tweak but to tweak it so you could get it to work properly for you.'

He rubs his hand across his forehead.

'Is that why you volunteered for the trial? So you could earn some money and spend the time getting it to work on you?' He doesn't answer. 'That's okay, though.'

240

He stands. 'I'll get your Revisit ready.'

'Thank you.'

He hesitates by the door. 'Sometimes, though, I wonder whether Revisiting isn't that different to Rachel spending hours on her phone scrolling through her old photos. Neither are real life. But yeah, I get it, real life isn't that great at the moment. But anyway,' he slaps the door jamb. 'I'll go and get your Revisit set up.' He gives a rueful smile. 'See you in five minutes?'

'Five minutes,' I say.

When he's gone, I go into the kitchen. Like yesterday when I got the ice for Yahiko, it is sparklingly clean. And like the staffroom there are no windows, so I put on the light, and take my time to look around. It is all silver metal units: an industrial-sized microwave, the meal-delivery cart, open metal shelving containing cardboard boxes of paper napkins wrapped in plastic, others with sachets of salt and pepper. A silver workbench with a built-in sink, all of it spotless like a hospital kitchen should be. I hear the buzz of the overhead light, the hum of a fridge. I open it to see that it's empty. I open the freezer and take out one of the packaged meals: meatballs in gravy with mashed potatoes and carrots. Another: prawn curry and rice. I take out another and another. Piper was right: they are all meat or fish. I'm going to starve, or I'm going to eat these, or I'm going to go outside and get more food. Or I'll have to leave, and what then for the rest, when they run out of food? I close the freezer door and with my hand on the light switch look back to make sure I've left the room as I found it. On the wall is a large electrical switch – an override perhaps to turn the microwave off. And below it is what seems to be another, small and black and taped over with three plasters. DO NOT

REMOVE someone has written on them with the marker from the whiteboard. I pick at the top two strips and peel them back. The air-conditioning controls are underneath. I hear the door to the staffroom open and Piper appears in the kitchen doorway.

'Are you okay?' she says. 'I'm really sorry about the curry. Not telling you.'

'What's this?' I ask, pulling again at the plasters.

'Yahiko stuck them on. I think there's something dodgy with the wiring. He didn't want anyone getting electric shocks.' She presses the plasters back down, gently pushes my hand away.

'Maybe I could fix it.' I know nothing about electrics but I'm sick of being cold.

'I doubt it. Yahiko knows what he's doing. I came in to get some ice.' She goes to the freezer and opens the door. 'Do you want a piece? It's good for making you think you're eating.'

She takes out an ice-cube tray and taps a couple of cubes on to the counter and gives me one. 'Try it. Imagine it's a Murray Mint. Remember those?' Her own ice cube is already rolling around her mouth, hitting her teeth. 'My dad always had a packet in the car. My mum would complain about how boring they were, she'd go mad for chocolate eclairs. Do you have a favourite sweet?' She sounds overexcited, like we're eight and our parents have told us to get to know each other. I notice she's talking about hers in the past tense for the first time. I crunch down on the ice and swallow the shards.

'Lemon bonbons. Before I was vegetarian.'

'Let's get you another lemon bonbon.' She laughs and

opens the freezer again. 'Are you going for a Revisit? Do you want to take one for Leon? If you hurry, it'll still be frozen.'

Dearest H,

I didn't exactly plan it or at least I didn't think through what I would do or how it would work. It was more that I'd gone a little mad. Grief or guilt or shame, or something. I went through the days like an automaton, doing the tasks I had to do, speaking to Margot, avoiding Justin. One evening I was the last to leave the aquarium aside from the security guy. At my locker I put on my jacket, pulled out my bag and slung it over my shoulder. I saw my sandwich boxes which I kept forgetting to take home. A set of boxes with click-on lids. One of them was big enough to fit a decent-sized circular cake inside that I'd had to use when I realized I'd left all my other boxes at work. I took it out and looked at it, and then I closed my locker door. I went back to your tank and undid the catch. You came to me immediately, and I didn't stop to think about the consequences of what I was doing. All that was in my mind was that I wanted to save someone, something, finally. I scooped up some of your water and you climbed in the box. You tucked your arms in neatly as though you knew, and I snapped on the lid and put the box in my bag – a roomy, cloth bag. I had a little chat with the security guy about the weather and what he was going to have for his tea. I went down to the sea and I released you.

Neffy

When I get to Leon's room he's standing at the window staring out. He turns.

'You okay?' he asks.

'Here,' I say. 'Have a lemon bonbon.'

'Your mum will be sorry she missed you,' Justin said, hopping from one foot to the other in the doorway.

Oh, Justin, I think. *And I've missed you.* I want him to stay still, motionless, so I have time to move around the scene without it speeding on, to look again at my beautiful Justin from every angle.

His fingers were rammed into his jeans pockets and his hair was messy as though I had caught him napping. We were in a storeroom behind Clive's Dorset house. Maybe it was once going to be an office or a laundry but now it was filled with things that didn't suit the rest of the house with its clean lines and minimalist spaces: a black chair on castors, a tall unit for CDs, an old-fashioned standard lamp.

'She said to give you her love and to say again that she hoped it went all right in Paxos. I wish you'd have let me come with you. Jeez, it's fucking freezing in here.' He had on his *Back to the Future* T-shirt.

'I know,' I said. 'She called me from Copenhagen.' It had been one-hundred-and-twenty-two days since Baba died; sixty since I'd returned to my work at the aquarium, stolen an octopus, returned it to the sea and been sacked; twelve since I'd returned to Paxos where Margot and I had scattered Baba's ashes in the sea; and one day since I'd been back in England. Justin and I had messaged often and called but I'd managed to keep him at arm's length. I needed some time to work things through and I'd come back to Clive's and Mum's house for clothes I'd stored here after I was sacked from my previous job. I still hadn't told Justin about what I'd done at the aquarium. He'd mentioned on his last message that he'd be in London today but now I was wondering if he'd planned to ambush me all along. We hadn't kissed; I'd managed to shimmy around him, sliding out of his arms, although all I wanted was to have him hold me.

'It seems a funny place to go to in January,' I said. We were making small talk about our parents. It was ridiculous.

'Dad's got some big commission. He won't even tell me what it is. Top secret, although apparently they might have to stay for months.'

'Months?' Mum hadn't told me this.

'Do you want a cup of tea?'

'No, I'm fine, thanks.'

I want to give that old Neffy a kick in the shins. It's tea! This is Justin, have tea with him, don't be such an arse. But I carry straight on.

He was right, it was freezing. The cold came up through my jeans where I was kneeling on the concrete floor. I'd pulled out a wheelie suitcase that I thought was an old one of Mum's. It certainly looked familiar, although I wasn't sure. 'They didn't invite you to go with them?' I unzipped the suitcase and opened the lid. The jumpers on top were folded with their arms behind their backs. I realized that Justin hadn't answered me and when I looked up at him, he said, 'I told them I couldn't go.'

'What?' And then I got it. 'You didn't have to stay in

England because of me. I'm fine. Absolutely fine.' He looked at me. 'I just need some warm clothes because it *is* fucking cold in here.' I rummaged through the jumpers.

'It's warm in the house.'

'Nice thermal performance,' I said sarcastically.

'*Very* nice.'

I didn't mean to be sour; it just came out. Before I could apologize, he asked, 'You are going to stay tonight, aren't you?'

'Well, actually, I booked a taxi to the station. I'm going to London tonight.' I lifted up a jumper the younger me didn't remember owning – black with a round neck. *Put it back in the case and go and have tea with Justin.*

'Don't you have to go back to work?' I heard his feet shuffle on the concrete floor.

'Work is off.'

'Off? What do you mean, off?'

'They sacked me.'

'Oh shit, Neffy. What happened?'

'I stole one of their octopuses and released it into the sea.'

'What?'

'I stole one of –'

'I heard what you said. But why? Why would you do that?'

'Because it needed to be free.'

'But your job.'

'I didn't like it anyway.'

'When did this happen?'

'Two months ago? A bit less.'

'And you didn't tell me? Christ, Neffy. What have you been doing for money?'

'You sound like my mother. Actually, you sound nothing like her. She's never worried about money.'

'Because she's always got a man who'll pay for her.'

I pulled my head back. 'Ouch.'

'Sorry. Sorry. I didn't mean that. But I don't understand. Why didn't you tell me?' He squinted in that way that made him look sweetly short-sighted. 'This is a load of old shite.'

I sat down properly and looked at him, and the concrete instantly numbed my backside. I knew he didn't mean the clothes in the suitcase.

'I don't know why you're doing what you're doing but it's a fucking load of crap. Your father died and you weren't with him. I get it. You've just scattered his ashes and that must have been terrible, but this is crap.' He swept his arms wide to take in me on the floor, the suitcase, the other discarded items, and everything I was doing.

I shook my head to try to dispel the film of tears forming in my eyes.

'Let me help you,' he said more gently, and he slowly squatted down in the doorway, still a few feet from me as though I were a creature that could be easily scared. 'Stay here, with me.'

'And be like Mum?' My throat was closing with the effort of not crying.

'I shouldn't have said that. I'm worried about you. Where are you going to live?'

'I'm going to stay with a friend.'

'What friend?'

'You don't know her.'

'Whereabouts?' He had red patches high on his cheeks which he always got when he was excited or agitated. Like a young farmer, I used to tease him, *ruddy Justin*.

'South. South London. Yes, south. Peckham.' I held the black jumper against me. It smelled of the cold.

'I don't believe you.'

'Well, you can believe what you like. It's true.'

It was only true in so far as a friend of a friend had tentatively agreed to let me sleep on her sofa for a couple of nights until I sorted something out.

'Were you ever going to tell me? Or are you doing a very poor version of ghosting? One where you only sometimes answer my texts and only turn up at the house when you think I'm not going to be here.'

I glared at him. So this was an ambush. I could have told myself that at the beginning of this Revisit.

'Of course I was going to tell you.' I was shivering now in my summer jacket and, even though it was thin and loose on me, the idea of taking it off to put the jumper on was unbearable.

'When?'

I hugged my knees, put my head on them. I could smell the denim, unwashed.

'I just can't do it any more.' My voice came out cracked and squeaking.

When I looked up again Justin crawled on all fours the few feet across the floor and hunkered down in front of me. I covered my whole face with my palms.

'Neffy, please.' He took hold of my wrists and gently pulled my hands away. 'Please, look at me.'

I stared sideways and down where the contents of the suitcase were strewn about. My cheeks were wet. The palms of my hands were wet.

'Don't do this,' he said.

I shook my head.

'I love you,' he said. He knelt and took my head into his shoulder. I couldn't bear the smell of him, there was too much comfort in it. He stroked the back of my head and I opened my mouth wide but nothing came out, no scream, no cry. The knots of my hair where I hadn't brushed it slid over my scalp, under his palm. 'It'll be all right.'

I pulled away from his hands and rubbed at my eyes. 'No,' I said. 'I can't see you any more. I'm sorry.' I said it in the hardest voice I could find.

He sat back and looked at me without speaking and I was sure he was remembering too: that room, that bed in Cow Hollow, San Francisco. I remembered the feel of him inside me. I remembered the sounds we made. I never sent a text to tell Baba I would grow him a kidney. Of course I would have been too late but he never even knew. And what about pleasure? To be feeling the kind of pleasure and joy I'd been feeling when your father is dying was a serious business.

'It's not that,' I said, although Justin still hadn't spoken. I shook my head vehemently. 'It's just . . . It's just that it's not possible. You and me. We shouldn't be together.'

'Yes, we should.'

Yes, we should, I echo, inside my own head.

Justin and I went inside the house, and he set about making tea while I sat in a chair and not on the sofa. The house was its perfect temperature but I was still cold. I slipped off my jacket and pulled the black jumper which I'd brought in with me over my head. It was baggy and had dog hairs on the sleeves.

'What do you think about this stuff that's happening in South America?' Justin called from the kitchen as he opened cupboards to take out teabags and mugs.

'What stuff?'

'A virus. Causes swelling in humans apparently. They're talking about an epidemic or a pandemic or something.'

'I haven't been following the news.'

'Probably nothing.'

He came across the room with the two mugs. 'You must have opened the wrong suitcase.' I looked down at my jumper and saw a penguin on the front wearing a Christmas hat. I'd never seen this jumper before. Some of the sequins were missing. 'I'm pretty sure that was my mum's. Dad has a photo of her wearing it. I didn't know any of her stuff was still in there. It was supposed to have gone to charity years ago.'

He'd told me about his mother. She'd died of cancer when he was four. She'd had a cake-making business, designing and baking them for people's birthdays and for weddings and anniversaries. Justin once said that the last cake she made was for herself, knowing it would be her final birthday. Even though it was for her, she decorated it with a little footballer kicking a ball. Justin had wanted to eat it, the little boy footballer who looked like him. His mother said he wouldn't enjoy it, that marzipan was for big boys, but he insisted, and he bit the head off the boy and spat it out. He remembered her anger and the horrible taste, but he couldn't really remember her. I told him that was natural, normal to only remember some things and not others. Another time he'd shown me a picture of her, and I'd thought she looked very like my own mother although I hadn't said so; it was too fucked up already.

Justin came to kiss me, and it took all my willpower to turn my head away. And now I hate myself for that turn of the head. *I will learn from this*, I tell myself. I will do the right thing from now on: I will always kiss the man I love; I will go outside. I'd hoped the chair was too small, too tight with its wooden mid-century arms for him to squeeze into it beside me, but like an old familiar Labrador which still thinks it is a lap-sized puppy, Justin climbed on to me, squashing me into the chair, a knee in my groin, my face in his chest. 'This is grief, Neffy,' he said. 'It's awful and terrible, and it will never truly leave, but you will learn to live with it, and you have to let me help you.' And he held me as I cried.

Dearest H,

In the disciplinary meeting I was told that I had to pay back what I owed to the aquarium for the loss of an octopus. They said it would be for the cost of buying and transporting a new white-spotted octopus from Turkey, even though you were a curled octopus and could be found in UK waters. Either I agreed or they would call the police.

My manager took my pass, and I was escorted from the building through the gift shop, past the goggling parents and their kids. The security guy had provided me with a cardboard box to empty the contents of my locker into like they did in American films when someone is dismissed. While he watched, I put in a paperback book, pages wrinkled, and the half-dozen empty sandwich boxes which rattled with dry crumbs. One was missing. I suppose I'd left it on the rocks beside the sea when the local mental health team arrived. Someone must have called them after they spotted a woman standing knee-deep in the water. They drove me home and told me to make an appointment with my GP. I never did.

Neffy

Day Twelve

Rachel's room is tidy, the bed is made. Since I was last in here, she's shifted her furniture around and now her desk with all its make-up is in front of the window. Maybe thirty or forty items in tubes and bottles are laid out, as well as a circular mirror. Margot had one just like it, the kind you can flip for a magnified view. I own a single lipstick and some mascara which I brought with me although I can't remember the last time I put either on, but I know it wasn't while I've been in the unit.

Rachel comes out of her bathroom holding a pair of scissors. She's dressed in the usual jeans, hoodie, robe and platform trainers, but her cheeks are rosy from the shower and her face is free of make-up, literally washed clean. She has a towel wrapped around her hair, folded up high on her head so that her eyes are pulled at the corners making her, if it's possible, even more beautiful.

'Happy birthday, again,' I say.

Rachel raises her hand and snaps the scissors in the air, and I rear back. I still find her unpredictable and moody. Mum would have loved her, she would have called her *effervescent*. 'Your face!' Rachel laughs and sits at the desk. 'I gave myself a haircut for the party.' She unwraps the towel from her head and roughs up her hair, now a ragged bob with a high fringe that looks like it's been cut at an expensive salon. And the scent of honeysuckle from her shampoo wafts briefly in the room before it is dispersed by the air conditioning or my poor sense of smell loses it. Rachel picks up the mirror and holds it in front of her face. 'What do you think?' She moves it until our eyes meet. Her reflected face is the same as in real life. Most other people's faces in mirrors are curiously different, with crooked eyes, lopsided smiles, an evil twin, but Rachel's is perfect. Symmetrical.

'Want one?' she says, snipping again at the air. The scissors make a satisfying sound, metal sliding against metal. She laughs. 'Okay, maybe just a bit of make-up.' She jumps up and has me sit in her place while she pulls over the other chair. She holds my chin and turns my head towards her so she can examine me. I feel exposed and try to pull away, aware of my greasy skin, my plain round face, how much older I am than her. She lets me go and digs through the make-up on her desk, finally deciding on a half-used tube.

'Did you get enough to eat at dinner?' she asks, squeezing some foundation on to the back of her hand. Everyone had agreed that I could have two pots of porridge. No one had mentioned what I was going to do about food tomorrow or the day after that or the fact that I was eating their breakfasts. Rachel is trying to find out what my plans are, maybe Yahiko has even asked her to ask me, and I know I will have to go outside but I still keep putting it off. I can't ask any of them to come with me because I'm feeling panicky about the idea – risking their life as well as mine. I've been trying not to think about it because picturing myself on the street makes me feel light-headed and weak, as though soon I will be bodyless – remove each layer of my bulky clothes and there will be nothing left of me. I have already self-diagnosed anxiety, the beginning of a panic attack, maybe even agoraphobia, so I have stopped thinking about it. Tomorrow, I tell myself, I will deal with it.

'It's fine,' I say. 'I'll manage.'

Rachel tilts my head. 'I'll have to be quick, the light is crap.' She dots the foundation under my eyes and on my cheeks and begins rubbing it in.

'I got you a present,' I say.

She stops her work. 'Really?' She's as excited as a child.

'Well, actually I'm regifting it. And I thought we could share it.'

'A present!' She claps her hands.

'And I couldn't find anything to wrap it in except toilet paper.' I take it out from my robe pocket and hand it to her, watching while she unwinds the paper. She holds the sample pot to the window where the daylight is fading. She gives it a shake.

'It's a Matchmaker,' I say. 'Two halves of a Matchmaker.'

'I know what it is. Yahiko told me he gave it to you. It was the last one. You can't give me this. He said you were saving it for someone.'

'I want us to eat it, now.'

'No, you should keep it.' She hands it back to me. 'For whoever it is.'

I unscrew the lid and sniff and it's there, the heady breath of sugar, chocolate and mint which Yahiko described. 'Justin. His name is, was, Justin. He was on a plane going to Denmark but it got diverted to Sweden and they wouldn't let any of the passengers off. He sent me a video and I haven't heard from him again.' As I speak I feel in my gut that Justin and I have been disconnected, severed, and that however much I reach out, blindingly searching for a reply, none will come.

'Oh, Neffy.' She opens her arms and we embrace. It feels natural, easy; perhaps it's after trying to reassure Yahiko yesterday, or me eating fish by mistake, or what's been going on with her dad, or most likely, all of it. She smells of expensive soap and I wonder if Yahiko has shared out more of what he took from Jade's room.

When we break away I say, 'He was my stepbrother.'

'And?' Rachel says.

I screw up a corner of my mouth.

'You know that *step* means you aren't related?' she says.

I frown at her, confused for a moment.

'It's fine, you and him.'

'Thanks,' I laugh and tip the pieces of Matchmaker on to my palm and hold them out. Rachel takes one. She puts her piece in her mouth in one go, and I put all of mine in at once too and then we open our eyes wide at the taste of it, the delight, the notion that not everything can be saved.

Rachel continues with my make-up, applying eyeliner and mascara. 'How's the Revisiting going?' she asks. Her minty chocolate breath wafts across my face. 'What's it like? I'm glad it doesn't work on me. Sounds grim.'

'Really? You wouldn't want to go back to see friends again, your dad?' She sounds like Piper and I wonder if their insistence that they wouldn't want it to work is to hide their disappointment at it not working for them.

'God, no. I'm trying to forget all that.' She laughs.

'It is pretty intense.'

'I hope Leon isn't letting you do it too much.'

'What do you mean?' I don't want anyone else thinking I should do it less.

'You know the project got pulled?'

'Because it didn't work on enough people?'

'Because of the lawsuit.'

I shrink away from her hand, stare at her.

'Leon didn't mean to tell me about it.' She continues applying the make-up. 'But apparently some people, their testers or whatever, got addicted to Revisiting and then went crazy when they weren't allowed to do it any more. Fucked their mental health by the sound of it. And they sued the company, Leon's company, which meant, like, the investors had to pay, or their insurance, or someone. I don't think it went to court but the money was stopped, just like that.' She waves the mascara wand in the air. 'I think that must be why he volunteered – because of his debts.' I don't tell her what I think the reason is, which Leon as good as confirmed.

'And you? Why did you volunteer?' I feel I can ask her now.

'It's silly really. I'm embarrassed to say.'

'No, go on, it's okay.'

'It was just my dad being locked up. If I hadn't gone out with that idiot – the swimming coach – my dad wouldn't have had anyone's nose to break, you know. He wouldn't have been arrested, found guilty and sent to prison. So I thought I should be locked up too. Just for a little bit. Is that silly?'

'No, not silly.'

She puts the lid back on the mascara. 'So, you have to make sure you don't Revisit too much,' she says.

'I'm definitely not. It's fine. It's okay.' I don't point out the irony of how many hours she spends scrolling through old messages and photos on her phone since for the first couple of days after I woke up I would do that too.

She chooses a lipstick and dabs it on me then moves her own lips together to make me copy her so the lipstick will smudge. 'You know I said I wanted to come with you if you leave?' She moves back to assess my face. 'Well, you don't have to take me. Not any more. I think I'll stick with Yahiko, and the others. No offence. But I think Yahiko is getting pretty desperate about the food, you know.'

'I know.' I want to promise her that I'll go outside and find them some but the words won't come.

'Maybe the army will arrive after all.' She sounds as though she's trying to cheer me up, make excuses for me.

'For Piper.'

'Oh yeah. They'll leave us behind and just take her.' She sniggers.

'I've been wondering – how's the army going to know we're here if we're not allowed to put on any lights or move the blinds or put any signs on the windows?'

'Because they know about the trial. They know we're here. We're famous. We were on the news – one of my friends tagged me when she posted it. Someone high up will have the address.' Rachel sounds like she's come around to Piper's way of thinking and I wonder if it is something to cling to. She closes the lipstick and stands it name upwards with the others.

'If you did leave, where would you go?' I ask her.

'I don't know. Maybe we should find somewhere new, start again. Piper wants to go back to her house to see her parents. To be honest, Leon and I are sure about what she'll find but I suppose we'll have to check.' Rachel selects a tiny brush and sweeps my eyebrows upwards.

'And your dad?'

'No. I think, like your Justin, if he'd got out, if he was able to come, he would have found out where we were and he would have got here by now, and I'm not going to see. I don't want to look at that place again. The walls, the flood-lights.' She shudders. 'Thinking what it must have been like inside.'

'And how do you think Yahiko will cope with leaving the unit?'

'God, I'm worried about Yahiko. He's definitely losing it. You were so good with him yesterday. So calm.'

'Maybe I should have stuck with medical school.'

'I didn't know you went to medical school.' She wipes the edge of my mouth with the tip of a finger. 'There.'

'I gave it up. Realized I wasn't any good at helping people.'

She's holding the mirror to my face but it's too dark to see.

'Yes you are. You signed up for the trial.'

'For the money.'

'No, none of us signed up just for the money. There were always easier ways of making a few quid. I did camming until we were in lockdown and too many other girls were doing it. I reckon you're pretty good at saving people, Neffy.' She looks at me critically. 'And you'd be pretty good at camming now I've done your make-up.' We laugh and while she applies her own mascara by touch and scrunches her new hair, I think again about Justin and how he was always trying to save me – financially, from pain, from grief about Baba's death – and I wonder if Rachel is right: maybe I didn't only sign up for the money but to try to return those kindnesses by having the vaccine and the virus. And with the possibility of saving myself, I might save him too.

'Come on,' Rachel says. 'It's party time.'

In reception, we hear voices coming from the staffroom and when we go in the lights are bright and someone has hung loops of toilet paper from the ceiling with plasters. I can still smell a whiff from the waste chute but no one comments on it. The table has been pushed under the whiteboard and there are five mugs on it and a bottle. Piper isn't wearing her hat and for the first time I see her hair – undercut at the sides and the top styled up. I almost don't recognize her except that she's wearing her slippers. 'Happy birthday,' she says to Rachel. We saw Rachel this morning at breakfast and at dinner, but we'd agreed we'd celebrate this evening. They comment on her haircut and my make-up, Yahiko making us turn one way and then the other. Leon has made Rachel a card – I recognize the paper from the notebook he took from my room – and Piper gives her a string of origami cranes folded from pages torn from a novel, which Rachel coos over and drapes around her neck. Piper, I learn, is spending her days making a thousand paper cranes for good health or good luck. Yahiko gives Rachel a phone case, the back decorated with a donut design. We all admire it, discuss how realistic each donut looks and which one we'd eat. Yahiko and Rachel squeal and clap their hands when they pick the same one and I try not to think about the person who left this in the unit.

'Look,' Leon says. 'Yahiko did have more alcohol.' He goes for the bottle.

Yahiko reaches out and takes it before Leon can touch it. 'Let me,' he says. He makes a meal of twisting off the top, bending close to the five mugs so he can see as he pours some into each one. Piper says she doesn't want any, but he insists. He hands around the drinks and we stand in a circle and chink the mugs together. 'Happy birthday, Rachel,' he says again. '*Kanpai!*' and we echo him and drink.

It's water.

Leon doesn't even pause before he says, 'Oh, that's good. What is it?'

Yahiko holds up the bottle – the same vodka that Leon and Rachel finished off, or at least, the same brand. Momentarily I wonder if he's only given water to me and somehow given vodka to everyone else, but Rachel says, 'I can't believe you saved some vodka for my birthday.' Rachel, who has always seemed to me the most candid of the group, can't quite carry off the lie.

'Cheers again,' I say and take a big slug, exhaling as though it's burning my throat.

Rachel laughs and Piper looks from one to the other of us worrying, like me, that the joke is only on her.

'Fake it till you make it!' Rachel says.

Piper continues to look confused.

I lean in and say quietly, 'Like role play, in HR.'

'Oh,' she says, getting it, smiling. 'I'm not a big drinker.' She sips. 'But this is nice.'

Rachel makes us put our heads together and takes half a dozen pictures on her phone and then flicks through them. Yahiko insists she puts the phone away and then he lifts her hand and makes her turn under his arm and they dance to Leon's muted trumpet version of Nina Simone's 'My Baby Just Cares for Me' – nose to nose, back to back, Yahiko's and Rachel's bodies are supple, mobile, mesmerizing. Piper refills our cups, knocking her drink back in one go. Her face is flushed and standing beside the table she sways to the music. Rachel catches her hand and makes her come forward to dance. Piper resists and then, laughing, joins her, and I finish my drink and dance with Yahiko, who now begins to blindly bounce off the table and the walls as the beat picks up, and then we're dancing together and laughing. I feel even dizzier than before, light-headed and happy. The mugs are filled again and Rachel jumps to pull some of the toilet paper from the ceiling and Piper helps her wrap it around her head like a crown. Everything is funny.

'This is the best birthday,' Rachel says breathlessly.

When I turn back to the table the bottle is full, and then emptied. Leon gets the hiccups and this is hilarious too. 'No more, no more,' Piper says, waving her hand above her mug as Yahiko tries to fill it.

Leon starts the music up again and we watch Yahiko and Rachel stagger around the room, pretending to be drunk, slumped over each other. With her hand, Piper is beating out the rhythm on the lockers. I sit on the floor with my back against a cupboard and my legs out straight and watch them dance. Then we're all sitting on the floor, Rachel lying with her head in Piper's lap with her paper crown wet and stuck to her hair. Piper picks out flecks of it and lays them on Rachel's cheeks like tiny pale tears.

'To the beautiful, sad, birthday girl,' Yahiko says, and raises his mug. He's the only one still drinking.

Rachel struggles up out of Piper's lap and all but one of the toilet paper tears fall from her face. 'To me!' she says, waving her hands in the air. 'And to Neffy.' She raises her imaginary mug. 'May she be our final girl!'

I lower my head in thanks. 'And to Piper,' I say. 'For her eternal optimism.'

Piper puts her hands together, bows over them. 'To Leon.' Piper also raises an imaginary glass. 'For the music!'

Leon makes a farting noise with his mouth. 'To Yahiko,' he says. 'For the vodka.' He blows Yahiko a kiss.

'Hooray!' Piper cheers.

Leon is still, quiet. He raises his mug again. 'To absent friends,' he says, and Rachel starts to cry.

Dearest H,

I try to put myself inside the mind of an octopus. A brain shaped like a donut with the intestines travelling through the central hole, a being that understands the world through arms and suckers, as much as head. How different would I be from who I am now? And what would I want? Does an octopus want? If you do, perhaps it would be the chance to mate, to play, to hunt, to choose freedom.

Neffy

In the darkness of Leon's room I'm wide awake, lying on his bed, my palms open, waiting. Rachel's party fell apart after she started crying, all of us too sober to pile into a tearful and self-pitying group hug. And now while Leon gets the Revisitor ready, I think of some of my own absent friends: Justin, Nicos, Margot. I wonder what the pandemic has been like on islands like Paxos. Would the virus have swept through the two thousand or so residents and decimated the place, or would its relative isolation have kept them safe?

Margot had been determined to stay on in the flat without my father, saying that her life and her friends were on the island even though her mother remained in California. She couldn't imagine ever starting again – didn't want to live in a larger place in the hope of finding someone new. Her biggest sadness she said often during the days when I was on Paxos for Baba's funeral was that she'd been unable to have a child with him. We'd phoned each other now and then but I'd missed her last call a week or so before I was due to go into the unit and had never returned it, had only ever replied with that picture of me with the peg on my nose. She'd left a message on that final call: 'I've been thinking,' she said. 'Maybe Oliver died on purpose before you could get back to the clinic, you know how people do sometimes die at a certain point when they feel everything has been completed. I know he didn't want you to do it, that thing with the kidney, so maybe he made sure it was all over before you got back. It only just occurred to me, so I thought I'd phone. Anyway, hope you're living your best life. Love you!'

'Ready?' Leon asks.

He puts the pebbles in my palms and I close my hands around them and think of Margot on Paxos. As ever, I am taken elsewhere.

The bottom of Mum's dress was wet, heavy with seawater and sand as she squatted next to the rock pool. I knelt beside her. 'Everything A-okay in there?' She tapped the goggles which she'd spat into and crammed over my face, and she waggled the snorkel in my mouth. This, my first snorkel and goggle set, was lurid pink and I loved it. 'A-okay,' I said. The word seemed to come out from the top of the snorkel tube.

The exceptional heat of that English August sun comes back to me now, to my older self – Mum has forgotten the sun cream again and I remember that tomorrow my seven-year-old shoulders will come up in blisters so sore I'll have to sleep on my front. In a few days the blisters will dry and, in the caravans it's Mum's job to clean, I'll sit reading and absent-mindedly reach over my shoulder to peel off the skin in long, satisfying strips.

On the beach, Mum grasped the straps on the back of my swimming costume, bringing them together in one hand. The fabric stretched across my chest and dug into the front of my shoulders. 'Ready?' she said. We had been coming every day to the rock pools when the tide was out, after she'd finished work. Up until today I had only scooped out the sea creatures with my see-through bucket, examining in close-up a hermit crab, a shanny and a common prawn – identifying them from a sheet we'd picked up from the tourist office. Mum had been paid earlier, in actual notes and coins, and she'd seen the snorkel set in a shop window on our way to the supermarket. 'Who needs food,' she'd said as she'd paid.

'Ready,' I said. I grasped the sides of the rock I was kneeling on, held back by Mum's grip on my swimming costume, and lowered my face into the water.

And I looked down into another world.

Mountains and valleys, chasms and rockfalls, swaying fields of grass. The light was sallow, the colour of Mum's green tea, and the sound was of tiny scrapings, bubbles and my own breath. My hair floated in the edges of my vision, a fronded weed, blonde at the ends where it had been bleached by the sun. I watched a prawn with its insides on show backing into a clump of cloudy seaweed, legs forever galloping like the legs on a fairground horse. A brownish crab carrying white eye-spots crept sideways into a dark space and then burst forward as though something had spat it out. I stared at the overhang where the crab had been. I watched and I watched until something orange with suckers, smaller than my little finger, felt its way forward. I held my breath and then abruptly I was yanked backwards up into the land of humans and noise and light and sound.

'I thought you'd forgotten to breathe!' Mum said, laughing. She took the snorkel out of my mouth, the goggles off my face, and hugged me, not caring that I made the front of her dress wet.

'I saw a tentacle!' I said. 'A tiny tentacle uncurling out of the dark.'

'Did it have suckers all the way along it, even at the tip?'

'I think so.'

'Then it was an octopus and what you saw was an arm, not a tentacle.'

We held hands and swung our own arms as we walked back to the caravan where we were staying, and she told me about an octopus she'd fallen in love with when she was eighteen.

'I met him in Greece,' she said. And my adult self recalls the octopus – now, I realize, the second octopus I ever met – that I fell in love with when I was twelve.

'Where Daddy lives?'

'Exactly,' she said. 'In fact, on that very beach where you go each summer.'

'On the beach? Not in the sea?'

'Well, on the rocks. Near a rock pool like the one you just looked in.'

'Can octopuses come out of the water?'

'They can.'

'Did you see its arm and its suckers? Was it orange?'

She laughed a lot then. 'I saw his suckers later. He was a male octopus and exceptionally handsome. He liked to sing opera. I loved him very much and I think for a while he loved me too. But we couldn't be together, not for very long; we lived in different places, we ate different food and we wanted different things.'

'What does an octopus want?'

'Oh, I don't know. Freedom, maybe. A different octopus?'

'And then what?'

'Then what?' We were walking across one of the patches of grass at the caravan park, mown to a crewcut. She bent down and flung her arms around her head, elbows sticking out, wrists circling and fingers tickling: an octopus. I squealed as she shouted, 'Then what! We made a beautiful octopus baby.'

Leon doesn't ask me any questions after this session, perhaps he has enough answers. I know I need to stop Revisiting; the joy of being with the people I love again, so alive and vital, has begun to be overshadowed by the pain I feel returning to reality. I don't speak to Leon about how this Revisit went but I can see from his face that he thinks this should be the last time. Perhaps he is thinking about the court case and the other people who became addicted. The people Rachel talked about had seemed anonymous at first but now I wonder whether they'd lost someone too. Am I addicted to Revisiting? I only want to go to my own bed to mourn my mum in private – the woman she was then, and the woman she was in the future. Leon and I say goodnight, both of us subdued.

In the night I try to imagine going outside, properly this time: not simply standing in the doorway as I had with Boo, but stepping out into the street, walking down it, going into another building. It's too terrifying. But we can't stay here without food, and I can't keep Revisiting. I think about the empty streets, the dead, the virus all around, and whether I could even manage to find a supermarket with food – and I curl up on my side, trembling. What if those packs of dogs come back or one of the groups of men finds me? What if the supermarkets have all been ransacked like Rachel said or I have to walk miles to find one? I try to replay the drive to the unit when I sat in the back of the car and looked out at the streets of London. I was counting the people, not paying attention to what buildings we passed. Did we go past any of those mini-markets or corner shops? I don't even remember turning on to the street where the unit is. I stretch out my legs, lie on my back. But there is a way to see what we passed. I can Revisit the drive, notice the shops this time, find a mini-market. But no Revisit has ever taken me back to where and when I've been thinking of, and I would have to persuade Leon to let me do it one final, final time. Would he let me, even for this purpose? I'm not sure he'd believe that I'm being honest, he'd just think it was a ruse for me to get to see Baba or Justin again.

Another half an hour passes and I can't think of an alternative. I get out of bed, put on my robe and go down the corridor to Leon's. The unit is quiet and dimly lit. I tap gently on his door and when there's no response, I open it and go inside. He's sleeping, slow heavy breaths, with the moon shining in through his window. I go around the end of his bed and slide the silver box out from underneath. Leon doesn't wake.

Back in my room I open it and take out the apparatus. One piece goes on my forehead, another on my chest. I remove the pebbles from their compartments and hold them in my palms. All of it connects wirelessly with a screen in the box's lid. I switch it on as I have seen Leon do many times. I have a good reason for this Revisit, I think, it's a sensible thing to do, I tell myself. I lie back on my bed thinking about being driven to the unit and how I looked out of the window counting pedestrians, trying to remember whether I saw a supermarket. I close my eyes.

I drift down through the blue as always, through the buzz and the hum, and I am not in the car; I am lying on my bed in the unit, where I am now.

The walls were too white, too bright, and I felt my pupils

constrict to the shape of a letterbox, swivelling independently towards the darkest corners of the room. I don't want to be back here, sick in my bed, the virus working through me. Not again! I struggle against this Revisit, trying to will myself to rise out of it.

I hear the slow shutting of a door, and the suction sound as it pulled closed. Under the duvet I was shivering but in the next moment I was too hot, kicking my covers to the end of the bed.

Pills were put on my tongue. 'Swallow, Neffy,' Boo said gently, her hand cool and ungloved behind my neck. The touch of a human. My head was lifted above the waves for a mouthful of air. I was rolled by the sea, one way and then the other, my stinking sheet tugged out from under me and replaced. She lowered the interior blind like curtains drawn around a death bed.

'I have to go, Neffy. I'm sorry,' Boo whispered in my ear. Me too, I thought. Me too. 'Take these but not too many. Eat this when you can. Drink.' Brown eyes above a blue cloth mouth.

I surfaced at what might have been two hours or two days later to silence, inside and out. And then there was knocking. I turned my head towards my door, why didn't they just come in, but the knocking was not from my door, it was from behind my head. Feeble knuckle raps from the other side of the wall, from the Irish girl who laughed a lot. *Tap, tap, tap; tap tap.* On and on it went, sometimes urgent, sometimes faint. And then voices in the corridor, urgent whispers, the sound of shoes squeaking on the vinyl flooring. A single 'No!' and the voices moved away. The tapping continued and I sank again into my fevered sleep.

Dearest H,

Most octopuses live one to two years although some species survive for only six months, while the giant Pacific octopus can live for as many as five years. I used to wonder why you have such short lives when you're so highly evolved. All that power and intelligence, for what? But perhaps you perceive time, which is only a construct anyway, differently. I hate to think, though, that you lived the equivalent of fifty years or so in that tank. A curled octopus can live up to three years which means you might have only had a few more months in the open water. Would it have been better to let you grow old and die in captivity?

Neffy

Day Thirteen

'Hey! The power's off!'

And I rise fast from my Revisit, bubbles in my blood-stream, shocked upwards back into the unit, like a night-time doorbell jerking you awake, only for you to grasp that you dreamed it. And I remember I should have set an alarm like Leon said. I wait for the shout to come again as I try to work out what happened in my Revisit. What was it I heard?

It's bizarrely quiet in my room and I listen for what's missing and realize I can't hear any air-conditioner hum or feel its breeze. Its absence is like its own noise. But replacing it are smells – a ripeness which might be my socks and train-ers, the stink of the waste chute pervading the whole unit, the limey deodorant I use, the bedtime odour of myself.

'Hey, guys! The power's off!' comes again from outside my room. Rachel, I think.

I hurry out of bed and into reception, letting my eyes adjust to dimmer than usual light. The temperature is defin-itely warmer. Piper and Rachel are crowding Yahiko, who has his hand over his heart and is groaning.

'He's having a panic attack,' Rachel says. 'And the lights won't work. The power's off.'

'I think I'm going to be sick,' Yahiko says weakly.

'Go and get a bowl,' I direct Leon, who has joined us. 'One of those cardboard ones from the treatment room. Quick. And prop open my door so that we get a bit more light. Come and sit down,' I say to Yahiko, and take him to the sofa. He's pale and sweating. Rachel sits beside him, her hand rubbing circles on his back.

Piper stays standing, her hands pressed together as though she's praying. 'Oh no,' she says, and I can hear the terror in her voice. I think she's worrying about Yahiko but she adds, 'The food in the freezer. It's still days until the army arrives.'

Yahiko moans, puts his arms about his head and begins to rock. 'Breathe,' I say, the feeling of control and authority coming back to me. I squat in front of him and try to get him to look at me. 'Slowly in, slowly out.' Rachel begins to breathe with me.

'We won't be able to boil the water.' Piper taps her fingers on her lips.

'Maybe the air-con controls in the kitchen have tripped something.' I stare up at her. 'Didn't you say some of the wires were loose?'

When she looks back her eyes are wild. 'Oh fuck. The air conditioning.' I haven't heard her swear before.

Leon returns with the cardboard bowl, sliding the last half-metre in his socks. 'It won't be that.'

'How do you know?' I take the bowl and pass it to Rachel, still sitting beside Yahiko.

'The air con isn't broken,' Leon says.

'But it's off.'

'Fuck, oh fuck,' Piper says and begins to pace.

'I thought you said it got stuck when Yahiko tried to fix it? Why are there plasters over the controls, then?'

'Breathe,' Rachel says to Yahiko.

'Trust me,' Leon says. 'It's not that.'

Once again I sense something else going on below the surface. 'What is it, then?'

When none of them look at me or answer, I say, 'Has

anyone checked whether the generator has actually stopped? You know, listened down the waste chute?'

Leon follows me to the staffroom and stands in the doorway, watching. I open the chute; the smell coming up is bad, but the whole place smells rank. We're both silent, listening. There's no noise.

'Maybe the fuses have tripped,' Rachel says when we're back in reception. 'The fuses were always tripping where I used to live. We'd put a light on and everything would pop. We'd have to vote for who would go down to the cellar and switch them back on. Does this place have a fuse box?'

'Consumer unit,' Yahiko says, muffled. He grabs the bowl from Rachel and puts it on his knees, his face over it.

'Okay,' I say. 'So where will the consumer unit be? In the basement?'

'With the generator?' Rachel says.

Piper puts her palms on her red cheeks.

'Well, let's go down and see,' I say. I am surprisingly calm, logical. This feels like something I can solve: soothe Yahiko, get the generator going again.

'It'll be locked,' Leon says.

'You and Yahiko got in. Didn't you go down and check it out just after Day Zero? We'll probably need Piper's key card. Anyway, the doors must have some override mechanism otherwise how would anyone get out in an emergency?'

'Maybe,' Leon says.

'What about the food?' Rachel asks. 'How long will it stay frozen?'

'Maybe we don't want it to stay frozen,' I say. 'Can't cook it. No microwave.'

'But the air con,' Piper wails.

'You'll come to the basement with me, won't you?' I say

to Leon because he's sat down on a sofa and looks as though he plans to stay. Reluctantly, he gets up. I don't understand his hesitancy.

Piper pulls the key card out from under her jumper and there's a strange moment as she vacillates about who to hand it to, Leon or me, and then she passes it to me. It's disturbingly warm and I shove it in the pocket of my robe. Yahiko lies on his side on the seating, knees to chest, and seems a little calmer. We leave Piper hovering, and Leon and I push open the emergency exit door next to the lift. The stairs beyond are concrete with a metal handrail, and while the inside of the unit is all sleek surfaces and fancy lighting, no money has been spent behind the scenes. It's like stepping off a stage into the wings. Here is the rough underside, the revealing reverse of the scenery flats; the unpainted, knocked-about parts that make the fakery seem real. There are no windows and only the light from our reception area illuminates half of the upward flight – to the door to the roof, Leon says – and a couple of steps of the downward flight. The rest is too dark to make out – the final step might end in an infinite drop that we'd fall off, never reaching the bottom.

'Is your phone charged?' I pause on the threshold.

'No,' Leon says. 'Why?'

'For the torch. Mine neither.' I hear embarrassment and guilt in my voice because I have forgotten that someone might call, that I might be able to call someone, one day. 'Rachel, yours must be charged?' I say to her. She's just behind us.

'Mine?' she says.

'Yours is always charged,' Leon says.

'But if you use the torch, it won't stay charged for long.'

'Get your fucking phone,' Piper spits and we're silent while Rachel goes to fetch it.

When Rachel returns she switches on the torch and hands it to Leon grudgingly. 'You know you're not supposed to go into the basement.'

'What?' he says.

She lifts her arms above her head, makes her hands into spiders. 'Don't go down to the basement,' she says in a ghoulish voice. I see Piper close her eyes behind her as Rachel laughs a little crazily.

We make Piper stand in the doorway, propping the door open so that we get as much light as possible, and Leon and I go downstairs. He goes first, holding the phone high with its torch illuminating the stairs ahead of us, around the first corner and down another flight. Piper's and Rachel's conversation, and Yahiko's moans, fade away. Leon continues on past the first door, down the next flight, and I am left in darkness.

'Wait,' I say and he turns back, directing the light at me, and I see that this door, marked 1, is ajar. I press on it with my fingertips and it swings inwards. 'The electricity going off must have released the lock.' Some light in the first floor's reception area spills in from the office windows.

'Come on,' Leon says. 'It's the basement we need.'

I'll come back, I think. See if there's anything useful. I go down the stairs, holding on to the rail, feeling each step with my foot, trying to keep up with Leon. The door to the ground-floor lobby has been released too and I push it open as I pass. It provides some light which fades as we turn one more corner of the staircase to the basement. Here is another door like the others, plain with a curved bar for a handle, but this one doesn't swing open at my touch. Leon shines the torch on the reader and I pass Piper's card across it back and forth but no green light comes on. I hold it against the box but it stays dark.

'It's not going to open,' Leon says. 'It must have a different security setting to the other doors for when the power goes off, probably the same as the door to the roof.'

'But you and Yahiko got in with the card.' I slam my palm on the door. It doesn't even shudder.

'No,' he says. 'Yahiko and I never went into the basement.'

'But you saw the generator. What was it, state of the art? That's what Yahiko said.'

Leon moves the light on to me. 'We didn't even reach the basement door.'

I squint and hold my hand up to block the glare. 'I don't get it.' I want to see his face, understand what it is he's telling me.

'We used the card to get into the first floor on our way down to the basement, just to see what was there. Food, water, you know. People had gone in a hurry but it wasn't just bags left on desks and chairs turned over.'

'A flock of parakeets?' I step out of the light. 'Or was it crows?'

'Crows,' he says and lowers the torch. 'A few people must have been too ill to leave but they'd opened a window. We saw them in a meeting room, through the glass walls, some were still sitting in their chairs. Yahiko went up to the glass and banged on it, and the birds were in there too, flapping and squawking. Feasting. We got out as fast as we could.'

'Oh God.' I think about Lawrence Barrett in his suit and green tie and I hope that he was at home when he did his television interview – in his kid's bedroom and not in his office. And I can't help but imagine that floor below ours. Did the virus spread too rapidly for them to even leave their meeting or did those that were sick agree to go into the meeting room to keep away from their colleagues? Or did someone lock them in?

'And then neither of us could face going further down,' Leon continues. 'We sat on the stairs and waited until we thought enough time had passed.'

His face is in darkness but his tone is one of guilt, regret, embarrassment. I reach out a hand and it finds his arm and I give it a squeeze.

It's clearly time for confessions. 'I was Revisiting when the power went off. I went back to when I was ill, you know, in my room and feverish.'

'You were Revisiting?' Leon sounds confused.

'Yeah, sorry, I came into your room and took the box. But listen, it was weird, I heard –'

'Did you set an alarm?'

'Rachel's shouting woke me.'

'You shouldn't have taken it.'

'I know, but –'

'That was meant to be the last time, last night in my room.'

'I'm sorry.'

'You're addicted, Neffy.' His voice is serious, even angry.

'I'm not. Really.' I'm scrambling for words, for the justification of taking the Revisitor. 'I just needed to go back to the route the driver took to bring me here. I can limit myself –'

'And did you?'

'Did I what?'

'Go back to the route the driver took?'

'No, I –'

'No, of course you didn't. That's just an excuse. You're addicted, Neffy, and you need to stop.'

'I will, I promise.'

'Anyway, we're going to have to go outside now,' he says with authority. 'We're going to have to leave. We don't have any power, no clean water and the food's defrosting.'

'I'll go.' The words are out of my mouth before I've thought them. 'I'll get us some bottled water and some food. None of you should be going inside places. Not yet. Like you've all said, I'm probably immune. And after that, we can all leave together.'

I look out through the glass doors where I had stood only three days before with Boo. Her shoes are still lying on the pavement, together with the small collection of litter and leaves which dance in the wind under the building's over-hang. My stomach tells me it's breakfast time but none of us have stopped for that; anyway, we only have dry porridge. When I press the door's exit button nothing happens and then I remember that the electricity is off and that's why I'm heading outside with the empty rucksack that Leon fetched for me from Yahiko's room. I push the door and it opens.

Outside it smells even more like autumn in the country-side than it did before. Leaf mulch and bonfires. I have a feeling of something starting, that internal churning I would get when I was a child on the first few breezy days of return-ing to school in September, where if I opened my mouth the wind would take my breath and my words away.

First, I walk right, past the car, the bus and the ambulance without glancing at them, and when I'm far enough from the building I turn back and look up at Rachel's window. I left Piper sitting next to Yahiko, who was sleeping, but both Rachel and Leon are at her window. They wave at me and I hold up the scissors and smile in what I hope is a positive, brave movement. I don't feel positive or brave and I can't imagine using the scissors for anything other than cutting open a packet of plasters. Both had wanted to come outside with me; Leon said he would wait on the street and when I said he couldn't, he said he'd wait in the lobby and watch me through the glass to check I was okay. I said he couldn't do that either and we nearly argued about it. He gave me the pair of pointed scissors – as a weapon or tool, I wasn't sure – together with a mask and gloves which I put in the rucksack. I said they could watch me from Rachel's window.

There are only a few shops at this end of the street before the row ends in railings and what must be a block of flats beyond. I have no intention of going into where anyone lives. I remember they all told me that before everything fell apart people had been instructed to stay home, lock themselves in and not to answer the door. Food parcels that were going to be distributed never came.

Two disintegrating cardboard boxes lie in the middle of the road next to a scattering of clothes including a pair of orange corduroy trousers dropped with one bent leg as though running.

I walk back the other way along the opposite pavement, past the mobile phone shop with the smashed window, and the three shuttered shops: Charlie's Casual Wear, Miz Nails and Easy Carpets & Flooring. Grass is sprouting from a blocked drain.

Then I am beyond the end of our building, and I can see down the alleyway which my room looks out on, with the bollard at the end and Sophia's building opposite. I walk on. The silence, the emptiness, is unnatural, and I look behind me as often as I look forward. I glance above the shops – the upper storey of what once were probably houses, now flats or storage rooms, all a little shabby: peeling paint and grubby net curtains. I pass London Travel, which looks like it might have closed a long time ago, High Power Sunbeds and Rayz Barber. A bicycle rests on its side in the road, one wheel crushed, the other spinning slowly in the breeze. Rachel said she thought she remembered an Asian or Polish mini-market further up this way when she first arrived but she wasn't sure.

On the other side of the road is Chicken Bites – no shutters down, no broken windows, door closed. I look both ways before I cross. In my pocket I grip the scissors tightly, warming them. I'm scared but I'm not sure of what. There are no bodies on the streets, or I haven't seen any yet. Perhaps the dogs took them or the foxes and the cats. I don't think I'm scared of the dead themselves: I don't believe in ghosts or that anything happens to us after we're dead. I am a scientist, I say to myself as though this might help. Observe, record, question. Am I really immune? If I *was* immune, am I still? From the edge of the pavement, I look up at the net-curtained window above the chicken shop. No, this is what I'm afraid of: the living. Did the curtain move? Of course it didn't. At the plate-glass window of Chicken Bites I look in, shading my eyes, and see a small, high counter at the end, an area for the till, an empty drinks chiller. It's bottled water I need really but there could be food in the back. Not chicken, obviously, or I hope not chicken. Maybe bottles of water or cans of Coke. Does a chicken takeaway sell any food that won't have gone off? Tomato ketchup. I wonder if the back room is connected to the upstairs. This place isn't worth it, I decide. I need to find the mini-market with shelves of pickled vegetables and tubs of salted nuts. Still, I push the door. I'm surprised to find it's unlocked, and suddenly my heart is jumping. I take one step inside. Just one step and the smell strikes. It's not chicken. I turn about, gagging, and pull the door closed.

Now, I hurry. Past Pizza GoGo, William Hill bookies, and slowing at the Cosy Home Café and then dismissing it, wanting only a supermarket where the goods will be in tins and jars and packets. The empty rucksack bangs about on my back and I grip the straps. The litter and rubbish on the street is greater here – a child's buggy on its side, clothes and books, a dog's bed, sodden and leaking stuffing. I see the supermarket from a little way off – its blue canopy and faded lettering. All Day Mini Market I read as I get closer, and a phone number that still starts with 0171. The shutter is half up and buckled; someone has been here before me. The door behind the shutter is open. I wait from a distance – maybe it has only just been broken into; maybe the person who did this is still inside – but after a few minutes I don't hear any sound, don't sense any movement from within.

I crouch low and shuffle so that the rucksack doesn't catch on the shutter. It's shadowy inside and I wish I'd thought to bring Rachel's phone. I take the scissors from my pocket and point them forward. The shop smells of overripe fruit, soft vegetables sprouting, nothing worse. It has been looted but maybe not everything has been taken. Rachel gave me a list of food she thought Yahiko would like, as though I'll be walking around with a basket over my arm checking the calorific value of each item before I decide to take it. I accepted the list only when she told me that Yahiko's Japanese grandfather had starved to death after the Second World War. She said she didn't know the details.

I should be logical and look first for water but behind the till I see the cigarette locker. The cigarettes and the alcohol have gone but there are lighters and matches and I take off the rucksack and tip them in. In their clatter as they fall to the bottom I think I hear a sound from the back of the shop. I pause, stay still in my agonizing bent position and listen. Silence. No one is here, I tell myself. 'Is anyone here?' I shout it and my voice sounds dead. There's no reply, no sound. I go up the first aisle, holding one of the lighters to the shelf labels. 'Rice and pasta' they say, but the shelves are empty. The chillers are empty too but on the floor is a single tin and I pick it up and hold the lighter to the label. Plum tomatoes. With a ring pull. I sit on the floor and open the can and tip a whole plum tomato into my mouth. It's juicy and meaty with a sourness that makes me squint. I squash it into the roof of my mouth with my tongue and swallow, and then I wipe my sleeve across my mouth and drink from the can. As I'm eating the rest, I see that pushed to the back of the bottom shelf are other tins, and I get on to my knees and pull them out. I don't look at the labels, just shove them into the rucksack and hope they aren't dog food, hope there are vegetables or fruit amongst them. I move through the shop filling the rucksack with packets and tins from the bottom shelves, but I don't find water. I'm about to cram a jar of what looks to be beans into a side pocket when I hear a noise. Definitely a noise this time. I stop once more, listening. Once more crouching with my thigh muscles burning. The noise comes again, a rustle.

And I see the rat. And another rat, and then more, along the shelves, running across the floor. How could I have missed them? I drop the jar and it explodes, white beans and brine and glass shards flying outwards. And I grab the rucksack and I run.

Outside I carry on running, the rucksack clonking painfully against my legs until I heave it on to my shoulders. I can hear myself whimpering. I go past three or four shops before I slow and finally stop in a doorway, panting. I put my hand to my heart and feel it thumping under my palm, still not fully recovered from the virus. When I force myself to look behind, there are no rats, no movement on the street or from any of the windows.

I have stopped outside a letting agency with a display of houses and flats for rent. I go to move on, back to the unit, but see beyond the pictures in the rear of the office a water dispenser with one of those keg-sized water bottles on top. From here it's hard to tell how much water is left in it and, when I rattle the door, it's locked. I look up and down the street. Nothing has changed. I slip off the rucksack, rest it against the window and take out a tin. It's chickpeas. I stand back and throw the tin at the door, and the edge hits the glass with a crack. The sound seems tremendous, echoing back at me. If anyone is in the upstairs rooms, they will be looking now if they weren't before. It's a slow job to pull my hoodie down over my hand, shield my eyes and use the tin to smash away enough glass for me climb through. A column of plastic cups is attached to the side of the water dispenser and I drink and drink, sitting in a swivel chair behind a desk as though I'm hoping to let a house or a flat. I open the drawers and find chewing gum and a mostly full packet of Marlboro Lights, which I put in the pockets of my hoodie. I can only get the half-full water bottle off the dispenser by pushing the whole unit over, and then I discover in a back office two full ones, which I roll to the front. I can't get them across the door frame no matter how much I shove and pull, until I discover under another desk a footrest which I use as a ramp. When I'm back in the street with the rucksack and the three bottles I realize there's no way I can move them to the unit in one go. I sit on one to rest and now I have stopped moving I don't want to get up again. How are we going to take the bottles with us anyway? I had imagined leaving on foot but now I realize if we do these bottles can't come with us. It's hopeless. I sit for maybe ten minutes, undecided about what to do. In the end I take only the rucksack. Maybe I'll come back for the bottles. And then when I have hoisted it on to my back and walked a little way, I'm worried that someone – who? – will come along and take them. When I look back, I think I should have disguised them in some way, found a jacket and thrown it over them.

When I reach the alleyway, my alleyway, I look up at my window – it's high and at an angle and I can't see in. Opposite I can just make out Sophia's reply to me still stuck on her windows in big black letters, and I remember the radio I saw on her windowsill one of the first times I looked over at her apartment. Was it there the other times? I can remember what it looked like – one of those pretend vintage ones with big dials and a front grille. How badly do we need a radio? How useful might it be? Someone could be broadcasting about a vaccine that works, a central meeting point out of the city, something about other countries – Sweden or Denmark. I'll ring Sophia's doorbell, I think, just to see. There are three buzzers for her building and I'm debating which one to start with when I realize the door to the block is unlocked.

I push on it with my fingertips and, like the doors in the unit's stairwell, it swings slowly open. Inside is a wide modern staircase, a road bike locked to it, a row of post boxes and a handwritten notice asking residents to throw away the junk mail. It could be a normal entrance to a normal block of flats in a normal London. Except that the door is unlocked and London is not normal. I remember what Yahiko or Piper, or maybe all of them at some point, had told me about people watching from outside, about not lowering my blind or putting my lights on. I'd not really thought through what it meant about who had seen what, it just seemed to be another rule the group had made without me, but now I wonder if one of them saw someone buzz at Sophia's door and somehow get let in. She'll surely have left, I think, hesitating on the doorstep. I can just get the radio and leave. I go up the staircase.

There seems to be one flat on each floor and Sophia's must be on the second for her windows to be level with mine. When I reach it, her door is also ajar, unlocked. I knock. It seems the right thing to do. I am aware of the pulse of my heart, the muscle of it working, my dry mouth. This door too I swing open.

'Hello?' In front of me is a short corridor with parquet flooring, coats and jackets on hooks to my left. Under them is a bench with shoes below, all lined up, heels out. I wait and I listen and I sniff. I can't smell any bad odour, just a mustiness, stale air, old perfume. 'Sophia?' I call, and feel myself blush at my mistake, even while I sense the place is empty. No body. Nobody.

I lower the rucksack, prop it against the wall and move

into the apartment. I pass a bathroom on my right and on my left the corridor opens out into a beautiful sitting room with a high ceiling. It's peculiar to be inside this space which I looked across to so often. The parquet floor of old polished wood continues in here under two powder-blue sofas and a large rug, a 1950s sideboard and standard lamps. The line of Crittall windows that looks over the alleyway has a deep white sill scattered with cushions. It is tasteful, artfully arranged and tidy, but there is no radio. Beyond, the kitchen has polished granite surfaces and expensive equipment and also no radio. I move through the apartment silently without touching. Everything is perfect. No mess, nothing has been disturbed, and although I should be relieved, I am not. One more door, back towards the hall. I open it cautiously – it is to the bedroom – and here is the carnage: a duvet dragged across the floor, pillows strewn, the bedside table knocked over, broken glass and smashed china on the rug, a potted fern spilling soil, blood on the sheets. Even when most people were trying to stay away from others because of the virus, some would still take advantage of an unlocked door or a buzzer that's answered.

I close my eyes; I cannot search this room for the radio, and instead I turn back to the beautiful sitting room and the windows with the view across to my room in the unit, except that Sophia's message to me is still blocking it. I can see the lettering where the light shines through the sheets. The words are reversed but I know what they say: YES, I'M HEAR.

But she isn't here, no one is here. And I have a terror of being alone, in this building, in London, in the world – I don't want to be Rachel's final girl, the last human. I want to be with the others, back with Rachel, Leon, Piper and

Yahiko. I go to the windows and press my hot face to the glass and look at my own room across the alleyway. The light falls in such a way that I'm able to look inside and see the chairs and the bed as well as the door to the corridor and the interior blind. I imagine seeing myself rising from the bed, walking across the room and sitting at my desk to write. I look at Orla's room, with our beds back to back, and I think about my last Revisit, the knocking and the whispering in the corridor. I move along Sophia's window to the far right and stare into Orla's room, the one I've never been in because it's locked. I look harder. I stare until my eyes water, and then I run to Sophia's kitchen, stretch across her sink and open the window. The unused room with the faulty plumbing is next to Orla's, which makes Stephan's room too far along to the right to see into from here, but Orla's empty room is now directly opposite. I can see her chairs, her door, her blind, her bed. Her bed which I am now certain is not empty. Not empty. Not empty at all.

I sit on one of the powder-blue sofas. My head is full of the things I've seen and been told and I try to reassemble them into coherence: the air conditioning always on, the plasters over the controls, the locked doors, Rachel crying for absent friends, the knocking. I lie on the sofa and then sit up again, press my head to my knees. I go to the bathroom and dunk my face in handfuls of cold water to wash away Piper's horror at the air con going off, how I was locked in my room for seven days, but Orla's knocking goes on and on. She didn't leave like Yahiko said and probably Stephan didn't either. Too ill to get out of bed and move her blind, too sick to call out – or too scared of the people who had locked her in. The smell of the unit this morning comes back to me viscerally and I gag over Sophia's sink. *Fuck*, I say to myself in Sophia's mirror. *Fuck*. I think about my promise to Leon to find food and water and to leave with them. I wanted someone to save but I wonder if these people are beyond saving.

In Sophia's hallway I heft the rucksack on to my back, the tins and jars clanking, and I take the stairs at speed. In the alleyway I look up at the unit but no one is looking down from my room. At the main road I pause before stepping out. The three water bottles are where I left them and only now do I think about my options. I will need these and the food on my back to survive on my own. To my right is the front door of the unit and, beyond that, the accident on the corner with the car, the bus and the ambulance. I jog under the overhang of the building, checking no one is in the lobby before I pass it, and when I reach the corner of the building I pause again. If Leon and Rachel are standing at her window waiting for me to return, they'll see me, but perhaps they have given up and anyway won't be expecting to see me from this window. We'd said that we would start out on foot with the idea of finding a vehicle along the way, having dismissed the three we could see from the unit: the car's bonnet is too crumpled even if the key is in the ignition, no one wants to get on the bus, and Piper, who told us she liked to watch those series about paramedics and emergencies, had said it was a sackable offence to leave the key in the ignition of an ambulance and it wouldn't happen. I take a deep breath and run out from the unit, slipping between the car and the bus, and stopping behind the double-decker. I edge forward again and look up to Rachel's room. They aren't there. I stand on tiptoe and stare in through the bus driver's side window.

In front of the wheel is a complicated-looking panel of buttons and switches and I'm almost relieved that I can't see a key. Before I lose momentum and all confidence, I step out from the safety of the bus and scuttle under the weight of the rucksack around the back of the ambulance. Its rear doors are still open but the cab's are closed. I look in the driver's window, and in the ignition is the key. I remember what Rachel said about the paramedics with their swollen faces, not remembering what they were supposed to be doing. I try the door and it opens and I take off the rucksack, shoving it ahead of me and across, over into the passenger side. I am not thinking, I am only doing. When I'm in the driver's seat I pull the door to, check the handbrake and that the gearstick is in neutral. Mirror, signal, manoeuvre.

I put my hands on the wheel and look straight ahead. Dorset is that way, probably. The empty house. Clive's and Mum's and Justin's empty house. I know they won't be there. Two of them are somewhere in Denmark and the other is dead on a stationary plane in Sweden. I check the gearstick again, the handbrake; I lean across to the passenger seat to see up to Rachel's window, but the angle is too acute. I turn the key and the engine starts first go. I check the mirrors, flick the indicator stalk, press on the clutch pedal and find first gear. The ambulance hops forward, and I move it into second. It is so loud, I might as well be shouting, Yes, I'm here! But it moves, and when I get to the water bottles, I brake too fast and slam myself over the wheel. 'Seat belt, seat belt!' I shout. I turn off the engine and now the silence is deafening. When I get out of the cab, I see that I've left the back doors open.

One of the water bottles is cradled in my arms when Leon crashes out of the unit's front door.

'Neffy,' he calls. He comes towards me and then stops when he's still some distance away. 'What's going on? Where are you going?' Piper comes out of the door next, followed by Rachel. Yahiko steps out too in mask and gloves and apron, but he stays beside the door with one hand on the glass as though the shock of the outside is too much.

'I know what you did,' I shout.

'What do you mean?' Leon asks.

'To Orla and probably to Stephan too.'

Piper is beside him now.

'You left them to die. They got sick and you locked them in.' The water bottle is heavy and cumbersome but I clasp it to me.

'We had no choice,' Piper says hotly, tossing her head. She comes forward and Rachel and Leon follow. Yahiko keeps close to the window of the unit, inching his away along.

'Like you fucking locked me in too.'

'You were all infectious,' Yahiko shouts. He has lowered his mask. The others turn to look at him and then back to me.

'And you lied,' I shout back. 'You told me they left. You said the air conditioning had broken.'

'Of course we had to lock you in,' Piper says; she's close

290

enough not to have to shout but through her aggression her defensiveness shows. 'And anyway, we thought you were dead.'

'We had no choice.' Rachel chokes on her words.

'We had a choice,' Leon says. He stands forward, just ahead of Piper. 'We always have a choice.'

'They weren't dead,' I say. 'I heard Orla!'

'No,' Piper says.

'She was knocking on the wall behind my bed. I heard her.' Rachel begins to cry, wiping at her eyes.

'And I heard you too,' I say.

'No,' Piper replies, bluntly.

'You were in the corridor whispering with Yahiko or whoever, outside Orla's door. You heard the knocking and you left her to die.'

'What else were we going to do? She was infectious. Orla and you and Stephan were infectious,' Piper says like a terrier baring its teeth.

'You could have put food and water through their doors too. You could have searched harder for a hazmat suit. They're probably in the fucking basement.'

Yahiko moves his head from side to side. 'No,' he says.

'The most important thing was to keep the rest of us safe and well,' Piper says.

'What, so you could start the new super race?' I snort. 'Leon told me about your grand plan.' My arms are aching from the weight of the water bottle.

'Leon voted that we should go into your rooms,' Rachel says. She puts her hands over her eyes, tries to get control of her gulping. 'And check on you, and Orla and Stephan.' Leon touches her arm to stop her.

'You took a fucking vote?' I say.

'Two to one we keep the doors locked,' Yahiko shouts. 'I saw what had happened in that office below us.'

Rachel stares at him, not understanding. 'Four days' isolation,' she says.

'And in the end,' Piper says, 'Rachel abstained.'

'And I abstained,' Rachel says softly, agreeing, guilty.

'Four days' isolation?' I yell. 'That's what they said on the TV, didn't they? Four days. And when did you hear Orla knocking? Because you did hear her, didn't you?'

Leon rubs his hands across his face, washing something away.

'Day Five,' Rachel says.

'You're monsters.' I'm trembling and I can feel the water in the bottle tremble with me. 'I don't know where your humanity is. You let them die. Who are you to choose who should be saved? Maybe Orla and Stephan should have been the ones to be saved – maybe they would have been immune. For the past week I've been trying to work out what was going on between you all, what it was you weren't telling me, but I never guessed their fucking bodies were in the rooms I passed every day.' The words are pouring from my mouth and the others only stand and watch, not trying to interrupt. 'I thought I was going to die. I thought I was alone in the unit and I was going to die alone. Can you imagine how that feels? Can you? And do you know how I found out? I went into the flat opposite mine across the alleyway, just now, to get us a fucking radio which wasn't there anyway. And I looked out of the kitchen window and I saw into Orla's room. I saw! You're fucking monsters.' I chuck the water bottle at them but it's heavy and my arms are weak, and it goes nowhere, only landing between us and rolling crookedly away.

Rachel lets her tears fall and Piper says, 'And what else did you see in that flat? Did you notice what the woman who lived there had put on her window for everyone to see? Who's responsible for that? Who should take responsibility for inviting those men to where she lived so she could be dragged out screaming into the street? Whose note was she answering?' There is a long silence broken only by the cooing of a pigeon on a nearby roof.

I wait in the driver's seat of the ambulance while the others settle in the back and Leon slams the rear doors. I put my hands at the top of the steering wheel and rest my forehead on them and think about Sophia and her reply to me with its spelling mistake and whether that meant she was already forgetting. Maybe she didn't understand fully what was happening when she was taken by those men? I know I'm only trying to assuage my guilt. And I think about the four people I have agreed to go to Dorset with, what they did, and whether it was reprehensible or understandable, or even forgivable. When we had finished with the shouting and the crying, we had sat together, silent and exhausted, in the middle of the road. Maybe we are as bad as each other, or maybe not; all I know is that I don't want to be alone while I work that out.

It's a squash in the back with five rucksacks and cases plus the one with the food, the bottles of water and three people. I hear Rachel suggest that they bring the defrosting food from the freezer even if it will have to be eaten first and none of us knows how we'll cook it. I try to remember the oven at Clive's house – is it gas or electric, will that make a difference? Or wasn't there a barbecue down at the swimming pond? Maybe we'll have to build a fire in the garden. Yahiko argues for bringing some of the things he's collected from the other rooms but is persuaded to leave most of it behind.

I reach across the passenger seat to push the door open for Leon. 'Piper's parents' house first, yeah?' he says. 'Just to be sure.' He places the silver case by his feet and I waggle the gearstick, check the handbrake is on and start the ambulance.

Day Six Hundred and Eighty-Five

I rise slowly, lifting through deep blue and turquoise to a dusty light, leaving behind the ambulance and the sight of the road out of London, though the cough of the engine repeats as though the vehicle has stalled and I'm forcing the key forward, turning the engine over and over. The light brightens and I take a gulp of air, breaking through the surface of the real world.

'Mmmmm! Mmmm!' I hear the sound that had infiltrated my Revisit. I place the pebbles, as I still think of them, on my bedside table and look at my alarm clock, one of those old mechanical wind-up types, and see that the alarm I'd set isn't due to go off for another twenty minutes.

The July sun comes in through the windows, dancing the shadows of the silver birch leaves across my bedroom walls. The repetitive chant changes to a quiet burble of nonsense and I wonder if I'll be lucky enough to get five more minutes in bed. I'm surprised the Revisit took me back to the ambulance. Firstly, I'm strict with how often I allow myself to Revisit. Once or twice a week at the most, and if it starts to creep up, I take the case and I lock it in the outbuilding with Justin's mother's suitcase. And secondly, these days I'm more skilled at controlling where I go and what I see, and I hop around in time and place to memories which have brought me joy: Revisiting the swimming pond with Justin in the early days of our relationship when our parents were away; eating ice cream with Baba when I was a child and giving him the end of the cone. And the one I go back to repeatedly: crouching beside my mum on that English shore when I was seven, dunking my head into a new world.

I'd driven the ambulance and all of us in it first to Piper's house, where I knew as soon as I opened their front door that her parents were dead. We stood in the road as Yahiko and Leon held her tightly in a double embrace while she wailed and struggled to get free and go inside. To reach Dorset we were forced to avoid the motorway and its silent and motionless lines of metal coffins which stretched for miles, and take the back roads, driving on pavements, making detours across fields where we had to, Rachel surprising us with her knowledge of how to syphon petrol.

'Mmmmm! Mammamm!' has started again, together with a rattle. The connecting doors are open to the bathroom and on through to the bedroom which used to be Justin's. I'd claimed my old room when we first arrived at the house, which of course was empty. Yahiko chose Clive's and Mum's bedroom, Piper used the spare room at the far end, and Rachel and Leon had Justin's. At first, I wouldn't let them change anything. Justin's clothes stayed in his drawers and his wardrobe and Rachel lived out of her suitcase, and the same in the other rooms. I let them take Clive's books down from a shelf to read but they had to be replaced in the same spot. In those early days I sometimes dreamed of Justin, Clive and Mum arriving home, rushing in the front door to find their belongings in piles and strangers in their beds. They were always angry with me for not keeping everything the same.

The day after we arrived in the ambulance, I drove alone to the pub in the village and returned with bottles of beer and water and spirits, crisps and peanuts, and a radio. The pub, surprisingly, had no bodies in it, or at least not down-stairs, but the stench of death was everywhere I went and unlike in London, where the streets had been kept relatively clear, here, in the villages, bodies lay on the ground outside houses, at windows and sitting up inside cars – their mem-ories so quickly lost they had forgotten to drive home. I manoeuvred the ambulance around them and didn't stop.

Leon spent most of the next couple of weeks moving through the dial of the radio, and the house was filled with the hiss of white noise. A couple of broadcasts were still going, one repeating the same message that people should stay home and food would be delivered. The other was, we thought, a station broadcasting in Arabic – also a message repeated again and again although we never worked out what it was saying.

Piper decreed that the meals we'd brought from the unit had too high a risk of food poisoning to be safe so we sur-vived for a few days on the tins and jars I'd found in London – no dog food – and what Clive and Mum had in the house. When these were finished, I got back in the ambu-lance and drove to the next village which had a shop. The smell inside made my stomach heave even though I'd tied my hoodie around my nose and mouth and I was in and out in less than ten minutes. Eventually I came to know the best village shops in the area – those with no bodies and plenty of food. It was a month before I risked an out-of-town super-market and an optician's to try to find some glasses for Yahiko. We cooked on the barbecue which we wheeled up from the swimming pond and I raided a local garage for more gas cannisters. I brought home packets of seeds and garden equipment ready for the spring. These forays kept me out of the house for most of each day and for that I was grateful. It was a long and slow acceptance on my part to come to terms with what they'd done, and what I myself had done.

The house is warm and even through the winter was snug. Probably all that sheep's wool or whatever it was that Clive insulated it with. And there's electricity. Soon after we arrived, I found a generator at the farm Mum and Clive had gone to for the gig. It was on wheels but still it took me hours to push back to the house. It's used for cooking, firing up the immersion for hot water and for an electric radiator when it was really cold during the winter. But running it requires me to go and find fuel. All of it is hard work.

Day Twenty-one came and went without any sign of the army or government although we had left a notice on the front door of the unit with our Dorset address. I'd agreed that if anyone was determined enough to find us, they were probably safe to meet.

I pack away the pebbles and the rest of the equipment in the silver case and leave it in front of the window to recharge, and go through the bathroom to Rachel's and Leon's room. The baby has hauled herself up and is clinging on to the bars of her cot with her pudgy hands, swaying on bent legs. She smiles at me, proud of her success and in the joy of it, and then lets go and sits down with a thump of surprise on to the mattress. Her face crumples but before she can start to howl, I lift her out.

'Come on,' I coo, settling her on my hip. Many things surprise me about the baby – her dense weight, the solidity of her, and how at ten months she is already her own person with likes and dislikes – but mostly I am surprised at the overwhelming love I feel for this new human being. 'What's up?' I say. 'What's up?' I pull out the back of her sleepsuit and peer down, taking a sniff. No poo but her nappy is bulky and I lay her on the changing mat on the chest of drawers and give her a toy to play with which goes straight to her mouth.

For seven months I'd been careful every time I went out. I wore gloves and a mask, I left my shoes outside the front door, I showered before I spent time with the others, and I wiped down the things I brought in with me. All this, even though we were beginning to think that Leon, Rachel, Piper and Yahiko had maybe escaped the virus since in all that time I hadn't seen another living person on my journeys, and therefore we thought perhaps there wouldn't be any hosts for the virus to survive in.

Rachel caught the rabbit in the garden. It was one of those beautiful April days, bright-blue sky, and warm. The first intimation of summer. Apparently, she launched herself across the grass and must have broken its neck when she landed on it. Or so I was told – I was out in the ambulance getting supplies, having to drive further to search out the list of things we needed. It was Piper who skinned and gutted the rabbit, and Yahiko who stewed it in a pot with some herbs and a tin of green beans. They did it before I returned so I wouldn't have to see. Leon tried a mouthful and said it turned his stomach; the others finished it off. We learned the hardest way that the virus still lived within animals.

Piper was the first to become ill. And although we tried to isolate her, and when her memory went, ironically locked her in her room, within a couple of days it had spread to Yahiko and then to Rachel. Leon was the last. They were all dead in less than two weeks.

I would have lain down and died myself if I could. Every day when I wash the baby or change a nappy, I check her for swollen limbs or a distended stomach, for bruising, for the telltale bulging eyes. So far, I've seen nothing. But how do you check whether a ten-month-old is forgetting?

I was a poor nurse. Impatient and, yes, sometimes rough. It had been easier to deny the suffering, tell the sick – or Yahiko at least, who was so distressed – that they would be up and about soon, than to have to face it. Those two weeks had been relentless, brutal, devastating. If I thought I'd make a terrible doctor I never knew I had it in me to be any kind of nurse, undertaker, mourner and midwife.

Every day I marvel at the baby and long to have someone to exclaim about her with, to notice every tiny milestone, someone to show my imaginary and never-ending baby pictures to.

I unzip her sleepsuit and change her nappy quickly and efficiently, already an expert, and dress her in a woolly baby-gro. It's tight around the feet and soon, I know, I will have to drive to town for more clothes and baby items which an occasional raid of a village shop doesn't provide for.

I put her in the baby seat which is clipped to the kitchen island and while I boil the kettle to make a cup of tea, I push spoonfuls of tinned mashed vegetables into her mouth where it mostly oozes out, then scrape it off her cheek and post it back. I spread Marmite on crackers and eat them standing in the kitchen where Mum once stood. While the baby is distracted by her spoon, I pick up my notebook and read what I started writing earlier. It still needs finishing.

Dearest H,

I can see smoke across the valley. It's coming from the chimney of the cottage on the hill opposite, and yesterday when I was outside in the vegetable garden and the wind was blowing towards me, I thought I heard children's voices. Should I go and see? My mind plays with the dangers, thinking about the virus and how the others died. I try to tell myself it might be a family, ordinary, friendly people who will welcome us, but sometimes at night my mind spirals back to the others telling me about the men who took Sophia. Last week my Revisit delivered me to the moment when I released you into the sea, and I saw again the way you paused in the shallows for a second as though you were tasting something you remembered from long ago and then how you were off with a single pulse of water, not stopping to say goodbye. As it should be. But I knew the dangers you would face even if you didn't: predators, overfishing, habitat destruction, pollution. Does freedom win over containment, even with all its risks, including death? And now, I again have someone else's life to consider,

I'm not good at sticking to a routine. If the baby is awake and happy let the baby be awake no matter what the time is and if we're hungry we eat, whatever the hour. When I was a teenager, I thought the way Mum and I lived was dis-ordered and chaotic but now it feels like spontaneity, flexibility, fun. I'd like to apologize to her for my anger about the missed meals, the school meetings she forgot to come to and the sleepovers where I was the last girl to be collected. And how I compared her to Margot, in my head at least, and found her lacking.

When the meal, if that's what it is, is finished, I wipe the baby's face with a wet flannel – oh how I remember Mum doing this – and fish her out of her seat. With her returned to my hip and my cup of tea in my other hand, I stand at the sliding glass doors which look out over the garden and down the valley. I see the smoke trailing into the sky from the chimney of the single house in the distance and think about choices. Rachel told me what had happened in the unit after Boo and everyone else had left, and the vote which Piper made them take. We were sitting side by side in her bed – Leon somewhere else in the house – holding mugs of real tea.

'It was a nightmare,' Rachel said. 'Literally, a nightmare. I couldn't decide anything. I didn't know whether to leave or to stay and I had no clue about what we were supposed to be deciding. I know that sounds like an excuse but it was so hard to believe any of it was really happening. I just stayed in my room for as long as I could under the duvet with the blind down. But then I got so hungry I had to go out. Leon and Piper were in the staffroom I think or going through the food in the freezer. We all ate so much at first – Yahiko must have eaten four of those meals in one go. We didn't think about what was going to happen next, and then Piper started organizing us and I was just happy for someone to take charge. You know, making sure the food would last, boiling the kettle for the water, all that stuff. And then she called a meeting about you and Orla and Stephan. We knew you'd all been given the virus and Yahiko was sure none of you had left. Your blinds weren't up and your doors weren't open, so Piper made us vote. Whether to keep the doors locked for four days, that's what we were voting for. Leon voted to go in.' Here, Rachel started crying, sobbing and rocking, and when she finally calmed, she said, 'I didn't

302

really abstain, I'd never even heard of that word. I just couldn't decide. But anyway, Piper and Yahiko voted to lock the doors. It was the only thing they ever agreed on, and eggs.' She gave a sour laugh. 'They put the air con as high as it would go and we knew it was to try and mask the smell although they never said it. And then on Day Five Yahiko heard knocking coming from Orla's room. Leon said he was going to go in because it was past the four days' isolation but Piper was the one with the key around her neck and she wouldn't open the door. And eventually the knocking stopped. The next day Yahiko saw that your blind had moved and Leon insisted Piper let him push some food in on a tray and the day after that he went into your room.'

'Why didn't you tell me, as soon as I was better?' I asked. 'I might have understood if you'd explained it from the beginning.'

'What? About hearing Orla knocking and us ignoring it?' Her voice was full of horror. 'Yahiko slept in my room that night so he wouldn't have to hear her even though we never said that was the reason. We never talked about it. None of us mentioned it. We couldn't tell you what we'd done cos we'd done it to you too.'

I sometimes try to think which way I would have voted and I'm still not sure, although I often torture myself about what happened to Sophia and how responsible I am in that. I believe she had the virus – I think about the misspelling in her last message – but perhaps without my questions and her replies she would have stayed in her apartment alone but safe.

303

I stare out of the doors at the smoke and say to the baby, 'What do you think?' She makes a happy sound and I look down at her dark and tufty hair so like her father's and her mad eyebrows just like mine. Leon named her Nina before he died, although we had no idea whether she would be a girl or a boy.

Only a month or so after we'd arrived, Piper's grand plan came to seem sensible and practical to all of us. Even Rachel was happy with the idea when she understood what it would – or rather wouldn't – involve. I think too that she carried some guilt for the enormous repercussions of her second thoughts on having the vaccine when she arrived in the unit.

Like Piper had wanted, I worked out when I was ovulating and on one of my trips to a supermarket I found that old cliché of artificial inseminators everywhere: a turkey baster. We were successful surprisingly quickly. Leon often discussed what future he'd like for his daughter, the same things I suppose any father wants for his child: happiness, good health, for them to be loved and to have someone to love in return. He taught me to use the Revisitor sparingly but he never expressed whether he would be happy for his daughter to use it when she was old enough. Perhaps because he thought he would have time to decide in the years to come. We all thought there would be more time.

We'd done a lot of preparation for the birth, read the books, got as much equipment as I could find, although I refused to go to the nearest hospital to see what they had that I might need. Piper was going to help me with the delivery and Leon would be there to cut the cord. Rachel said she'd like to be in the room but Yahiko said he would pace the corridor outside and smoke a cigar when it was over. In the end I had to do all of it alone. There was pain and swearing and blood and crying. And, finally, a baby.

I talk to Nina a lot about her father and the others, telling her what Leon was like and about those memories which he shared with me. It is too little. And I'm conscious of the new memories I'm creating with her, making sure we have fun amongst the work. I sometimes find myself talking to her about my own recollections too, not only to hear an adult voice in the house but to have her know about the people I have loved and I know she would have loved too: Nicos, Margot, Clive, Justin and her grandparents. I've kept the five hospital bracelets in a box of mementos which includes Rachel's phone with the pictures of her party and of Leon. One day soon I will be reckless with the generator, charge it up and show them to her.

Looking at the cottage across the valley, I ask, 'Shall we go and say hello?'

She reaches out a hand and plants it flat on the door: a small brown starfish stuck to the glass. Juggling baby and tea, I unlock the door, slide it sideways and step out.

Day Nineteen Thousand,
Seven Hundred and Ten

Nina opens her palms to the sound of jazz on the radio, lets the two pebble-like sensors cool and her mind rise through the blue.

Acknowledgements

Huge thanks to Tim Chapman, Indigo Ayling and Henry Ayling. To Ursula Pitcher and Stephen Fuller, and the rest of my family for their love and support. Thanks to my early readers: Louise Taylor, Judith Heneghan, Amanda Oosthuizen, Rebecca Fletcher and the rest of The Taverners including Richard Stillman, Paul Davies, Claire Gradidge and Susmita Bhattacharya.

Thanks to everyone at Lutyens & Rubinstein including Fran Davies, Lily Evans, Anna Boyce, and in particular Jane Finigan, who makes everything happen. Thanks also to the lovely David Forrer.

Thanks to all at Penguin and Fig Tree (and beyond) including Jane Gentle, Ella Harold, Ellie Smith, Karen Whitlock, and especially Helen Garnons-Williams, for her patience, vision and perception, and for being a joy to work with.

Thanks to my Tin House family including Win McCormack, Craig Popelars, Nanci McCloskey, Elizabeth DeMeo, Alyssa Ogi, Beth Steidle, Alice Yang, Becky Kraemer, Jae Nichelle, and most importantly, the brilliantly insightful Masie Cochran, who has helped me through another book.

Thanks to everyone who has assisted me with research and advice: Clare Baranowski, Simon Fraser, James Crowley, Luke McMaster, Jane Hudson, Louise Allcock, Colin Johnson, Stephen Fuller, Indigo Ayling, Henry Ayling and Neal Hoare. Any mistakes or crazy ideas are my own.